DECEITFUL
INTENTIONS

DECEITFUL
INTENTIONS

NELDA SUE

TATE PUBLISHING
AND ENTERPRISES, LLC

Published by Tate Publishing & Enterprises, LLC
127 E. Trade Center Terrace | Mustang, Oklahoma 73064 USA
1.888.361.9473 | www.tatepublishing.com

Tate Publishing is committed to excellence in the publishing industry. The company reflects the philosophy established by the founders, based on Psalm 68:11,
"The Lord gave the word and great was the company of those who published it."

Published in the United States of America

ISBN: 978-1-62994-475-3
1. Fiction / Contemporary Women
2. Fiction / Romance / General
13.12.05

PREFACE

"You are delusional and I am hallucinating. I am in a hospital bed for God's sake. This isn't really happening. It's not real, and you're deceitful," she replied with puzzled wrinkles formed on her forehead and a raised tone to her voice.

"No you are not. And no I am not. It's very real. Here I'll pinch you so you can feel I am real and really here talking to you," he said raising his voice trying to keep it pleasant at the same time. Then he reached out and gently pinched her upper arm in a place where he saw no bruising, cuts or scrapes.

Trina jerked her arm away from him and scooted down in the bed pulling the cover over her head almost yelling, "Will someone wake me up. This can't be happening."

Alejandro reached and took hold of the sheet pulling it down from over her face. He bent and gently kissed her forehead. "You are so beautiful when you think you're getting your way. How could I ever not love you?" he asks her remaining bent down over her.

CHAPTER ONE

Trina Wright caught her long curly blond hair in the hands of the tall cherry wood coat rack as she turned herself about in a furious attack. Her eyes of baby blue turned into pools of dark glassy glares. Her full lips of pink formed her words with careful thought just as her medium built full breasted body came to a sudden halt. She screamed at the pull of her hair from what felt like huge metal claws to each side of her head. She snarled and took a step backwards mumbling under her breath, "Damn coat rack."

George couldn't hear what she was saying, so he dismissed it and got up from the big cushioned chair where he sat and walked across the room to release Trina's hair.

"Now Trina, calm down. You've been the best journalist I have had for my paper in over six years. You write the best stories, you take the best pictures, you dig the deepest to find the diamond in the rough story and you know you're the best one for this job. On top of being the best darn journalist anyone could ever ask for you're my favorite niece and you need some rest. Go and take it easy and enjoy the beach. Maybe meet a young man, get wild and have some fun for a change," he pleaded as he released her captured mane.

Despite the fact that Uncle George had always been there for her when she needed a shoulder even before losing her parents she just couldn't let him dip into her personal life. She knew he only meant the best for her and was trying to help but all she really wanted was to be left alone. She didn't want a relationship with anybody because she just didn't think she could handle being broken hearted all over again. She had always looked up to her uncle George and loved him almost as much as she did her own father. However when it came to her personal life she felt she had to stay stern. So she quickly and sharply snapped as she turned," Uncle George, that's enough. My personal life is none of your business. And I would appreciate it...if you...would stay out if it."

George laid his hands on Trina's shoulders and gazed at her with an allude expression. He was trying to persuade her, not really for a story but for a vacation which she much needed and couldn't see herself. She was his niece and he had promised his brother on his dying bed he would take care of her.

Ever since Trina's parents had been in a fatal car accident five years back George had noticed that she had withdrawn from social interaction. The one time she tried having a relationship it had failed and left her in a deep dark hole. To George, it seemed she was covering herself deeper and deeper everyday. He was concerned about his niece. He wanted her to have the best life had to offer and he felt it up to him to teach her how to try and get it and encourage her where he saw fit. He thought putting her in positions where she had to meet and greet the public in her own age range just might fix her relationship hole. At least he had hopes it would and sending her on this fake trip for his paper' The Open Chronicle' he thought would put her in her age group.

George was going to teach her the best he knew of success; he had promised not just to his brother but to himself as well. Trina needed a young man she could be fond of in her life, and Uncle George was going to do everything he could to see it happened. He knew Trina wouldn't agree to just taking a vacation, so he planned this scam with hopes of encouraging her to go. Trina was a beautiful, intelligent young woman with a lot to offer some nice young man, and George had hopes of her meeting him on this trip, so she could start living her life again.

"Trina..." George pleadingly spoke, "Listen to me, just hear me out, it's all I ask. Sweetheart, you have stressed yourself more than you realize over some man who didn't deserve you anyway. You've stopped sleeping, you've stopped dating, you've deserted all your friends and you're getting overly tired. You need rest! We both know you are the best for this job. Common honey, I need the job done. It's July 1, 2008 and its lovely out. You can take the month, that's not a big rush. Take it from Uncle George you need this Trina. Come on baby girl, what do you say?"

Trina bit her bottom lip to keep from displaying her anger. Uncle George had to bring that awful man up. She didn't care about that man who she dated for over two years, who she thought she would one day marry, whose children she thought she would be having but she knew Uncle George didn't understand that. She wasn't sure she did herself. All she knew was when she found out he was already married it had crushed her heart and turned her away from ever wanting to be in another relationship. She chewed her lip hard and folded her arms around her waist as she walked across the large room and come to a halt in front of the huge picture window. She gazed out across the busy street below as she thought about what Uncle George had said. She knew he was right, Randy, her ex-boyfriend had worn her nerves and crushed her heart more than she was admitting and she knew she needed the rest. George wasn't going to give up on her and she knew he wouldn't. So she decided she would go and enjoy the peace.

Trina sighed deeply as she turned to face George and ask, "You need just a story meaning a story on whatever I see fit?"

George smiled a face spreader and said, "Yes."

"Alright, I'll do it! Just to get away from you for a month." she rapidly replied.

She swiftly walked across the room and flung her arms around George's neck giving him a tight hug and kiss on the cheek. She then walked over to the big mahogany desk which George took much pride in and picked up the flight ticket.

She hurried out the door with a good-bye thrown towards George as she quickly exited with a little bit of a cocky grin on her face.

Once she had arrived to her small apartment which consisted of a tiny kitchen, living area, and bedroom with a connecting bathroom. She cautiously picked out clothing to take on the trip with her. She was glad George had talked her into taking this job.

Her thoughts were interrupted by the loud ringing of the phone.

She dropped the clothes she had in her hand inside the case and hurried to the living area to answer.

"Hello" she quietly answered on the third ring.

The voice on the other end of the line eagerly returned her response.

"Trina, Hi, I've been trying to reach you all day. Let's have dinner tonight." The deep voice replied.

"Oh, Jim, It's you. I can't tonight. I'm off in just a few minutes on assignment." She politely told him.

Jim was a nice man she dated from time to time. He wanted to get serious with her but she was not interested in that kind of relationship.

She had told him over and over, but he still insisted on seeing her and he was fun to be around. He had been the only friend she had really had much to do with since her break up with Randy. However she wanted nothing more than friendship and wanted to keep that much at a distance.

Jim sadly replied, "Oh, well maybe when you get back."

"Yes, I would love to then." She said into the receiver.

Jim teasingly asks, "How long will you be gone this time?"

"I'll be back in one month and we'll have dinner then." She told him not wanting to upset him. She was embarrassed thinking that she hadn't even considered giving him a call before she left. Although her business really wasn't his business he had been nice to her and she couldn't honestly deny that.

"Really, that long? Where are you going?" Jim asked in a surprised voice.

"Yes, Uncle George needs this special story for his paper and he thinks I'm the only one that can do it. We'll get together when I return if you wish," with a little sigh she told him and avoided telling him where she was headed.

"Then I guess I have no choice but to let you go, I'll miss you. You will call me won't you?" He asked her just as she hung up the receiver.

She had needed a rest for a long time now, but was too stubborn to take it. By taking the assignment she had no choice, she had to go. She smiled at the peaceful thought of having to as she gathered her bag's to head out for Westwood airport.

Once outside her apartment, she flagged a taxi cab to the curb. Butter Wing, Wisconsin where she lived was not too big a town. The population consists of twenty thousand, and it was easy to catch a cab. So Trina utilized the convenience of their service all the time.

The driver got out, greeted Trina then retrieved her bags and placed them in the trunk of the car. When he returned to assist her with the door, she had already gotten in. She was in a hurry and wished the taxi driver would get that way too. Once he was behind the wheel again, Trina eagerly told him, "Take me to the airport and hurry. I have only thirty minutes before my flight takes off."

"Yes, madam," said the cab driver and Trina spoke no more words to him on the short drive to her destination. She got out of the cab and asked the driver to carry her bags to the check in baggage point for which she would gracefully tip an extra ten bucks. He was happy to assist her and delivered her bags in a speedy manner. Trina got on board the plane and found her resting area for the next five hours. She leaned her full blond haired head back on the rest of her window seat as she got comfortable for her flight to Paradise Islands in the Bahamas. Hot beaches, warm sun and all the casino fun she could possibly want. She did need this time and she would work on the story George needed at the later part of the month.

She couldn't understand why he needed a beach story anyway. However, the first two weeks she was going to enjoy all to herself, then she would worry about George's story for his paper. The thoughts of all the things she wanted to do while she was on the island danced throughout her head. She was a thrill seeker. She wanted to bike the dirt trails, go horseback riding, enjoy from a balloon high in the sky's breathtaking views of the land, right down to swimming with the dolphins. She especially enjoyed activities that made her heart pound with excitement.

"Excuse me," said the passenger next to Trina. His voice jarred her thoughts back to the present.

"Yes, did you need something?" She asked the young man.

"Do you know how long until we arrive at Paradise Island?" He politely asked her.

Trina looked down at her cheaply made fake diamond watch. It was twenty minutes until arrival time. "Twenty minutes," she told the young man getting herself and all her things together.

Once the plane landed, she would be eager and ready to make her exit.

Trina was getting excited as the plane landed in a glide and slowly rolled towards docking. She couldn't keep herself still in her seat. She wiggled squirming and leaned herself into her young neighbor in the seat next to her.

"Oh, I'm sorry. I'm just getting excited." She told him as she started to sit herself up.

The young man just grinned and offered her assistance for which she graciously accepted. Taking his hand, she pushed herself up straight in her seat thanking him with a big smile.

Finally the plane stopped and the okay for exit had been announced. She had all her belongings gathered and with eagerness moved behind the other passengers up the isle to the exiting door. Once off the plane and out front of the airport she once again successfully flagged for a cab.

Trina was headed to her hotel, The Eternal Sunrise. She had a snarl on her face at the thought of that name, and wondered about the combers of the beach and if they were the ones to give the hotel its name. Maybe she could look into that and use it for George's story but for right now she was not going to think about it.

Finally arriving at the hotel and standing out front she was shocked to find it was actually attractive. It stood nearby the beach and had the appearance of a castle. It shown off purple, yellow blue and pink pastel colors that sparkled like diamonds in the ocean's water. Yes, it was very attractive and she knew right away she was going to enjoy this job.

To top off the beauty of the hotel she was welcomed by the most handsome Cabana boy she had ever seen. Her imagination was instantly captured by the glance she had thrown his way. He was tall with a dark complexion, gorging muscles and dark piercing eyes. His hair was shoulder length and formed beautiful dark ringlets which blew in the wind. He retrieved her bags and motioned for her to follow him to the desk for check in. Trina ashamed of herself for such thoughts grabbed her purse and swiftly took off walking in front of him.

"What's your name?" She asked him from over her shoulder.

"I am Alejandro, madam..." he replied.

"Trina...and call me by my name," she scornfully said to him over her shoulder again and quickly applied speed to her east-to-west-hip-swinging stroll to the front desk. She found this man surprisingly captivating in his looks alone so she felt she had to display an attitude of sternness' to maintain control over her own self while on the island and for sure if he was going to be around.

"What do you mean you have no reservation for me? I have the whole top floor on reserve. I want to see the manager. Get him for me now!" Trina spit out the orders angrily.

"Ma'am, we do have your reservation here I see. I apologize for the misunderstanding." said Max the desk clerk and manager as he was handing the key to the top floor over to her.

Trina bit hard as she swiftly turned towards the stairs after snatching the key from Max's hand. "Have your cabana boy deliver my bags in five minutes," she told Max. Then off she went slipping her purse strap once again over her shoulder.

Once inside, she looked around a room that consisted of a dining area, a kitchen and a very large sitting room. She couldn't see the bedroom from where she was standing so she thought she would get to it later. She was admiring the space of the sitting room when a knock came on the door.

"Baggage," called the cabana boy.

Trina yelled back at him "Come in and put them in the bedroom." She heard the door open and the cabana boy come in and walk across the floor. He never spoke a word, once he was inside. He hurriedly delivered her baggage and quickly threw them on the bed.

She turned as she heard him coming back out of the bedroom. Seeing he was a different boy than Alejandro. This boy was skinny and unattractive, and Trina felt he was ill-mannered by not speaking when he came in, and she felt he deserved no compensation.

"No tips for you today." she sarcastically said to him.

"Thank you," the cabana boy said as he left the room shutting the door tightly behind him. His thoughts being to hurry up and get away from this bubble headed beach blond. He didn't take the time to ask if there was anything more she needed. He just wanted to get out, so he made as quick an exit as he possibly could.

Trina was tired from the long trip she had just embarked upon. Her legs hurt from sitting on the plane for five hours without straightening them for more than a few minutes at a time.

Her relaxing thought was of her everyday bath oil Tip-anon she had packed and brought with her so she without hesitation decided on a long hot bath as soon as she possibly could get to it but she would have to find the tub first.

The first doorway she came to and entered lead to the bedroom. The bed was king size and covered with a bright satin red comforter. The four large posts were accented in shimmering red shear satin flows of yardage. It flowed beautifully from a sharp point in the center top of the bed. The two large billowy red satin sham covered pillows laid out side by side finished the overall bed with a glamorous appearance of peaceful comfort. The bed's luxurious elegance was inviting her to jump in. However, in the center the cabana boy had just thrown her bags, and it was now a mess.

Trina's blood boiled, she was very picky about her bed. She couldn't stand it to be messed up like this. She quickly stomped her feet over to the desk across the room, picked up the phone and summoned for the cabana boy to return to the room, and straighten it and do it now, she had told Max.

"Yes, right away madam." Max eagerly said and hung up the phone.

"Alejandro," he called out. "Room, top floor and make the bed quickly."

"Yes sir." Alejandro said as he zestfully took the stairs two at a time. Reaching Trina's suite Alejandro knocked lightly and called out, "Room Assist, madam."

"It's about time, Come in." Trina yelled through the door.

Alejandro recognized the lady's voice. He had met her cab earlier when it arrived.. He drew a long breath and turned the door knob thinking he would just get the bed made and exit quickly.

Stepping inside Alejandro looked around and found Trina facing the window across the room. Her light flowing curls of blond nest softly on her shoulders. Her body stance gave her the appearance of a princess exhibitionist. Trina moved her position and Alejandro quickly drew his attention towards the bedroom.

"Room Assist madam, I'm here to prepare your bed," he said as he scurried into the bedroom.

Trina drew a long breath and stared out the window. It was beautiful, clean and clear pale blue air in the background of her reflection. She thought her breast of ample stood firmly and her blond hair fell graciously around her face, while her sensuality stood out like the innocent young woman she thought she was.

"Stop that, Trina," she bashfully told herself. Then swiftly turned and headed towards the bedroom.

"You should have..."Trina came to a sudden stop in the middle of her sentence when she stepped inside and saw Alejandro from the backside leaning over the bed. Her eyes of blue turned to sparkles of stars. Her eyes feasted upon his muscled firm backside, draining the womanly passion right out of her soul. She barely caught herself before letting her tongue slip, and asking Alejandro if he would like to stay for awhile. Instead she quickly turned around, and made an exit without him seeing her.

Her face was warm and blushed to deep pinkness. Her heart was pounding and her mind was running passion and desire through her entire body. Her legs felt like some limp noodles as they were folding her down onto the couch. She quickly picked up the remote and turned on the television. She needed distraction and she needed it now.

Alejandro entered the room and asked "Would you be having a need for anything more, madam?"

Keeping her back turned to him, she eagerly waved her hand in the air towards the door.

"Very well, madam and good evening," Alejandro said to the back of her head as he desirably escaped the dreadful woman.

Trina jumped into her desired bath quickly as soon as Alejandro had left and then headed off to bed. She was tired and tomorrow was going to be a big day for her. She was going to enjoy herself and just relax. Maybe read a good steamy book on the beach. Breathe the fresh air and watch the waves as they pull the embedded footprints back out of the sand. See the sunrise over the eternal waters and do just whatever she felt like doing for a change.

She pulled the satin comforter and sheet back on the bed. Took from her bag a soft white skirt flowing teddy and slipped it on over her cold tired body. She slid into bed and pulled the cover up over her tucking it in around her neck. Resting her head on the big billowed pillow she closed her eyes and drifted off into a worn out sleep thinking about that hunky cabana boy with the tight butt.

CHAPTER TWO

Morning brought the wake-up call Trina had previously requested of Max at seven in the morning sharp. She sprang out of bed and flew to the window to peer out. It was a beautiful Saturday morning. She was looking forward to a day on the beach relaxing while catching some much needed sun rays.

Trina quickly dressed herself, stood in front of the oval body mirror to decide on the looks of her choices. The pink laced bikini top pushed her full breast up and rounded them into a perfect cleavage. Her slightly tanned skin glistens of smoothness down her sides. The bikini bottom's pink lace fit snug and outlined her curves attractively. Over her bikini, she wore a white see through sleeveless fishnet cover that flowed to mid thigh. She slid her pink nail-covered toes into sandals that fit between her feet tightly. Trina grabbed her bag, which she had previously packed with reading material, towels, lotions and a few personal items, and swiftly moved towards the door.

Alejandro was standing in the lobby at the foot of the stairs beside some palm trees in barrels when he looked up and saw Trina coming down the stairs. He quickly moved behind the tree and watched Trina as she cautiously took the stairs down one by one. She moved past him so fast that he could smell the luscious sweet rose-scent left lingering behind in the air. Alejandro watched as she strolled her preppy rounded butt across the lobby with a swing of her hips from east to west. His mind was captivated with the surprising effects this crazy woman was having on him. He couldn't stop thinking of how stunningly lovely and desirable this wild woman was. How his heart raced when he saw her. How his desires started to rush through his veins without notice. Embarrassed at himself, he quickly turned and headed up the stairs.

Trina walked out into a bright, warm-sun-shinning day. The air was dry and the wind blew lightly on her up turned pretty smiling face. Closing her eyes and taking a slow deep breath and then releasing it she sucked in all the fresh sweet smelling air her lungs could muster. Over and over she breathed the air in. Finally, she felt completely refreshed from the hotel's many different aromas and opened her eyes. Standing before her was a young nice looking cabana boy offering her guidance on the beach. He was tall, dark and handsome with piercing eyes resting on her bosom. She felt chill bumps forming in a running pattern from top to bottom on her spine caused by his glaring eyes. "Just show me where thirteen Cabana is," she told him.

He politely motioned in a westward direction and said, "Follow me, madam," then headed down the beach strolling while talking loudly. "The cabana is fiber built and sits in one of the best spots on the beach. It has its privacy and it is close to cold drinks. The view of the ocean is clear this morning, the smell fresh and air crisp. You have a cushioned reclining chair and I think you will find it quite pleasing."

"Excuse me young man, what is your name?" Trina asked him, nearly running to keep up with him.

"Blas and here we are now" The boy said as they arrived at the cabana.

Trina stopped in her tracks pleased that Blas announced they had arrived. Her sandals were full of hot sand and her legs tired already. The sand was deep; it must be at least five inches and feels like an inferno on her soft tender feet.

The cabana was a half-dome shape of brilliant purple colors. The haze faced the ocean with a magnificent view of beauty. The sun was high in the perfectly clear sky of pale blue and the clouds billowed in the summer wind. Rays of warmth enveloped her body. Trina removed her bikini cover and placed it over the back of her chair. She took a large white fluffy towel from her bag and spread it over the thick soft cushions of bright yellow which filled the reclining chair.

Blas stood and watched as she prepared her nest for comfort. He was enjoying every move she made. Viewing her beauty and wishing he could approach this dove of a woman with special offers of himself. Trina was a vision of everlasting lust and caught glance from the male species of all ages across the entire beach.

"What are you looking at?" Trina screamed at Blas.

"I want a different boy and I shall report you for your misconduct. Now go and have your replacement bring me a cold drink, one of them with the little umbrella in it." Trina firmly snarled after Blas as he was walking away.

Blas came to instant halt, turned and stared at Trina with an inquisitive frown on his face.

He was just about to ask her to repeat her order when she started yelling at him again. "What now? Can't you understand a simple order?" She asked and gasped for air to refill her lungs.

"Right away," Blas said with a smirking smile on his face. His mind wandered as he strolled to get her drink. This is a beautiful woman who needs a firm man alright enough. Blas hysterically laughed out loud as he was arriving at the drink cabana.

Alejandro walked up to the cabana as Blas was explaining to Max that Trina wanted another cabana boy and also wanted a cold drink with a little umbrella in it. Blas and Max laughed frantically as Max prepared the drink. Then they both turned and looked at Alejandro at the same time.

"Guess the job is yours Alejandro." Max said. "Take the little lady her drink and be her boy for the day."

"Ah, yes sir," Alejandro groaned out as he headed out to the cabana with the cool drink on a small silver tray and covered with a pink napkin.

Trina lay stretched out on the soft comfortable folding chair that was provided. "Where is that boy with my drink?" She asked herself. Then, she thought about how the boys gaze upon her bosom actually disturbed her and sent goose bumps up her spine. Shrills of pleasure was jetting through her body like lightening streaks as she slid her small hand inside her bikini top. She knew she had the burden of sexual frustration and was tempted to satisfy herself right here on the open beach.

"Here is your drink madam." Alejandro said as he offered and saw Trina's hand resting inside her bikini top.

Trina jumped, sat up, and turned with urgency to face Alejandro. Her eyes met his bright wide glare. She could not move her lips, or make her mouth form her words. She mislaid in the pools of Alejandro's eyes with her own. Trina was irrecoverable.

"I shall place your drink on the table here," he told her as he set the glass down gently.

"May I be of any further assistance?" Alejandro hesitantly asked her. His eyes eagerly scanning her beautiful upturned face down to her pink toe nails without moving an inch. Alejandro felt the urge to reach his hand and run his finger tips down her cheek. Instead, he started slowly backing away from the purple cabana with the pink bikinied desirable woman inside. He saw a vision of a miraculous sunset over eternal waters of endless lust in this woman!

Trina smiled to herself as he backed away from the cabana. She knew he had gotten nervous and quickly made his exit. She lay back on the reclined chair and thought to herself, *"I'll give him an hour and then I will order again."* Her face glowed with the reflections of her devious thoughts. She placed her dark glasses over her closed eyes as the heat from the sun warmed her body in tune with the relaxing warm breeze making her sleepy.

She drifted off with her devious thoughts running wild. She was trying to think of a way to get the handsome cabana boy's attention. She built her ego on getting the attention of attractive men and Alejandro definitely fit the order.

"Hey!" Trina screamed from the rude awakening of being popped in the forehead.

"Oh, my goodness, are you alright ma'am?" The man said from just outside her cabana.

Trina sat up rubbing her forehead back and forth. "What was that?" She asked looking into the face of who was nothing more than a strange beach bum to her.

"I am so sorry ma'am. It was my beach ball. The wind caught it and whipped it this way. I'm so sorry, are you alright?"

"Well...I guess I'm alright, if I don't get a headache from it," She whined What's your name, unless of course you want me to call you a strange beach bum."

He offered her a hand to stand and said "My name is Donald Denison. I am picnicking right over there on the beach near the water. The wind caught my beach ball and flung it over here. Why don't you let me buy you a cool drink? What would you like?"

"Oh, well thank you, I think I would like that. How about some fruit punch" and she started laughing out loudly. "Do you get it?" She asked him.

Mr. Denison stood in silence with a confused look on his face. What was this woman thinking, running through his mind over and over again.

"For goodness sake, man," She said. "Punch, you know, hit in the head and fruit punch." But he continued to remain silent with a puzzled look.

"Never mind then," Trina squeezed out in a nice way with a big smile on her face. "Yes, I would love some fruit punch." She said withdrawing her attempt at cracking a joke. It was corny anyway so she dismissed it quickly.

Mr. Denison very politely responded with "I will get it for you. You just rest now."

"Thank you" whispered Trina as she leaned back in her chair.

He left the cabana in a hurry.

It was not more than five minutes before Alejandro arrived with the fruit punch and a cool cloth for her head. "Mr. Denison told me what happened. I took it upon myself to bring you a cool cloth for comfort to your forehead. I hope you don't mind." Alejandro said with a concerned look on his face.

Oh, now what am I going say to him was all that was going through her mind. *Do I just thank him, or do I say it was not alright or....oh, what do I do?* She tortured herself in search of the right words. She rose from the chair and reached for the cloth that Alejandro held. Her fingers gently ran across the back of his hand as she slowly pulled the cloth towards her. Her eyes locked to his and she felt weak. She didn't understand why this man had such and effect on her, but she could see in the depths of his eyes that he was just as interested in her as she was to him, but she would not let it be known that she felt his vibrations.

"Thank you, Alejandro" she softly said turning her back to him.

"Madam, might I suggest you lie down and take it easy for a little while before you roam around the beach," he pleaded over her shoulder.

Trina slowly turned to face him once more. "Yes, I will thank you again. I won't be in need of anything more at this time. You can go now unless you would like to sit and cool off a bit first." She calmly replied. Alejandro turned about quickly deciding to take her up on her offer with nothing more than concerns of her well being in mind. This woman had already shown a bad attitude in which he really didn't want anything to do with. However, she is a guest at the hotel where he works so he felt responsible to look out for her. Besides she had just taken a hit on the head and that was warrant enough for him to stay for a short bit.

"Here you can sit on the foot of the recliner," she said as she gently patted the cushion with her hand.

Alejandro took a seat and turned to face her asking, "Are you feeling alright madam?"

"I'm alright for now, "she said. "Say did some lady get hurt earlier today? Shortly after I got here I saw some men carrying her off the beach on a board and I was just wondering."

"I don't know," he replied. "However I guess with your just arriving on the Island a short time ago you hadn't watched any news or anything."

"No I hadn't," she said. "Why would you say that?"

"There's been a few ladies come up missing yet to be found and some who say some man took them and they escaped him by some miracle chance," he told her.

"Oh..., I don't want to talk about this anymore. How long have you worked for the hotel?" she asked changing the subject.

"A few years," he replied.

"How many is a few?" she asked.

"I reckon I have been around since I was a young boy. I started getting paid about ten years ago when I was in my teens," he told her. "How about you, what is it you do for a living? He asked.

"I'm a journalist and I am here on assignment. I'm supposed to get a story for the newspaper I work for back in Wisconsin." She chuckled a little and then continued to say," A beach story," peering at Alejandro in the face.

"May I speak freely madam?" he asked. He needed to get away from her because he didn't need her to see how attracted he really was to her.

"Yes, of course, go ahead," she replied anxious to hear what he had to say.

"A story might be hard to come by if you keep up that attitude you had when you arrived yesterday however if you stay as sweet as you are right now, you just might get what you want," he told her as he stood to leave feeling comfortable she was alright. "I'll get back to work now. You seem like you're going to be alright."

Trina laughed out loud feeling like he was leaving because of his attraction to her. Actually she felt like she knew he was attracted to her. She could tell it, she could see it in his face and his eyes. So she just smiled behind him as he walked away feeling she had won the attraction battle between them this time because she wasn't as uncomfortable being next to him as he seem to be by being next to her.

He delivered her one more fruit punch before his day was done.

She seemed fine by the end of the day and he felt relieved knowing she was alright.

Nightfall laid Alejandro on his feathered mattress covered in blue satin sheets. His hut was small and only bore room for a bed, chest, and a comfortable chair for resting. The bed in the left corner, the chest in the right, and his chair on the adjacent wall, left a foot path just big enough to get through without tripping. He looked about the hut and shook his head in anxious wants of a bigger one. His day had been exhausting. His manly empire had been invaded by an obnoxious and desirably attractive woman. His last experience with a woman buried him deeply into a sanctuary that only he could fill. He wanted nothing to do with a woman. Especially, women like Trina, as beautiful as she was, he wanted nothing to do with her, and he told himself many times.

He twisted and turned until he had his feathered mattress folding around his firm essence. Comfortable on his side with the feathered mattress soothing his tired body, he closed his eyes. His thoughts drifted back on the day's events and that dreadfully beautiful woman Trina. How could any man stand to be around that woman? She was an insult to the female race and a very pretty insult too. Warmth began to flow through Alejandro, as he thought of Trina and her beauty. Slowly Alejandro eagerly slid his big hand down to his maleness and squeezed gently. His thoughts of Trina's beauty let deep moans of pleasure escape his mouth. Feeling content with the pleasure which he bestowed upon himself Alejandro drifted off to sleep with Trina buried in his thoughts.

Meantime, nestling down into her satin sheets Trina thought of Alejandro. Twinges of pleasure shrilled soft moans through her lips of wine. Visions of roughened lust outlined images of him to her imagination. Passion burned vibrantly through her body in want of this heavenly creature. Sweetened sensations ran through her body making her quiver in lustful want. She was astonished at the sexual harmonics she felt with Alejandro. She softly released moans of heated pleasure from her inner depths as her vision saw him by her side. Feelings of radiant power raced through her as she expelled the tightness which welled inside. Her legs quivered and fell in limpness to her side. Her heart was pounding as visions of Alejandro enveloped her every being. Limp like a dish rag thrown to the side and feeling confused, Trina fell off to sleep with amazing satisfaction reflecting from her face and the indescribable want of him in her bed.

CHAPTER THREE

Morning raised Alejandro from an extremely relaxed night of rest. He showered and hurriedly dressed, then headed out to the hotel. He had walked more than half-way up the trail when he remembered that he had forgotten his keys, which fit all the doors.

"Darn," he said to himself. "I can't get in. I have to go back and get them," he continued to talk to himself and answering. He turned and jogged back down the trail quickly. He would have time to make it back to his hut, and then to the hotel before any guest arrived, if he hurried.

Trina on the other hand was as usual running late, and had to rush if she was going to catch the site seeing train, before it took off without her. She grabbed her bag and flew out the door. Down the stairs she scurried in a hurry catching a glimpse of Max who stood in the far corner of the lobby. When she reached the bottom she yelled towards him "I'm going to..." *Bump*, the noise sounded as Trina hit the floor landing on her rounded rump. She shook her blond head to and fro before verbally attacking the monster of a man who stood in her path.

"You're an idiot!" She screamed at the top of her lungs.

"Couldn't you see me?" She asked with fiery eyes.

"I could have been hurt badly." She said as she looked up into the worried dreamy pools of Alejandro.

"Are you alright, madam?" Alejandro quickly asked offering his hand at the same time.

Trina was struggling for words. All she could think of was her escapade the previous night with this handsome man in mind. "Well, next time watch where you are going." She managed to squeal out. All the while she was reaching for Alejandro's strong hand for assistance to get up off the hard floor.

Sweat formed on the palm of Alejandro as he eagerly watched Trina reaching for his hand. He saw her beauty escape her, and he felt desire rise in his every depth. He swiftly looked away from Trina, not wanting her to see the desire in his darkened eyes.

Once on her feet again, Trina quickly straightened her snug fitting dress of thin pink cotton. "Just watch where you are going." She snapped at Alejandro as she moved towards the door.

Max called out to Alejandro. "Come here, I need to see you Alejandro." He whaled loudly.

"Yes sir." Alejandro said.

"I need you to go into town and pick up an important order. You may have to wait just a little while but do not leave without that order. Take the jeep and go now. There's a map on the seat showing you where to go. Now go on, get going boy." Max sharply said handing Alejandro keys to the jeep.

Alejandro took the keys and hurried off to run his assigned errand. Slowly driving in the fresh sweet smelling breeze and the heat of the sun, he thought of Trina on that floor looking up at him.

"Such sweet sorrow surrounds that woman and she needs a man. A real man, that is." Alejandro's thoughts raced in his mind. He knew he would be happy when this crazy woman's vacation or whatever she was doing was done with and she was gone. Then and only then can he get sleep and breathe without her present to burn his every thought. Yes, that will be a glorious day for Alejandro. He is not allowed to mix with the guest, so he decided he would stay away from this woman completely. She was a danger to his emotions and his work.

Alejandro got to the train station mid afternoon to find the package had not yet arrived. He was told not to leave without it and so he would have to sit and wait. He took a seat on a hard bench in the corner of the train station. Looking around he spotted a newspaper on the table beside him. He picked it up and started flipping through it, when the clerk behind the counter called to him.

"Excuse me, your package will be three hours late at its shortest time. The conductor reported a hold up of at least that long." The attendant said.

"Thank you Sir." Alejandro kindly replied and quickly decided to take the sight seeing train along the beach. After purchasing his ticket, he got on board and found the most solitary seat available. The seat was in the very back row, which pleased Alejandro. Settling back into a comfortable position he closed his eyes, opened his ears and just listened to the hustle and bustle of vacationers boarding the train. He had three hours to kill and knew he would enjoy this ride.

"Move over, look what you made me do." The voice pierced Alejandro's ears.

He quickly opened his eyes and peered down the isle, and there Trina stood bent over picking up her bag from where it fell on the floor. Alejandro's heart pounded at the sight of her rounded rear-end stuck up in the air. Streaks of lusty desire shot to his groin causing a reaction that made him place an arm over his lap, watching Trina as she took her seat two row's up on the opposite side.

Trina pushed and pulled until she got the seat just perfect for her legs to stick out into the isle. She crossed them and made herself comfortable laying her head against the soft cushioned back of the seat.

The lined muscle's of Trina's tanned soft thighs and smooth calves made Alejandro need more than his arm for cover. He quickly turned his head and leaned back laying his jacket across his lap, then closed his eyes and drifted off into dream land.

"Ah," Alejandro moaned at the feel of Trina's dreamed breath against his tightened skin. Heated quivers shot through his veins. Her breath left path's of warm sensations as she moved her moistened lips across his tender neck.

"Yes, Trina baby your lips burn me like the heat of the sun. My body throbs in want of your gentle touch. My tongue searches for your sweetened taste. Show me your deepest desires." Alejandro moaned his words seductively.

"What are you doing here?" Trina rudely snapped at him bringing him to his senses and shocking him.

"Ah, well I am on my work." He finally said. "And do you get paid to take train rides and sleep?" She sarcastically asked. Not giving him time to say anything, she said, "The ride will soon be over with. The train stopped five minutes ago for the last shopping stop and someone took my seat before I got back so move over." Alejandro slid over to the inside seat wondering what in the world this woman was going to do or say next.

"If you were doing your work then you were sleeping on duty. I could have you fired for that." She had a small smile spreading on her face as she hurried to take the seat beside him.

Alejandro shook his head in disbelief of his napping thoughts of Trina. They were far different than his waking thoughts. He wanted her, he wanted to make love to her, but he could never do that. He would have to keep it to himself through her time at Paradise Island. She will not know how badly he desires her. It's against his work policies and he couldn't take that chance no matter what.

Trina interrupted his thoughts with yet another question. "What is your position at the hotel?" she asked.

"What's with all the questions," he asked in return.

"I told you before I was here to do a beach bum story and you have become my target," she said with a chuckle.

"I suppose you wasn't going to let me in on that little secret of yours either," he replied with a sigh following.

"Well of course I....," she hesitated peering past him out the window. Alejandro turned to see what it was which brought her words to an end.

"There is another body," she said. "It's all over the place here." Two rescue workers were rolling a gurney out of a nearby ally with a drape over the top of something rather large underneath.

"Yes I see," Alejandro said turning away from the view. "Come on, don't watch them." He told her as he placed a hand on top of hers giving it a squeeze.

Trina peered down at his hand over hers. She felt warmth pass from his hand to hers which gave her a feeling of being safe and secure from any harm.

"Now when exactly did you have planned to let me in on this beach bum story you keep talking about?" he quickly asked as he moved his hand away feeling the same warmth as she.

The train came to a stop and Trina quickly excused herself feeling it had come to a stop at just the right moment because she was feeling weak towards Alejandro and could have easily broken down giving into him. She could have said some things that might have been the biggest mistake she ever made. All she could think was, "*I don't want a relationship with anyone.*" Then her thoughts would change to, "*Alejandro probably wouldn't want anything to do with you anyway. Just get your story and go home.*" She struggled back and forth, back and forth with he wants me thoughts to he don't want me thoughts.

Trina laughed innocently as she turned the hot water knob on the big oval Jacuzzi tub in her hotel room telling herself, "I got that cabana boy. I got him good. He couldn't even speak." as she grabbed her bath oil beads." Her tip-anon oil was a sweet smelling rose oil bead. They dissolved quickly as she threw them at random into the tub. Trina thought to herself "*I'll have to watch my step, or I'll slip getting in there.*" And she watched the oil dissolving in the steaming hot water. She undressed slowly giving the bath water time to peak at her desired level. It was late and she decided to not get her hair wet, so she picked up her brush and brushed through her long strands, then carefully tied the ringlets up. She then took a large pink fluffy towel from inside the closet and strolled back to the tub side. Laying the towel on the tub's ledge, she gently lowered herself down into what felt like massaging paradise to her exhausted body. Once completely settled into the tub, Trina began to relax resting back on a pink air pillow that was complimentary of the hotel. Her body was exhausted, but her mind was running a mile a minute. She thought of the rise that she couldn't help, but notice on Alejandro. She leaned her head back all the way and closed her eyes. Her thoughts went instantly to the look on Alejandro's face when she woke him. There was something about that look that melted Trina in more than one way. He looked cuddly and babyish while at the same time strong and firm. His eyes pierced her into discomfort, and his smile seduced her womanly needs. Trina sat up and retrieved the bottle of liquid petal soap. She squeezed a generous amount into her hand and gently rubbed her small palms together. For a quick instant, she wondered what Alejandro was dreaming of to give him such an enhanced bulge. She couldn't think of that cabana boy in such a way. She was tired and wanted to rest with moments of peace. Besides, he was not even close to her type of man. Trina stretched her body until her nose was just above the water level. As she took in a deep breath, the warmth flowed through her body from head to toe. One by one, she felt her muscles start to give in to the heat that now enveloped her worn body. The comfort began to ease her thoughts of Alejandro. Tomorrow she would avoid him and catch the bus across town to the Dolphin show. After all, she wanted to swim with the dolphins. She had wanted to since she was a small girl and now she had the opportunity to fulfill that dream, and she wanted to do so before returning home. With those thoughts in mind she quickly bathed and scurried off to bed.

It seemed like the night was the longest Trina had seen in some time. She was excited as she stood and waited for the sales office to open up at Waterloo Dolphin Park. She had left her hotel room early to avoid running into Alejandro. He was the one person she didn't want to see. She was not going to let him mess up another one of her days on Paradise Island. Swimming with the dolphins and playing with them was almost more than she could believe. It was a childhood dream and now it was coming true. If the office personnel would hurry and get in, she could get started with a thrilling fun-filled day.

Trina pushed her nose upwards towards the sky and closed her eyes. She took in a long deep breath. The sun was high and radiated hot streams across her face. A light blowing warm wind brushed her blond ringlets across her forehead and all she could think was how her young dream is about to come true.

"Ladies and Gentleman" the man's voice came over a loud speaker bringing Trina's head down out of the clouds. "Welcome to Waterloo Dolphin Park. We aim to give you the dolphin adventure of your life. Please adhere to the safety rules which your guide will instruct you on. Thank you for joining us and have a pleasant dolphin day."

Trina felt her heart skip a beat and the tears start to build. This was a big day for her. A day she would not have anyone to share with. Maybe she could tell Jim, whom she hadn't even given a thought of since she had arrived. She quickly excused the thought and wiped her cheeks dry.

"Admit one?" The clerk at the desk asked.

"Yes, thank you." She said eagerly.

"That will be $250.00." The clerk replied.

Trina quickly pulled the cash from her bag and handed it to the clerk. She took her admission slip and followed her handsome guide to the dolphin pool.

"Now," her guide said once arriving pool side.

"The first thing I need to do is make sure you can swim Miss..."

"Trina, call me by my first name if you don't mind." She quickly told him cutting his words off.

"Great, Trina it is and you may do the same. I am Jose." He nicely replied and continued to speak."Swimming is a requirement to getting into the pool with the dolphins. If you can't swim your money will be refunded." He told her.

"Oh, I can swim." She said smiling from ear to ear.

"Great, then if you would please just slip right down there in that pool and show me how good a swimmer you are. The dolphins are not in yet." He upwardly and politely said while pointing towards the pools steps.

Trina dropped the deep purple jacket that covered her lavender one piece snug fitting suit and her bag on a nearby bench and then slid into the warm water of the pool. She swam from side to side and end to end of the rectangular pool before he called her back.

"Are you ready for your dolphin adventure?" He asked not giving her time to answer. "You get hands on experience with the dolphins in this interactive program. You can watch them swim underwater, and you may wish to have a photo taken of you with the dolphin giving you a kiss. You may choose to have a dolphin belly ride or maybe even lie on the boogie board and let the dolphin push you around the pool." He took a deep breath as he hesitated in telling her the options of her about to be adventure.

Trina took the chance to speak and asked "Do the dolphins have names? Are they male or female? Can I learn their anatomy by swimming with them?"

"Hold on, hold on." Jose finally spit out. "Yes, you can learn their anatomy and you'll get splashed by them, you can even feed them. I'm sure you'll find interacting with Lacey (female) and Casey (male) a grand adventure." Jose quickly expelled before she could ask any more questions.

"This is going to be so much fun." Trina squealed out like a small child holding her hands to either side of her face as she jumped up and down in the pool. She was overwhelmed with excitement. "Let's get started. Where are the dolphins? Let them in now." The words escaped through the wide smiling face of excited Trina.

Alejandro hid himself behind the rose bushes at the far end of the pool watching Trina. He had seen her as she climbed aboard the bus back at the hotel. He watched and waited for her to take her seat three-fourths of the way down the seat row. He quickly got aboard and slid into the first seat behind the driver. Alejandro had called off work. He had followed Trina and he had kept her from knowing he was anywhere around. The rose bush filled the air with sweet smell that lingered around his nostrils. He swung around to the other side of the bushes and took a seat in a cushioned lawn chair and prepared himself for a joyful day of Trina's inner and outer beauty. He patiently watched her as the dolphins were released into the pool. The look on her face amazed Alejandro as the dolphins slowly approached her. She seemed like a small child in a candy store. He could tell from afar, he was in for an exciting day watching beautiful Trina and the dolphins perform high energy behaviors as they play, dance and kiss in the warmth of the pool. Alejandro laughed out loudly watching and enjoying these curious animals face to face as they glided effortlessly in the water pulling Trina along with them. Her smiling face melted the hardness that had encircled his heart for several years. Alejandro was shocked at his behavior as he watched her getting her photo taken with the dolphin kissing her. He wanted to reach out to her and take her in his arms. He wanted to let her know he was watching her and how she pleasured him with her happiness. Instead, he exited without her knowing he was within her sight for the entire day. He quickly headed back to his cabana exhausted and unseen by Trina.

Once back home Alejandro sat with his feet propped high in the air. He was tired from all the sneaking around, following Trina, and his aching puppies felt as though they were going to fall off. He was worn to a frail and all he could say to himself was, "She didn't even know I was there." He had shared Trina's big dream day without her knowledge, and he would hold it dear for eternity to come. Why, he could not explain, he just knew he would. With a smile on his face Alejandro leaned his head to the back of the soft cushion on the chair which he sat. Visions of Trina kissing the dolphin flashed through his mind. How he wished it had been him. He fell asleep in wishful contentment.

Trina laid snuggled between the satin red sheets and comforter that hung over the sides of the bed across her. She was excitedly exhausted from her day. Her eyes felt like they were as big as half dollars. She couldn't stop thinking about her childhood dream coming true. The thrill of her day in the water with the dolphins warmed her heart. She only wished she had had someone to share it with. Trina repositioned herself to her side, tucked her pillow and changed her thoughts to Alejandro. She had made it through the day without even so much as a thought of him.

"Why now?" She asked herself as she slowly slipped into a questionable sleep with no answers. She rolled onto her back as she moaned in her sleep. She was dreaming vision's of Alejandro walking along a deserted beach. No shirt, white snug fitting jeans rolled half way up his calves. With no shoes on his feet and his long dark curls blowing in the soft warm breeze. His shadow was vibrant in the shimmering moon light which encircled his magnificent tanned build. She softly whispered "I want you Alejandro." And she slept with joyous dreams of togetherness all through the night.

CHAPTER FOUR

The ringing of the phone the next morning sprang Trina out of bed and into the shower.

Today, she would go horseback riding and see the beautiful foliage that surrounds the beach, and she again would stay away from Alejandro. For some odd reason he was a threat to more than just her womanly desires. He made her feel strange in ways she never felt before. When she was around him her heart raced and her mind wondered. He was a danger to the continuance of the single woman's profile of life. Which is the way she lived and she would avoid him for the rest of her stay on the island.

She quickly slid herself into a pair of sky blue shorts with a wide band of yellow around each of the legs. The snug fit felt of comfort to her so she then went for a blouse. She chose a bright yellow spaghetti strap with a full bodice which displayed the curves of her medium sized waist. Trina stepped in front of the mirror and gazed at herself for a few moments and decided her clothing would be a good choice. She walked across the room and pulled open the door that led into the closet. She had multiple pair of shoes and it would be easy to find a match for her outfit. She carefully looked through each pair and then chose a pair of blue tie ups and slid her feet in them one by one. She then pulled each side of her long blond hair back and placed a band around a small tail to hold it securely in place and let the rest of her hair fly free. She took her small hands and patted at the bottom of the curls which lay in ringlets upon her tanned shoulders.

She slowly turned and strolled into the front room and found the breakfast she had ordered the previous night for this morning. There was a small bowl of fresh mixed fruit and a glass of coconut milk. She was pleased the kitchen had gotten her order correct and delivered soon enough for her to sit and enjoy before time for her horseback ride. Trina took the breakfast tray and sat down at the sturdy built stem table covered in a white lace cloth. In the center sit a tall, full and clear vase of two dozen gorgeous pink roses. The aroma in the air was stunningly sweet and pleased her sense of freshness. She picked up the napkin, removed the silver ware and then carefully spread it across her lap. She stuck into the bowl and pricked her fork into a red grape and gently placed it inside her mouth. She bit down and it shot her mouth full of sweet juice. It was plump and delicious. She enjoyed eating fruit and found it hard to believe how fresh this fruit was.

She let her mind drift into thoughts about her previous night's adventures with Alejandro. She was embarrassed to admit it even to herself, and this would be a Paradise Island secret to hold inside from not only him but everyone. Trina drank up the last of her milk and left to be sure she catches the transit bus for the riding stables. She told herself that she would clear her mind of Alejandro on the way there. Feeling satisfaction with her decision she moved even faster towards the transit stop.

Alejandro scurried around his hut quickly slinging his clothing on. He was late for work. He had called off the previous day and that was enough to upset Max alone.

"Damn...damn, damn, damn." He said out loud to himself. "Why do I let that dreadful woman cause me problems?" Inhaling a much needed breath he spit out his words. "I should never have called off and followed Trina like I did. It's her fault, I'm late. She's a selfish, spoiled brat." He told himself out loud on his way out the door in a hard run. He was working the riding stables today and had only an hour to get the horses prepared for the guest of the day. At least, there he wouldn't have to see Trina and that would keep her out of his mind. Maybe then she would cause him no more troubles.

"Hey, dude!" Buzz excitedly said as Alejandro approached the stables. Then waited and continued when Alejandro was standing in front of him.

"Everything is ready man, except for these few horses and they will be shortly. Max has already been by checking. I told him you had an upset stomach and was in the toilet.

"Said, I hoped it wasn't catching. That scared him off in a hurry." Buzz told him as chuckles of laughter escaped him leaving tears in his eyes.

"Oh man, you're a life saver. Thank you." Alejandro managed to say out of breath.

"No problem dude, you owe me one. Are you making the opening speech today dude?" Buzz asked him.

Alejandro spoke simultaneously with his head as he turned his face east to west. "No, I'm working the back stables. I am only in today for questions. Probably will be a boring day like always." He softly said then headed off walking down the trail that leads to the back entrance. Once inside he quickly started coffee to brewing. He knew it would be a long day. He hated doing this job; there were never any complaints or problems. And that made for the long day. The trail rides were pleasant and in some cases even romantic. The visitors enjoyed the rides and left the stables with smiles on their faces. After his escapade yesterday he would need the coffee to keep him awake and help him make it through a long drawn out, quiet, lazy day.

Alejandro could hear Rubin when he came over the loud speaker. "Welcome to the Come Back Riding Stables. Horseback riding is incomparably soul satisfying. The horse as we all know is one of nature's most magnificent creatures and you will be allowed to choose the one you ride on this tour. We ask you choose from the front line of stables if you are a first timer, as the back line is for the more experienced riders. Please abide by the safety rules of your guide. Ladies and gentlemen, if you are ready, would you just follow the line for assistance in choosing the best horse for you. Thank you and have an everlasting enjoyable tour." Rubin told the group of vacationers and then excused himself.

Alejandro sat down in the desk seat and leaned his chair back propping his feet up thinking, it's going to be a long day!

Trina followed the slow moving line around to the entrance of the stables. She was excited about her ride and wanted the best horse they had to offer. So she shoved herself up the line. "Excuse me, let me past you." She said as she pushed her way forward. "Good only two more in front of me." She happily told herself out loud. She felt good about what she had done to get there.

"Welcome to Comeback Stables. My name is Bernard and I'm going to help you choose your horse for today," he drew a long breath as he finished his words to Trina.

Bernard was a tall good looking man. He had a dark complexion with firm muscles of grapefruit size. His eyes shone as dark glass. His long, straight, burnt-brown hair accented his skin glow of radiance.

Snapping back to reality Trina charmingly said "Hello Bernard, Please call me Trina. I do hope you will be joining us on the ride as well."

Bernard looked Trina in the eyes and said "I'm sorry Madam Trina, I do not take the rides. I stay at the stables. Please step this way." He pointed towards the entrance leading into the stables where the horses were awaiting.

Trina stepped carefully in the direction that Bernard was pointing. "It's too bad you don't take the rides. You would be a nice view," she softly said as she moved past him.

Bernard stood there, hands on hips watching Trina as she moved towards the stables. He shook his head in dismay and quietly followed behind her.

Trina rushed inside and went straight for the back stables. Bernard called to her, "Madam Trina those horses are for the experienced riders only."

"Oh, I know how to ride a horse." She said and smiled as she spoke.

"Then let me see your certificate certifying you for this row," he quickly told her.

She turned and looked at him in surprise. "What do you mean certificate. I don't have a certificate. I want this horse, tell me what his name is." she said as she searched of how to open the stables door.

Bernard drew in a long breath and said "Madam, I cannot let you have that one if you do not have a certificate."

"I tell you what" she formed her words with care, "I will let you decide on my horse if you go on the ride too and ride beside me." She teasingly told him.

"I don't go on the rides Madam Trina." Bernard regretfully told her.

Trina quickly asked "Why can't you?"

Bernard smiled and said "I am a stable boy. Not a guide."

"You know how to ride don't you?" She asked him bluntly. Without giving Bernard a chance to say anything Trina continued speaking. "Do you have a manager or something on duty?" She asked him.

"Madam Trina, he would only tell you the same thing. You cannot take that horse without a certificate." Bernard hastily said starting to get aggravated.

"Oh, very well then show me the best one there." She disappointingly said pointing across the stables to the other side.

The line of roomy individual stalls ran the entire length of the stables. There were mingled, spotted, black and brown colored horses. Some were short and some tall.

Trina knowing she knew nothing about horses pranced herself up to a black one and said "I think this one will do."

Bernard walked over and placed a hand on the side of the tall horse's neck. He rubbed up and down as he said "Ah, Blackball, nice choice if you can handle him, he likes to gallop his path and he will without proper guidance. Don't know if you are woman enough to handle him. Maybe you should make another choice."

Trina stood straight sticking her chest out as she said "I am woman enough to handle him. I want this one."

"Very well," Bernard reluctantly said. "Remember he will gallop without proper guidance. If you feel you cannot handle him after the tour begins tell your guide. He'll take care of you." Bernard led the previously saddled horse out to the starting point of the tour.

"Put your foot in my hand and I will help you climb aboard." He politely offered Trina after bringing Blackball to a halt.

"Give me a minute." She said.

"Is this the only job you do?" She asked him with eagerness.

"No, I work at the drink hut in the afternoons." Bernard said with a grin.

"And what time do you finish that job?" She curiously asked him.

Bernard was grinning from ear to ear as he said "We are not allowed to mix with the guest Madam Trina."

"I do not think I caught what time you said." She told him sequencing her eyes as she spoke.

"Five Madam—" Bernard barley said before she cut him off.

"Good, now I know who to ask to deliver my afternoon drink at, shall we say, five minutes before five." She said winking at him at the same time.

"Mount up." Jasper the guide yelled across the path.

Trina turned to Bernard and said "If you will be so kind, I will take that hand now."

Bernard folded his hands together and locked his fingers in place for Trina to use as a step ladder.

She slid her foot into his hands and swung her body up on the back of Blackball with ease. From high on the horses back Trina smiled down at Bernard and said "See you at five." Then she urged Blackball forward.

Bernard stood there with one hand on his hip and the other scratching the back of his head as he watched Trina ride off. "What was that all about?" He asked himself as he headed back to clean the stable Blackball had been in.

The trail the guide led them on was beautifully landscaped. There were palm trees blowing in the wind. Patched wild flowers of exhilarating loveliness were placed in attractive stone lined beds. Large elephant ears were growing wild and stood their roll of beauty. Pastel colors of different species of flowers were located through out the trail thus far and the view was that of lovely captivation.

"What do you think about those flowers there Blackball?" She asked the horse while patting the side of his neck. "They are beauties, don't you think?" She asked leaning forward whispering in Blackball's ear. "I know you can't talk to me but you listen to me talking to you. I know you do," She softly said.

Blackball raised his ears towards the sky anxiously listening to Trina talk to him.

"The next site where I'm going to take you, we will dismount and enjoy for a short break. There are some picnic tables where we will devour the beauty over lunch." Jasper yelled as loud as he could so all the riders could hear.

Blackball followed as if he knew exactly where he was going and suddenly broke into a fast paced gallop.

"Stop, Blackball." Trina yelled as she pulled back on the reins. Blackball just kept right on going and she kept right on yelling. "Stop Black—ball stop!" She screamed holding on for dear life. Blackball headed galloping down the trail passing other horses as if they were standing still. He knew where he was going and he was in a hurry to get there.

Jasper positioned the horse he was on sideways and waited for Blackball to get close. He reached out as the horse neared passing and took the reins from Trina's hands. He pulled back and yelled loudly "Hold Blackball, hold."

Trina held tightly to the horn of the saddle as Blackball came to a sudden stop.

"Miss, I'll lead him to the next stop. He will be fine from there on in. He's just thirsty right now. Did the stable boy not warn you Blackball would do this?" Jasper asked showing much concern on his face.

"Alright, that would be great. Thank you." She softly told him in almost tears ignoring his question.

Jasper could see Trina was scared, so he tightened the rein of Blackball around his hand and walked him beside of his own horse for the rest of the trail to the lunch site. Jasper dismounted his horse upon arrival and turned to offer Trina a hand down off Blackball's back. Once she was on the ground, he took the reins from both horses and tied them around a nearby tie stake.

"Inside the packs which are attached to each horse's saddle you'll find your lunch. The picnic tables are located 500 yards down this trail, so you'll need to remove the packs from your horse. Today we have fried chicken, potato salad, and baked beans with home-made yeast rolls. For dessert there are freshly toasted pineapple rings. There's a zesty fruit punch for drink, or you may choose the canteen also attached to the saddle horn, which is filled with cold spring water. I believe you'll find lunch quite tasty. We'll move out in thirty minutes. Enjoy your meal." Jasper announced loudly as he removed the food packs from his and Trina's horse.

"Right this way little lady," He told Trina pointing towards the trail.

Trina followed along behind Jasper still trembling from her scare. "What's the noise I hear?" She innocently asked.

Jasper turned and smiled as he said "It's running water Missy and it's beautiful. Yeah nothing like nature in its own beauty. Just you wait and see you will dearly love it. Now come on, put a smile on that pretty face of yours and let's get going."

Trina formed a small grin and followed Jasper down the trail watching each step she made. There were stones in the path and she didn't want to fall and embarrass herself even more than she already had. At the end of the trail there was a large wooden gate in the shape of a horse shoe. On the other side of the gate Trina feasted her eyes upon the most beautiful site she ever seen in her life. It was a huge mountain covered in different shades of greenish foliage and clear blue water rasping with strong force. Lying at random locations in the formed pools were huge boulders. They were covered in green moss that had the appearance of slickness. On top of some of the boulders were blossoms of some small lemon yellow four-leafed flowers which appeared as paths through the gorge? Halfway between the mountain side and the outer edge of the pool was an old dead tree turned on its side. The water rushed under the bottom of the tree in separation where the petrified limbs lay downward.

"I think I am going to skip lunch. I'm going to sit on that boulder there by the water's edge and wait for the rest." She told Jasper.

He watched Trina as she gazed at the beauty that lay before her and offered no discouragement.

Trina cautiously moved toward a large boulder sitting partly in the water. She climbed up on the top and crossed her legs. She placed her elbow on one knee and propped her chin on her hand. Her eyes were staring at a fall of tremendous amounts of cold water. She must be seeing at least twenty different waterfall areas. Each waterfall had its own story of natural beauty to tell. She focused on the great fall of pale neon blue. The rasping on the mountainside caused the water to have white caps and spring out into a glorious three dimensional appearance. The difference in the boulders heights made several paths of lovely blue white caped liquid stairways. She was hypnotized by the breathtaking beauty of nature as she sat at the middle-edge of the water atop a giant rock and all alone. The sunlight glistened sparkles against the clear blueness which reflected rays of bright brilliance all over the picnic area.

"Beautiful, isn't it." Jasper said from behind Trina.

She jumped at the sound of his voice before turning to face him. "Yes, the view is lovely. Almost like a dream world. I find it easy to get lost in the peacefulness it presents." Trina told him.

He could tell Trina had something on her mind or someone. It was nothing uncommon, it happened all the time here at this site. "If you don't mind my asking Miss, who is he?" Jasper cautiously inquired.

Trina looked at Jasper for a good long minute before she replied to him. "Jasper, can this conversation be between the two of us only?" She asked him finally.

"You can trust me on that, Missy." He said with a peaceful look on his face, giving her an inward peaceful feeling.

She smiled a little smirking grin at him and said "Thank you. Alright, can you or will you tell me what you know about Alejandro?"

"Oh, Missy, Alejandro is a tough one. He is a good man and I suspect someday he will make a good man for someone. He's a hard worker and takes pride in what he does. The last few years he has poured himself into his work. It's become his life. He was hurt badly in the romance department and never got over it to this day. You just be careful with him. I would hate to see you get hurt more than you are hurting now Missy." Jasper told Trina as he offered her his hand to climb down from the large boulder. "Now, we got to get back on the trail. Come on and you can ride beside me," and he was finished with what he was saying.

Although she didn't hear as much about Alejandro as she wanted she still felt the need to acknowledge Jasper's kindness.

For some odd reason Jasper made her feel as if she had known him all her life making it easy for her to trust in him. "Thank you, Jasper and please let's keep this between us." Trina said with a smile as she started to climb down off the boulder holding to Jasper's offered hand.

Jasper smiled in return as he said to her "Don't worry Missy, it's our secret."

With the comforting words of Jasper, she and Blackball headed down the trail to the stables in silence. Trina's thoughts stayed on Alejandro and how to get his attention. No matter how hard she tried to forget him, he always came back to her mind and it was quickly leading to her heart.

"What time is it somebody?" Rubin asked restlessly.

"Eleven thirty." Alejandro told him.

"Great, that means the tour will be returning in thirty minutes." Bernard offered to the conversation.

"If you two don't mind I would like to head on out just before they return," Bernard acquisitively told them.

"Is there a problem?" Alejandro asked him.

"No…well, maybe, I don't know but there is a lady on that tour. One I helped to mount. She started out being difficult. Demanding to see the manager, but then changed her mind when I told her that he would tell her the same thing I did. She argued over taking one of the experienced horses out. Anyway to make a long story short, she started coming on to me. I would just like to be gone when she gets back here." Bernard said with a confused look on his face.

"I bet I know which one she is." Rubin said as he chuckled.

"It's that Trina woman isn't it?" Rubin could hardly say due to laughing so hard.

Alejandro turned a quick upward look towards Rubin "long blond hair, real spunky like, and prissy but very pretty?" He thoughtlessly asked.

Bernard smiled real big as he said "Yeah, that's the one. Do you know her?"

Alejandro froze in the thoughts of running into Trina. All he could think was he had to get some help to the stables and he had to do it quick. He didn't know if he could handle another confrontation with her.

"Alejandro, are you alright man?" Bernard asked in concern.

"Yeah man, go, go ahead and go," He told Bernard as he quickly moved toward the phone.

"What are you guys freaking out about? She is a beautiful woman, who's going to say anything, have some fun." Rubin said excitedly.

Alejandro turned sharply to Rubin and firmly said "Don't ever let me hear you talk about one of the guest like that again, or I'll have your job. Now get out of here both of you," He then turned back to the phone.

Rubin and Bernard exited the office with disbelief of what they had just seen and heard. Once outside Bernard asked Rubin "What suddenly got into him? That's not like Alejandro."

"I don't know but if I was a guessing man, I would guess he knows more about that woman than he is saying," Rubin told Bernard with a serious look on his face. "I would watch what I said to him from now on about Miss Trina." Rubin said nodding his head front to back at the same time.

"Yeah, I think you're right." Bernard agreed.

"If I recall correctly, Alejandro's face turned upward every time her name was mentioned. I noticed it real quick. It's not everyday you see Alejandro act like a jealous school boy. It's been a few year since his last girl. Maybe that wild cat's bringing something out of him." Rubin said as he scratched his head.

Bernard quickly replied as they arrived at the hotel "I'm going to watch what I say about her to everyone," At the same time thinking to himself about what she had said to him earlier when he helped her mount Blackball.

Alejandro was just about to push the last button on the phone when Buzz came through the door.

"Hey man, the trail riders are coming in about fifteen minutes early," Buzz huffily told him.

Alejandro placed the phone head back down. "Uh oh," He exclaimed out loud.

Buzz turned swiftly, looked and asked, "What's wrong man?"

"I have to go now! Right now! There is a girl on that ride I cannot let see me. Bernard is already gone. I was just about to call for help. Can you cover for me Buzz?" Alejandro's words came out fast and clear.

Buzz smiled from ear to ear as he responded in a chuckle "Yeah man that will make two you owe me in one day. She must be some girl." He turned and headed for the door in smiling laughter.

"Thanks Buzz, I'm in your debt." Alejandro said with a sigh of relief. He hurried behind Buzz out the door but returned almost as fast as he had left and said, "I changed my mind Buzz. I'll greet her myself."

Buzz laughed until tears fell from his cheeks. While his mind peered over how Alejandro was acting. He was like a young boy finding his first piece. He hadn't seen him so interested in a woman in five years now. *"Alejandro's forgotten how to act"* He silently told himself.

CHAPTER FIVE

Buzz was smiling a huge grin when Trina's horse walked up to his stall.

"What's so funny?" She asked him eagerly.

"Oh, madam, nothing is funny." He told her still grinning.

"Did you enjoy your ride?" He quickly asked.

She looked puzzled at his answer, but quickly dismissed his reluctance to share his funny thoughts with her. She was in a hurry to get back to the hotel and wanted off the horse.

"If you can stop that stupid grinning long enough, I would like to get down from here." She rudely snapped at him.

Buzz now understood why Alejandro had wanted to take off so quick. This woman is outspoken, obviously spoiled and use to getting her way. This has to be the woman he is avoiding. She's beautiful and she comes across as being a very head strong stubborn woman. He laughed out loud as he thought, *She is just Alejandro's type.* Her words didn't bother him. He has been working the stables for ten years now, and he's seen and heard all kinds.

"Hey you, Mr. Grinner, I am the guest here. I'm ready to get down if you can hold your thoughts long enough to assist me," She sharply pointed out.

"Sorry madam," He kindly responded to her rudeness and then stepped aside as Alejandro stepped forward.

Trina reached to affix her foot safely into his hands to swing herself off the horse's back when she noticed the stable boy had changed to Alejandro.

"You keep turning up just about everywhere I go. What are you a jack of all trades or something?" she asked knowing she loved the idea of her assist coming from him.

Alejandro warmly smiled and locked his eyes on her face as he reached up and placed his large hands around Trina's waist lifting her and slowly sliding her down the side of the horse placing her safely onto the ground.

With both feet firmly on the ground she looked up at him and said, "Thank you." She then zestfully turned and scurried to catch the bus back to the hotel feeling warm inside from Alejandro's touch.

Once in her room, Trina quickly showered and dressed herself in a lavender Chiffon dress which free flowed around her hips. It was wide shouldered and sleeveless with a low dipping v neck in front and back. The lowness of the front left her mounded cleavage exposed to open view. Her smoothly tanned shoulders glistened like the glitter of gold. She peered at the delicate diamond framed watch on her wrist. Five minutes until Bernard was off work. She intended to use him to make Alejandro jealous at least she hoped it would work that way.

She walked over to the phone picked up the receiver and called to room service. "Yes, I want a bottle of your finest champagne and two glasses delivered to my room. I want Bernard to deliver it and don't expect him right back. I wish to speak with him." Trina quickly spit out the orders.

"Its five minutes until Bernard is off work madam, he would not have time to deliver. May I suggest another?" The clerk calmly asked Trina.

"No, I want Bernard to deliver. He can end his work on this delivery. He doesn't have to come back down to do so. All you have to do is send Bernard." Trina snapped her demands and hung up the receiver. She had full intentions of flirting with Bernard because she knew he would tell Alejandro she had. She hated using Bernard, but she had little over a week before her vacation was over and she would do whatever she had to do to get Alejandro's attention.

"Room service madam," Bernard's deepened voice rang out loudly.

Trina took the palms of her hands and lightly pushed upwards on the bottom of her soft blond curls. She pinched lightly at her cheeks as she moved towards the door. Slowly she reached and wrapped her petite hand around the glass knob of the door and pulled the door open.

She smiled as she said "Bernard, it's so nice to see you. Won't you come in?" She stood to the side of the door, tilted her head slightly, and floated her right arm in the air towards the inside.

Bernard drew a long breath and stepped inside carrying a large silver tray. On the tray were two etched crystal stemware glasses, a bucket of ice with a cooling bottle of Champaign inside. He walked over to the table and started to sit the tray down when Trina called to him.

"No not right there. Sit it on the table in front of the sofa," She quickly and eagerly told him.

Bernard turned and moved to the table in front of the sofa and sat the tray down. He then turned to Trina and asked "Can I open the bottle for you Miss—"

Trina cut him off and didn't let him finish his words as she quickly but elegantly flowed her body towards him. "Yes, please do." She said in a seductive voice.

Bernard rolled his eyes and tried to think of a best way out of this one. Trina was a beautiful woman and hard to turn down, but he had suspicions of how Alejandro was feeling about this woman. It was pretty oblivious from the way he was acting earlier. He wanted no part of it. He gently pulled the cork out, picked up one of the glasses and slowly poured.

"You do that so well." Trina said in a soft sexy voice from his side.

Bernard handed Trina the glass and said "Miss—"

She again cut him off. "One more glass for you and have a seat here on the sofa." She told him as she sat and pat next to her. She smiled up at him with big bright blue eyes.

Bernard's maleness kicked in and he almost forgot about Alejandro. He shook his head a bit to put his senses back where they should have stayed in the first place and said "Miss. I am not allowed to drink or mix with the guest. If there's nothing more I will be going."

"Nonsense your shift is over, now come on and take a seat," She sweetly said.

Bernard sighed and told Trina as he walked towards the door "No miss, it doesn't work that way. I am not allowed to mix with the guest if I want to keep my job." He reached the door, turned and gave Trina a firm serious eye to eye contact. He firmly said, "And I...want to keep my job." He opened the door and stepped out pulling it gently closed behind him not waiting for a reply.

Trina watched every move Bernard had made and when the door was closed all the way, she fell out laughing. Yes, Alejandro would hear about this. She was sure of it.

"Well, no need in wasting this pretty dress. I'll just go down to the pub where Alejandro will see me as well," she told herself aloud laughing all the way there.

She stepped inside the pub located just off the lobby of the hotel. The lights were low and the music billowing softly low. She scanned the darkened room and spotted Alejandro standing at the bar. She slipped quietly through the guest and behind Alejandro. She climbed up on the stool facing his back without him seeing her. She wanted him to turn into her face. She wanted him to notice her in a way that he would forever remember. She wanted to surprise him.

"Want me to—"The bartender started to ask when Trina put a finger to her lips and let a little air escape. She pointed towards the glass of wine the couple was having on the other side of her.

The bartender nodded his head in understanding and turned towards the other end. He returned in a short moment to Trina with a glass of chilled red wine.

She handed him a five dollar bill and shooed him with her hand gently floating.

He clearly winked at Trina and stepped away from the bar.

Trina sipped at the wine slowly while watching Alejandro as best she could without being to obvious. She would be ready to flaunt and bat her pleading eyes when he turned around. She twisted the stool back and forth making it squeak in hopes of irritating him into turning around.

"Nothing, he noticed nothing," She silently whispered to herself.

"What time are you going in the morning Alejandro?"Joanna softly asked.

Trina twisted her chair and stole a glance around Alejandro's side at the woman he was talking to. Fire formed flames in her eyes.

"Oh, it's going to be early Joe. So be ready by five, okay?" Alejandro told her with no hesitation.

"He's going off with her in the morning. I got to get out of here."Trina told herself.

She leaned in just a little bit further to see more of this woman that was getting Alejandro's attention. She leaned just a little bit too far and slipped off the stool falling into Alejandro's back pushing him forward. She fell to her knees on the hard cold floor with tears building in her eyes.

Alejandro caught his footing and turned just as Trina was coming up from her fall. Her tear filled eyes met his and projected a mirror of anger and hurt along with being embarrassed.

Alejandro reached for her arm grabbing hold to help her up and Trina jerked it away from him.

"Are you alright?" He aggravatingly asked her.

Trina shot lightning bolt glares into Alejandro's eyes, turned and ran out of the pub.

"Yeah, I'm okay." He replied in a rather low voice and sighing at the same time.

Joe took his hand and rubbed the back of it as she asked "Was that her?"

"What do you mean?" He quickly and sharply shot back at her.

"Oh, stop that. This is me, your sister you're talking to. I know you well and I saw that scene. She was jealous, it poured out of her eyes. The way she looked at you and then me and back to you. It was so obvious and it's obvious that you are concerned as well. Now tell me about it." Joe aggressively told Alejandro.

"No, it's not like that," He firmly said.

"Alejandro, look at me, come on look at me," Joe said as she turned him by his chin to face her. "I am very happy to see that you are getting interested in a lady. You can't go on not having what we all need. We all need somebody to share our life with. Just as we all need someone to love and someone to love us back. You have to stop believing that all relationships will be like your last was. I love you brother and I want to see you happy again. Will you talk to me, please? Let me help you understand." Joe said as tears fell from her cheeks.

Alejandro looked upon his sister as she spoke what he knew to be the truth but he didn't want to talk about it. "I love you too Joe, and it's time to go. Five comes early," He said sadly as he turned and walked away.

Joe stood and watched him as he disappeared across the room into the darkness.

Alejandro went out the door in the front lobby for a breath of fresh air and ended up walking all the way down to the beach. Much to his surprise he walked upon nobody other than Trina sitting on the water's edge crying. He wanted to reach out and hold her and tell her everything would be alright. But he himself

Nelda Sue

didn't understand or maybe he just didn't want to admit he did understand. He slowly approached her from behind softly calling her name over and over, "Trina…, Trina…, Trina…"

Suddenly she jumped up and turned facing him. "What are you doing here? Leave me alone," she yelled and started stumbling back towards the hotel with a vision of Alejandro and that woman in the pub together.

"Wait," he called out.

"Wait for what? What could you possibly have that I would want or need?" she asked through her tears. She wanted to wait and hear what he had to say but she couldn't. She couldn't take a chance on coming between him and that woman he was with earlier no matter how much she wanted to.

He didn't know why but her words ripped at his heart. He couldn't do anything but stand and watch her as she slowly walked away towards the hotel.

Joe took a seat at the bar and summoned for Vince by a wave of her hand. "Bring me a beer and a glass. I don't care what kind," She said frustrated.

Vince started pouring the beer in a glass in front of Joe. "What's wrong, you don't usually drink beer?" He asked as he started to wipe the condensed water from the bar counter.

"Oh, it's that brother of mine. He makes me so mad and he is so unhappy it just tears my heart out," She said in a whine.

"I saw that little happening just awhile ago. He likes that girl and she likes him too. It was easy to see," He told Joe capturing her full attention.

Joe quickly replied "Thank God, someone saw that other than me. I'm not crazy after all but he denies it to himself. He's so unhappy and has given his life to this job. I have to do something to help him see. I tried to get him to talk to me about it but he refused and walked away."

Vince took Joe's little hand into his looking into her eyes as he said "Miss Joanna don't let it worry you like this. Think about it.

56

She's interested in him and so is he in her. We saw that ourselves. It's been awhile since you seen Alejandro react like he just did, hasn't it? If it's meant to be with them two, it'll work it's self out."

Joe smiled up at Vince and that was thank you enough for him.

"Has anybody ever told you, you're too smart?" She softly asked him with a smirk on her face.

"Yeah Sweetheart, you just did," He said laughing out loud.

"Keep that up and you just might get my number one day," Joe almost seductively said and then blushed. "I have to go now, thank you for listening and making me feel better," She whispered as she stood from the stool.

"The pleasure is all mine Ms Joe and I'll take that number anytime you're ready to give it to me. I have a pen right here," He quickly replied not wanting to give her time to get away.

Joe smiled and took the pen from his hand and quickly wrote her cell number on a napkin stuffing it in his shirt pocket. She twirled around on one foot and gracefully left the pub.

Chapter Six

Alejandro lay tossing and turning on his usually comfortable bed. He couldn't get the look on Trina's face out of his mind.

"What did she think? Why did she act like that? She is so beautiful and fragile! Stop that Alejandro, all you do is think she, she, she and then you don't sleep. What's wrong with you? Get over it. You heard what she said. What could you possibly have that she would want or need." His mind just kept repeating these words over and over. He still couldn't stop thinking about Trina and her sad face with tear filled eyes. His heart ached at her pain and he didn't understand how this could be happening to him.

Trina lay curled in a ball on the end of the couch whimpering and sniffling with hurt embarrassment of her actions earlier in the evening.

"Why did you have to go to that stupid pub anyway? Why didn't you just stay here? Who was that girl with Alejandro? Was she his wife, his girlfriend, his fiancée, his lover? Who was she? I hate you Uncle George. This wouldn't have happened if you had sent someone else here. I told you I didn't want to come. Why couldn't you have listened to me for once?" Trina tossed these thoughts and words aloud back and forth, to and fro until she wore herself out completely and fell asleep without moving from the couch, or changing her clothes.

Vince cleaned the pub with a grin from ear to ear. He was happy he had finally gotten Joe's number. Something he had been trying to do for a long time. At least it seemed like a long three months to him, but he had it now and he was happy.

Joe fell off into her sleep smiling with visions of Vince dancing above her head and Alejandro with the strange lady hand in hand making her brother happy again.

"Joe, come on. It's time to go." Alejandro yelled as he loudly beat on the outside door. "Joe? Joe...Joanna. It's time to go," He continued to yell.

Joe jumped up out of her bed and flew to the door swinging it open.

"Alejandro, I'm so sorry. I'll be ready in just one minute." She told him almost out of breath.

"Hurry up. Where's your bag's at?" he asked.

"They are over by the chair." She yelled from the bedroom where she scurried around dressing.

"I'm taking them on down to the jeep. Hurry up and come on. I have to be back for work in two hours." He yelled towards the bedroom as he exited the door with her bags in hand.

Trina walked slowly across the lobby headed for the door when she looked up and saw Alejandro going out of it caring bags. She quickly moved behind the palm tree beside the door and watched through the window as Alejandro placed the bags in the back of his jeep. She had her eyes glued to what he was doing when her view was suddenly obstructed by that woman he was with in the pub. Trina ran her finger across the tear which rolled from the corner of her eye to her cheek. She watched the lady and Alejandro crawl into the jeep and drive away. Trina held her head up turning into the also emotional face of Jasper. When she saw him she couldn't hold it back any longer. She burst into hysterical tears and flung herself around his neck. He placed one arm around her waist and the other on her back where he patted her softly.

"Here now, I can't afford to be seen like this. Common, everything is going to be alright. I promise. Let's go get a cup of coffee and talk for a spell, my treat." Jasper very gently spoke into Trina's ear.

Trina pulled back from Jasper's grip, looked into his eyes with her big droopy red ones and nodded her head as she sniffled. Jasper took her by the hand leading her out to the front where he summoned for a cab. He opened the door and stepped to the side so Trina could get inside before him. She quickly sat down sideways and turned her body slowly sliding across the seat. Jasper got in and closed the door.

"Take us to Pepper's on Fifth Street," Jasper told the driver.

The short drive was speechless emotions as Trina dripped tears from her chin and whimpered the entire ride. Upon arriving, the driver pulled the car to the front entrance and stopped. Jasper opened the door, got out and offered Trina a hand. She took hold and slid across the seat exiting the cab. Once she was firm on her feet, Jasper turned and reached in his pants-pocket, pulled out a couple of bills paying the cab driver. He took Trina by the elbow and led her inside to a booth in the corner. She slid in on one side with him going to the adjacent.

"They have a fantastic custom made peanut butter coffee." He told Trina with a smile on his face. She gazed at him in amazement.

"Peanut...Butter?" She asked him dragging her words out.

Jasper laughed loudly and said "Yes, custom made just for me.

Best darn stuff this side of the earth. I tried to get them to sell it but they just won't listen to me."

Trina gave a small smile at Jasper.

"Was that a smile I seen on that pretty face?" He quickly asked her as he waved his hand in the air with a summons for the waitress.

"Yeah, I guess it was kind of one," Trina lowly spoke her words as the waitress approached.

Jasper looked up at the waitress and said "Two cup's of that fantastic peanut butter coffee and bring the little lady one of them there hot caramel buns."

"No, really...I couldn't—" She started to say and Jasper interrupted her.

"Yes, you can, your going to hurt my feelings," He told her and then turned to face the waitress again.

Jasper thought for a moment and said, "Heck, bring us each one of them there hot caramel buns."

The waitress nodded her head and left the two of them alone again.

"Now, what's a pretty little thing like yourself got to be so unhappy about?" He asked Trina with softness to his voice and taking hold of her hand.

Trina straightened herself and stared in a daze out the window. All she saw was yet another ladies body being hauled to an ambulance but paid no real attention to it this time. She had other things on her mind that was more important at the moment.

"That's okay little lady. Take your time. I have all day." Jasper said as he gently pat the back of her hand.

Trina turned facing Jasper and asked "What's a nice man like you doing working back in the woods on a riding trail?"

"Ah...Missy, there is nothing better than drinking in the beauty of Mother Nature. It's peaceful and completely relaxing. I love my job little lady." He said with passion expressed in his words. Trina saw that passion in his eyes and knew that Jasper was being completely honest with her. His facial expressions showed his love for nature and she felt completely relaxed at that moment.

"Here we go." The waitress said as she sat in front of Trina a steaming cup of coffee and a hot caramel bun. She then placed the same in front of Jasper.

"Thank you." Trina said looking up at her.

"Your welcome and enjoy." The lady said as she turned and walked away.

"Be careful, I think it's hot." Jasper teasingly told Trina.

Trina smiled and said "Thank you Jasper. This thing smells absolutely delicious."

"It's just what old Jasper prescribes to put a happy face on the little lady." He said with a spring to his voice.

Trina picked the cup up and softly blew to cool the coffee down some. She moved the edge of the cup to her ready parted lips and sipped a small taste of it.

"Mm...This is good. I have to admit. I didn't think it would be." She told Jasper.

"I'll never cease to amaze you, Missy. I like to live life to its fullest and enjoy the strangest things, but most of all I don't like seeing a beauty like you not smiling." Jasper sincerely spoke.

"I'm here with you. My shoulder is big and I got some big ears, see them?" He asked as he pointed at the side of his head.

Trina smiled a little bigger smile at Jasper.

"You're a wonderful funny guy Jasper. Were you ever in love or married?" Trina asked him in a soft voice.

"Alright now, my love life is not the topic here little lady. Tell me what's going on in that pretty little head of yours and start eating that caramel bun before it gets cold." Jasper grinned and told Trina.

Trina picked up the napkin rolled silverware and removed the fork. She pricked a small piece of the bun off and carefully placed it in her mouth. She chewed slowly tasting and enjoying the soft hot caramel moistness.

"This is really good." She said licking her finger from where she had caught the caramel when it dripped from the fork.

"Trina, talk to me. Tell old Jasper what's bothering you. It'll clear your mind where you can think straight. It will help you and I want to help you if I can." Jasper said with a caring look on his face.

Trina looked down at the table for a moment before she spoke. "I lost my parents both at the same time in an auto accident five years ago..." She started speaking.

"Oh honey, I am so sorry to hear that." Jasper interrupted to say.

"I too died inside. I was dating someone who I loved very much at the time. We had been dating for two years. The week after losing my parents, he told me he was already married." Trina sadly told Jasper as the tears whaled up in her eyes.

Jasper repositioned himself and leaned in over the table sure to not miss a word Trina was saying. "Go on sweetie." He gently told her.

Trina drew in a long breath and continued with her story to Jasper. "After the loss of all three so close together, I somehow changed. I became self centered, self absorbed and I gave my life to my job." She said as the tears ran from her eyes.

Jasper took from his shirt pocket a handkerchief and handed it to Trina. She accepted it and wiped her tears away.

"Thank you." She finally said to Jasper.

"My pleasure sweetheart, please continue." He carefully expelled his words.

"I didn't want any relationship with anyone. I just wanted to live my life independently and relationship free after all that happened. I couldn't love like that and lose again. So the best answer was to shut myself out. Completely out, from the rest of the world." She slowly told him. Trina picked up her cup of coffee and took a small drink to swallow the knot now developed in her throat.

"I closed myself off so far I believed my feelings to be true. I didn't realize how wrong I was for all the times I did the same thing to someone else because of it. I didn't realize that until now." Trina whimpered as she told her story.

Jasper placed his hand on his chin and propped his elbow on the table top watching and listening to Trina closely.

"I am just being silly." She finally continued to say.

"Nonsense, don't ever say that sweetie. If there is something that hurts you, it's not silly, it's important. Please tell me honey." Jasper told Trina.

Trina fumbled her cup of coffee back and forth one hand to the other. "Do you believe in love at first sight Jasper?" She softly asked him.

"Oh yes sweetie. There is nothing more beautiful than the realization of love at first sight." He said with a grin on his face.

Trina lowered her eyes to the cup in hand. Stared inside for a couple of moments and slowly raised her watering eyes back up to meet Jasper's. "Alejandro did something to me. When I first saw him I felt it and as time has gone on day after day I keep having some kind of experience or meet and greet with him. I saw him last night at the pub with a pretty girl. Then I saw him again this morning getting into his jeep with the same girl and drove away." Trina carefully chose her words and spoke softly. "I felt like my heart had been ripped right out of my chest. I don't know why. I know very little about him. The only thing I can believe is love at first sight with a few greet pushers in between." She finally finished her sentence. Trina again picked up her cup and took a small drink.

"But that is beautiful sweetie. Have you told him how you feel about him?" Jasper asked.

"No and I never will." She quickly responded.

"Why?" Jasper asked.

"He has showed no interest in me at all. He obviously has someone and I would not do anything to interfere with that." She told Jasper. "You have to promise me Jasper that you will not say a word about this to him. I'll be leaving in a week. Tomorrow I'm going for the dirt bike ride. I still have not taken the hot air balloon ride yet and..." She eagerly spoke looking Jasper in the eyes.

"Hold on, hold on." Jasper managed to get his words out. "It sounds like your planning all you can to avoid him. I understand the not wanting to interfere, but honey you have to have some peace with yourself about this. Your locking it up inside won't give you that peace. I'm no expert here but I know you can't have it being bottled up." Jasper said as he took Trina's hand in his. "Everything we speak about is forgotten as fast as it's said when it comes to repeating it. You can trust me sweetie. I'm here to listen and help if I can." Jasper continued to say as he gently squeezed her hand.

"Then I expect all will be kept in confidence no matter what my decision is." She quickly replied to him.

"It's no matter what you decide little lady. I'll stand by your decision." He told her with care.

"Good, then we are in agreement. I will not tell him anything. I will return home with him being none the wiser. But...." She was hesitant.

"Yes, but what?" Jasper asked.

"Jasper, if I give you my number will you keep me informed on how Alejandro is doing? You can call me collect anytime." She pleadingly asked him.

"I don't think that's the thing to do but if that's what you want, then that's what you get sweetie. Now, do you feel better?" He asked.

Trina wrote her name and number on a napkin and gave it to Jasper smiling.

"Yes, I do. You're amazing. Did you know that?" She asked him.

"I think I need to let you in on a little secret I have been keeping," he said capturing her full attention.

"What," she asked.

"I know your uncle George. We are good friends. Have been for years and when you accepted to come here he called me up asking me to keep an eye on you. Just to make sure you stayed safe. Your being in a strange place and all I told him I would be happy to. So you see I'm your friend always. I hope you can understand my keeping quiet about it," he told her as his hand continued to lie atop of her.

"Oh my uncle George, I am going to really bash him when I see him. I don't know if I will ever forgive him or not for this. First he sends me on a wild story chase just to run into a man he doesn't know and then I find out there is one he does know which he has watching over me. He can infuriate me sometime," she angrily said.

Jasper laughed out loud and said, "George loves you girl. He just wants to see you happy. He made a promise to his brother that he would take care of you and ole George will do what he says. Don't be too rough on him."

"In the end I probably won't. It might be different if he was sitting right here now but since he's not I have time to cool off," she replied with a little grin behind it.

"Ah, let's eat these here buns now and talk about something else." He quickly said trying to change the subject.

Trina and her newfound friend ate their buns and drank their coffee in projected sovereign.

CHAPTER SEVEN

"Hey, watch out for those holes." Joe hysterically yelled as she straightened herself up in the seat of Alejandro's jeep. "I smacked the glass in the door with my forehead when the jeep hit that hole." She told Alejandro as she gently rubbed her fingers across her head.

"Sorry sis, couldn't help it. Are you alright?" He cut his words short in reply to ask.

"Yeah, I'm okay but your not. What's your big rush anyway? Are you afraid you're going to miss seeing that lady from last night? Oh, yea, I saw it and so did Vince. You like her and denying it, just like she is." Joe exploded her feelings without any hesitation and then settled leaning back against the door to face Alejandro. She sat and watched his facial expressions which never changed. Joe sighed deeply and loudly as she asks "That's it? You're not going to say anything at all?"

Alejandro remained quiet as he pulled the jeep into the airport, where he would let Joe out. She was going to New York to take care of some business and wouldn't be back before Trina left, so he felt no danger and let his sister get her feelings out in the open as he pulled the jeep up next to the front door entrance. He got out and walked to the back to get Joe's bags out. Joe came around the side of the jeep reached and grabbed the bags from his hands and turned briskly moving away. He placed his hands on his hips and watched his sister knowing she was mad and he knew she would come back.

Joe suddenly made a quick turn and swiftly walked up to Alejandro pointing her finger at him. "You know life's too short to live with this egotistical stubborn attitude of yours. Do you know what a country girl like her would call you?" Joe angrily snarled her words at him.

"No, but I'm sure you're going to tell me." Alejandro said with a little bit of a grin on his face.

"Oh...you're impossible!" Joe angrily said as she twirled to walk off again. This time she stopped after taking six steps and turned to face him once again. "Butt, that's what. She would call you a Butt and do you know what a country girl's definition of a butt is? Of course you don't or you wouldn't have that disgusting smirk on your face. Why don't you think about that?" Joe yelled at Alejandro and started her brisk walk away again.

Alejandro shifted his position and got ready for one more attack from Joe. He knew it was coming.

Joe turned as Alejandro had suspected and zestfully flew across the parking lot screaming "Okay, I'll tell you. I won't make you have to use your brain for anything. There's no time for that." She said as she arrived in front of him one more time. "That girl's definition of a Butt is two cheeks wrapped around an asshole. If that's not enough said then I can't help you." Joe angrily said loudly.

Alejandro fell out laughing at his sister but he wasn't the only one. The entire surrounding area was full of folks watching, listening and now laughing. But Alejandro was the one who cared. He reached out and pulled Joe to him in a big bear embrace.

"I love you sis. I'm okay, really, don't worry. Now you go take care of your business and things will be just fine." Alejandro spoke while securely hugging his sister.

"I just want to see you happy, that's all. When I saw the reactions the two of you gave to one another...well, I guess I just felt hope for your happiness." She tearfully and softly spoke.

"I know, but you need to worry about you. I'm okay with the way I am." Alejandro firmly said pulling Joe back to look at her.

"I love you, brother." Joe softly said.

Alejandro winked at her and said "You better get going."

Joe disappeared in the now crowded parking lot of the airport and Alejandro got back into the jeep and headed towards the hotel. He was just a short distance down the road before he lost himself in thoughts of what his sister had said to him. He knew she was right. He just wasn't ready for a relationship with anyone. Or was he? Visions of Trina flashed before him. The glance she gave him when she first arrived. The look she had in her face when she had fallen to the floor after running into him. The embarrassment she showed when he caught her on the beach with her hand inside her top. Her happiness he seen at the dolphin park which brightened up his day and the hurt scared look in her eye at the pub. Alejandro's heart begin to beat faster and palpitate in his chest just thinking of the hurt he saw in Trina was almost enough to make him forget about his job and oath for no more relationships. There was something about her he just couldn't quite place what it was.

"A woman like that would never go for a cabana boy anyway." Alejandro told himself out loud. He remained self questionable for the rest of the ride back to the hotel. Alejandro went straight to the pub once inside the lobby. He took a seat at the bar and called his order to Vince. "Bring me a beer and a glass."

Vince laughed a little and said "Let me guess, it don't matter what kind, right?"

"That's right." Alejandro shot back at Vince.

Vince reached into the cooler and pulled out a long neck, grabbed a glass and took them to Alejandro laughing all the way.

"What's so damn funny?" Alejandro demanded to know.

"Like sister, like brother." Vince said chuckling out loudly.

Alejandro thought of Joe and started laughing with Vince. "Yep, that's some sister I got there." He told Vince with smile thinking about Joe's butt comment.

"You know Alejandro, I have intentions towards her." Vince said as he leaned down to prop himself on the bar.

Alejandro stopped laughing and focused on Vince and then asked "What does Joe think about that?"

"Nothing, I don't believe." Vince said.

Alejandro looked at Vince like he was crazy and said "Then your intentions are futile."

Vince started laughing again and told him "She doesn't know it. That's why I said nothing but..."

"But what, there are no buts." Alejandro quickly said.

"I've been interested in her for months and she finally gave me her cell number last night. She's some little gal." Vince said with a big smile on his face.

Alejandro smiled as well and said "Yes she is."

"Yeah, now tell your bartender about Madam Trina." Vince asked sticking his foot in the door as quick as he saw it cracked.

"She's some little gal Vince. Something else she is also." Alejandro said as he faded off towards the crowd.

"Hey, Alejandro, come back here." Vince yelled. Alejandro shook his head a little and returned to the bar.

"What can I get you Jasper?" Vince asked as he was taking a seat.

"Good evening." Jasper said nodding his head first to Vince then Alejandro.

"We have a beer glass don't care what kind special." Vince told Jasper laughing.

"That sounds good to me, Vince. Those riding trails were hot today. I'm thirsty." Jasper said as he pulled his cowboy hat and gloves off placing them in the seat next to him. Vince stepped to the other end of the bar and retrieved another long neck and glass. He returned with it quickly setting them before Jasper.

Jasper tilted the glass and poured the beer in slowly. When the glass was half full he stopped pouring and turned it up downing every drop. He sat the glass down and was about to pour the rest of the beer in when he was interrupted by Alejandro.

"Hey Jasper, your phone is ringing man." Alejandro told him pointing to Jasper's side at his cell phone. Jasper reached and pulled his phone from the holder attached to his belt.

"Hello." Jasper answered.

"George, how are you doing?" Jasper asked.

Vince and Alejandro just looked at one another and waited for him to get off the phone before talking more. They couldn't help but hear what Jasper was saying but tried to not pay attention.

"Ah, Madam Trina, she's a beautiful young woman George." Jasper sincerely spoke. Alejandro was the first to glare at Jasper when he heard Trina's name called. Vince was right behind him.

"Who's George?" Alejandro asked Vince.

"I don't know." Vince replied.

"She's okay, everything looks positive from this end. You may not get a story out of this trip though." Jasper continued to tell George who was a stranger to Alejandro and Vince. The two of them looked at each other with raised eyebrows of dismay.

"Story?" Alejandro asked Vince as he only raised his shoulders in reply as if he didn't know.

"Alright George, stay in touch." Jasper said and hung up the phone.

"Okay Jasper you can tell us..." Alejandro started. "Yeah, tell us." Vince finished.

Jasper wiped his brow and picked up his beer, poured the remainder in the glass and turned it up. He didn't stop until it was all gone. He fixed his eyes on Alejandro first and foremost for the longest and then Vince.

"You boys have a good night." Jasper said and left the pub with no further words exchanged.

Alejandro slapped the bar top and loudly asked "Why does everybody I see and hear talk about Trina? Why does she just keep showing up?"

"Oh, hey man, take it easy. There's a reason and you'll find it." Vince told Alejandro now with no doubt's that he was in love with Trina and in love with an almost stranger. He knew that was bothering Alejandro and didn't push it any further.

Alejandro stood as he said "Thanks man, I'm going to bed. Talk later." Then he swiftly took off.

Vince watched Alejandro disappear and almost felt the pain he was seeing in him. He was having a hard time with this Trina girl and Vince would be sensitive to the subject from now on unless Alejandro brings her up himself. Alejandro hadn't been gone fifteen minutes when Trina came in and took a seat at the bar.

"Beer, glass and it don't matter what kind. Am I right?" Vince asked her with a huge grin on his face. Trina just sat and watched him only nodding her head as if nothing did matter.

"Yeah...right...you got it." He said under his breath. Vince then started to sing out loud. "Confession day in the form of a circle..." He repeated the line over and over as he retrieved the beer and glass. "Here you go lady." He said almost sympathetically as he sat the glass down in front of Trina. She watched speechless as Vince poured the unknown beer into the fragile glass. "You know, this has been the favorite order for the last two days." Vince smiled as he told Trina.

"What has?" she quickly asked.

"Ah, the famous glass with an unknown beer," he said, grinning from ear to ear.

"Oh." Trina said as if she had no interest.

Vince watched Trina's reactions looking for the right moment to bring Alejandro up. He was curious, and he wanted to see what kind of disturbance he could stir up by letting her hear his name. "Yeah, there was a young lady and that head cabana boy, what's his name..." Vince hesitated. Trina turned her eyes quickly to his face straight into his eyes. Vince didn't have to go any further. He had found out what he wanted to know but he would go on anyway. "Alejandro, that's it, that's his name. He had the same thing you're having now. Yeah, it's been the special order tonight too." Vince said bothered.

Trina's mind started running in every which direction with wonder. Vince could see it in her face but he kept quite and kept right on riding it out. He was waiting to see if she would ask anything about Alejandro.

Trina picked up the glass and took a big gulp. She then turned to Vince and said "You really should get a new special. Good night!" She threw a five dollar bill on the counter and turned briskly walking away.

CHAPTER EIGHT

Outside the pub, Trina stopped and fell back against the wall, catching herself with the back of her hands. She then put a hand to her forehead and vigorously rubbed back and forth.

"Who is that woman?" she angrily asked herself. She opened her closed eyes and turned into the face of Alejandro. She sucked in a deep breath quickly and said, "Don't do that, you scared me." Then she stepped to the side of him in attempt to pass him by.

Alejandro reached and took her by the upper arm and held her back. She turned her head to face him and fell into a trance lost in the pools of his darkened eyes. "Madam Trina." Alejandro softly whispered her name.

Trina's insides started to burn with want of this man wrapped around her life like a safe with no combination. Her heart fluttered her eyes shown mirrors of his reflection. Then she thought about the woman she had seen him with and leaving with. She jerked her arm free and started walking small steps backwards never taking her eyes off Alejandro. Tear's built with every step she made. It took all the strength she could find to turn and swiftly move up the stairwell and out of sight.

Alejandro remained standing and watching for several minutes after Trina disappeared at the top of the stairs. His heart was aching in want of her. He didn't understand why, but he had given it a chance like his sister had told him. Trina had rejected him and now he could get on with his life without worry of her. He would put her out of mind and stay away from her if he had to call into work to do so.

Trina returned to her room and quickly closed the door behind her. She went to the bar and poured herself a brandy. She took a seat on the couch and sipped her drink wondering what her next move should be. She could still see Alejandro looking into her very own eyes. Tears dripped and she wiped over and over again. She had to forget him. She had to think of something else. It's another week before her return flight home. She still hadn't been on the bike trail ride or the hot air balloon tour either but...what if he was working one of them? "I can just take a walk around the beach on my own tomorrow. That way I can be sure and avoid Alejandro." She tearfully decided and told herself aloud. Feeling good about her decision for the next day's activities she took herself off to bed without any further hesitation.

While back at the pub Vince was grinning and laughing out loud to himself as he made a few final cleaning efforts for the night. "What a day!" He said aloud. "I don't know if I could handle another Alejandro attack." He continued to tell himself smiling and laughing. "Ah...but my Joe was the best of all." His smile turned innocent as the desirable words softly slipped through his lips. He then hurried himself to his room to bed never letting Joe's image leave his mind or his heart.

Morning brought Trina out of bed with swollen eyes from crying herself to sleep the previous night. She washed her face in cold water before stepping into the shower. She felt the tears start building as her thoughts of Alejandro tried to overcome her mind completely. She stood under the cold running water of the shower in a daze as the tears rolled down her cheeks.

"What am I going to do?" She sadly asked herself. She blankly stared at a white wall while standing under the running shower water. Her thoughts zoned out so far she didn't realize it was cold. Goose bumps formed over her and she stood staring without giving any recognition to how cold it was. Alejandro enveloped her entire mind and body. It was as if he had in some way hypnotized her. She was desperately searching through out her mind for the right answer to her acquired problem when it hit her like a light being turned on for the very first time.

"Go home early and get away from him. Spend the rest of your time by yourself. Find a happy medium with these messed up feelings you're having," she hurtfully said to herself. She would make the arrangements for the return trip today and she would say good bye to Jasper. Feeling content with her decision Trina feverishly finished her shower without paying any attention to the coldness of the water. She quickly dressed in tight fitting jeans, a dark blue tank top and slid her tiny feet into a pair of black air-walks. She brushed her hair and let it hang loosely on her shoulders and then grabbed her bag and headed out the door.

Trina didn't slow down to see who was in the lobby. When she reached the bottom of the stairs she flew out the front walk entrance just as the car pulled up and stopped. She grabbed the handle of the back door and jumped in giving order's to take her to the airport.

The gentleman in the driver's seat looked through the rear view mirror and smiled saying "Yes, miss." He then put the car into gear and drove away from the curb. He recognized her but she didn't realize it was Donald the guy whose beach ball had whacked her in the head earlier in the week.

"My name is Donald Dennison." He said to Trina through the rear view mirror. He was wondering if she would notice if he spoke but she still paid no attention. She seemed to be focused on something she wasn't revealing.

"Yea okay, just hurry and get me to the airport and when we get there, wait for me." She hastily replied to him.

"I'm driving as fast as I can." Donald jokingly said.

Trina sighing said "Well go faster. I need to get there soon."

"Are you late for a flight?" He asked anxiously waiting her reply because if she was he wasn't going to take her to the airport.

"No, I want to make flight arrangement hopefully for this afternoon." She eagerly told him. "I figure the earlier I get there the better my chances of getting one that soon." She continued to tell Donald still without looking up at him.

He smiled and softly said "I don't think I want to go so far as getting a speeding ticket for you. I think a ride to the airport is nice enough." He then turned the car into the main drive of the front entrance. He brought the car to a stop in front of the ticket depot. He got out and opened the back door for Trina to vacate his car.

"Here we go Miss, safe and sound at the airport." He told her as she swung her feet out of the car.

Once safely standing Trina reached for her bag from her side to pay telling Donald "Stay right here and wait for me. I will be right back as soon as I can get the flight scheduled." Donald pushed Trina's hand's from her bag and said "Miss, I gave you a ride because you seemed like you was in desperate need. I did it out of the kindness of my heart. I don't want your money, you keep it, buy yourself something nice. I will get my reward."

"What do you mean?" Trina frustrated asked him and at that moment realized who it was. "You're that beach bum whose ball hit me in the head the other day." She stood staring at him with her mouth half way hung open.

"Yes Madam, I'm not a cab service. You got into my car. You never asked nor did you see that I was not driving a cab. I went along because you seemed desperate." He firmly and kindly told Trina. "Now I'll wait on you if you want me to, but I don't want you treating me like I'm a service. I did what I did because I'm a caring man. I'd thank you kindly to take me that way too." Donald continued telling her.

Trina was at a loss for words. She was shocked at her actions. How could she have been so stupid? Her body began to shiver as if she was freezing and then she started sneezing repeatedly.

Donald pulled a handkerchief from his back pocket and handed it to her as he said "Bless you."

"Thank you and I am very sorry for this. I guess I was just not paying attention. I don't know what to say except forgive me." She embarrassingly spoke softly.

"Na, don't you worry about it at all. You looked like you needed a friend and I think I'm pretty good at it. I'll wait for you right here. Now, you go on and take care of your business. I'll be here. Besides I told you I would get my reward." Donald told Trina mentioning his reward again and then asking, "May I know your name, madam?"

She smiled again and said "Trina, my name is Trina and I will be back shortly."

"Very well Miss Trina. Donald will be here waiting." He said grinning from ear to ear while pointing toward the entrance.

Trina laughed and rushed inside to the counter. Out of breath she told the clerk "I want a one way flight for this afternoon for Butter Wing Wisconsin."

"I'm sorry madam, but there are no flights scheduling for two more days. I can set you up with one for then if you would like." He told Trina trying to push the flight for another day.

"Two days! Why?" She asked him.

"There is some work being done on the runway. It's going to be two more days before it is finished and flights resume regular schedule." He once again told her.

She frowned and asked "You mean I am stuck here even if I don't want to be?"

"I'm afraid that would seem so Miss." He said with an apologetic face. "Unless you..." His words faded out as Trina drastically turned and hurried back outside where Donald awaits her.

Donald had let his thoughts run wild while waiting on Trina to return. He was happy she had climbed into his car thinking it a cab. This gave him the chance to get to know her and her to know him a bit better. He thought she was a beautiful woman and that was something he needed in his life. He leaned back in the seat and rested his head staring up at the roof of the car. He sat quietly and soon closed his eyes. His thoughts of a woman turned into thoughts of his mother who he hated because she was mean and abusive to him when he was a young man living at home. She ragged him and made fun of him because he was a hefty young boy. She called him names and told him how he would never have a woman in his life. Especially a woman who had the looks of Trina! He had left home at the age of seventeen and struggled living in the streets of a town called 'Straight Arrow' out of Arizona. He found the street living easier than the living in the same house with his mean mother or listening to the tune she whistled all the time. He hated it too and now it's stuck in his head and he'll never forget it. He moved to the island three years ago and made a new life for himself but for some reason he hadn't managed to find the right woman to become his bride yet. He had encountered several but he couldn't really remember what had happened. Thoughts of his mother seem to always barge in when he tried to remember blocking his memory. Donald repositioned himself and said aloud in a hateful tone, "Look at me now my dear mother."

Trina brought Donald to an upright position when she suddenly opened the door saying, "Two days they are going to be working on the runway and I can't get a flight out for that long. I may as well just wait until my regular scheduled flight to go." Trina frustrated told Donald upon her return.

"Is that so bad?" He asked with a grin.

Trina turned and looked at Donald with a blank stare. The thought of what he said threw her into thoughts of having to avoid Alejandro that much longer and that terrified her.

"Are you alright Trina?" Donald asked as if he was concerned.

Trina sighed and said "Yes, I'm okay. I need to be getting back to the hotel."

"You turned pale and scared me. I thought you were going to pass out or something." He quickly replied in a seductive tone.

"I'll be fine after I eat something." Trina told Donald with a forced smile on her face. He held the door of the car open for her, and she got in with no more words spoken. Donald walked around and placed himself in the driver's seat beside her. He started up and drove to a nearby diner that usually had quite booth's available.

"Then let me buy you some lunch," he said and quickly opened the door not waiting for a reply from Trina. He walked around and opened her door then stepped to the side to allow her room to get out.

"I really need to be getting back to the hotel. I can walk from here." she said from sticking her head out of the car before turning and sticking her legs out to get out.

"No, no," he quickly said. "I can take you back to the hotel." He darted around the car crawling back in. "We'll go right now."

Trina watched and listened to what Donald was saying before returning straight into the seat and pulling the door closed.

Donald put the car in drive and pulled away from the curb.

CHAPTER NINE

"Afternoon, Alejandro." Max said as he entered the lobby of the hotel.

"Hey Max, how's it going?" He replied in a low voice.

"Ah, it's not too bad of a day. What are you fixing to be doing now?" Max asked puzzled.

"I've took the afternoon off Max. Don't you remember? I'm going to spend some time alone this evening. I'm on my way out right now. See you later." Alejandro said as he exited the front door.

Max stood and watched as Alejandro disappeared into the blue yonder of the beach. He had hoped to have a talk with him. He knew Alejandro was hurting and he wanted to offer his ear. Max had known his family for some years and thought maybe he could get Alejandro to trust in him enough to confide. Then maybe, just maybe he could see what path he needed to take and find some reassured comfort with whatever his feelings are.

"I'll just have to try another time." Max told himself as he went on about his business.

Alejandro walked along the warm waters edge of the far end of the beach. The end where nobody played, nobody swam and there would be nobody to bother him. He walked and he talked to himself, then walked and talked some more until he noticed that he had walked all the way into town.

"Oh, well hell." He said to himself as he looked around realizing where he was. "How did I get here?" He asked himself aloud and then thought. "Oh, it's that woman! Somehow she's got not only into my head, but my heart as well!" He aggravatingly said aloud. Loud enough that folks on the street stopped to take a second look at him.

A little old lady sitting on a nearby bench was the only one of all whom was around which spoke. "Go tell her young man." The little lady said smiling from ear to ear as she spoke.

Alejandro smiled at the little lady and said "Thank you, madam." Then he wondered off down the busy street trying to forget all which troubled him. He remembered the Plantation tour in the form of a buggy ride, on the south side of town and thought it sounded like a peaceful thing to do so he headed in the direction. The streets were very busy and he had to jigsaw his way through the crowd. He passed through the middle of a young couple arguing over their money. Young teenage kids on skate boards and bicycles and woman with their arms loaded with packages and bags. He bumped into someone with almost every step he made until finally he made it to the loading site of the tour.

Alejandro purchased his ticket in silence wishing Trina was there with him. He then took slow steps to the loading zone. The buggy was a large white open topped carriage with gold trimmings. The seats were placed to each end and covered in button tacked black leather. The coachman's seat sat high above the passenger seats. The carriage was to be pulled by five beautiful white Arabian horses. He admired the beauty of all before his eyes as he climbed on board the carriage. The tour would take the site seeing searcher's through an old fabricated plantation with the house of the land built to what the original beauty was. This was not the first time he had devoured this beauty nor would it be the last. He was sure of that.

The coachman yelled out "Lets go." and snapped the reins to the side of the horses. The carriage tugged, jerked and moved forward.

Alejandro listened to the other passengers talking among themselves. He didn't know how they could even understand one another. They were all talking at the same time and nobody was listening to anybody. He did hear something about some young lady in some diner somewhere which caught his attention but he couldn't hear all the two ladies were saying and didn't want to ask so he turned his attention to the views coming up instead.

The carriage was entering through a set of large white gates which lead into the fenced duplicated grounds. The young couple which sat across the carriage arm in arm started awing the beauty of the large oak lined drive. Alejandro smiled at the young love that sparkled between them and thought of Trina. He became impatient and jittery every time he thought about her.

He asked himself "Why, why can't I get her out of my head?" He twisted and turned in the carriage seat as if it was on fire. All the other passengers had stopped talking and were watching him. He hadn't noticed any of them. By the time he did, the coachman had started talking again.

"Welcome to the best fabricated Plantation tour you will ever see. The beauty alone will captivate you, but the history will throw you into empathic amazement. I am Juan and I will be telling you some of the known history. Obviously there is way more than I can tell you on this tour. Pamphlet's are available at the end of the tour." Juan's words were full of passion and touched Alejandro's feminine side, but he would never admit to it.

"Make yourself comfortable and get ready for an amazing tour of knowledge." Juan said and he took a moment to draw air into his lungs before continuing with his speech.

"Beautiful large Oak lined drives are not uncommon. Many of the Plantations have them. Much like this one we are traveling on. It's a half moon buggy trail with the large Oak's lining all the way around. It's just as it was in the era. Many folks think the plantations were cotton fields and that's all but that is in-correct the plantations were many other things and I am about to show you some of those things," he loudly said over his shoulder.

"They raise poultry just as many folks do these days. They have built and maintained a hen house to raise the chicken which they eat and they preserve all their meat in smokehouses they build themselves. The barn houses work animals, dairy cows and stables for their thoroughbreds. It also houses their tools and grain." Juan spoke loudly and clear so nobody would miss a word he was saying.

"This is just beautiful." The young couple said at the same time and then gazed at each other in astonishment.

Alejandro smiled at their loving sight.

"The workshops built near the barnyard are where the slave's craft horseshoes for their Master's thoroughbreds. Big barrels for storing things and the furniture the Master and his family enjoy. The female slaves hand weaves the cloth to be used on the plantation in these workshops as well. The masters of the slaves or the overseer appointed by the master see to it that the slaves cultivate gardens with ample of herbs and vegetables. As you can see to the right there is nothing about the vegetable gardens lacking.

Some of the larger plantations have a school for the white children while the slave's children slave and get a hand's on education of how to work.

The kitchen structures are almost all separated from the Big House, the planter's main housing mansion." The older coachman drew a long breath as he pulled the carriage up in front of a huge three story mansion before he started speaking again.

It was clear Juan knew what he was talking about. He was a new man and Alejandro was very much impressed.

Juan began speaking loudly once again "The mansion reflects the wealth of the planter family. In this three story mansion the front porch leads into a wide entrance hall which leads into a large dinning room, a parlor, sitting rooms and a library. The house is not open for entrance at this time due to some repairs on the spiral staircase. It will open soon for all to enjoy. I'll do my best to explain it to its fullest exquisite taste. The mansion is where the planter displays his wealth with imported artwork and European furnishings. Comfortable and luxurious decor compliments the upper floors. The bedrooms are not only where the Planter's family sleeps warm and snuggly but so do guest of other Plantation owners." Juan paused to breath for a moment.

Alejandro was wishing Trina was here with him. He thought she would enjoy this tour and the new guide was very wise. So he was sure she would have loved it. However he wasn't sure of how he knew she would. He just felt it.

Juan started speaking again and drawn Alejandro's attention back to subject at hand. He spoke loudly so all could hear "The uppermost floor is where you will find the nurseries. The servant stairs lead up from the back of the mansion and the slave women take care of the planter's children. It would appear to me the slaves would know more about the planter's children than the planter's themselves do." Juan's words came sadly and softly to an end as he stood and turned facing the mansion.

"Here is the centerpiece, ladies and gentlemen, of the entire plantation." He held his arms open wide as if measuring from one end of the mansion to the other. The passenger's all watched wide eyed and full of anticipation of the next words coming from this man's mouth. Juan stood and eagerly searched around the grounds of the house with wide passionate eyes. Not saying a word he admired the beauty which was displayed before him and detested the activities that took place in such a glorious era. Alejandro watched and listened to Juan in the amazement which he had spoken of at the start of the tour.

Juan sighed empathetically sadly before he spoke again. "Note the formal flower gardens which encircle the entire home. Yep, ladies and gents there is nothing the slaves can't make stunning with their blistered worn-out hands.

The office attached to the back side of the mansion is for the Planter or the overseer, so the slaves can be monitored closely. The slave's cabins are built not too far from the main house either. Never out of the monitoring zone. They are decorated with whatever they could manage to get and be allowed to have. Many of the cabins have dirt floors and box furniture. The economic study done indicates that less than twenty five percent of planter's employs white overseers or supervisors for slave labor and the overseers live in a modest home on the grounds in case of the absentee of the planter. So the slaves are always under some kind of supervision." Juan hung his head as if he was in prayer. His chest rose and fell as if he was sighing sadly. After a few moments of silence he began to speak again and Alejandro listened up.

"Not all plantations contain all the elements you see here. The crucial components are that of the master's home and the slave's residence. It's the different status that reflects the difference between the black and white worlds on the plantations." Juan turned and once again took a seat. "Let's go." He spoke to the horses and the carriage quickly urged forward. "I'm not going to go into the war. You'll find the pamphlets I spoke of earlier at the end of this tour which will tell all about it. Pamphlet's with stories that will intrigue you. So I'm just going to move right along.

Of the Southern families, almost a third of them own slaves! The capital value of slaves is greater than the value of the land. Slave auctions often break up the black families. Do you folks think you could handle being broke up from your family?" Juan quickly threw in a piece of his own two cent's as he often did and did not wait for any replies. "Yeah, slaves are known as res the Roman legal code, which stands for movable property." Juan said in aggravation.

Alejandro watched him in amazement. He was really getting into the story he told as if it was taking place present day.

Alejandro had never seen a guide of such brilliance. "Where are you Trina? You're missing out on some wonderful history." He said aloud in long drawn out words.

"Yes she is." The young man across from him replied while his wife smiled hugely at him.

Alejandro grinned again in amusement of his self and said "Ah, just lost in thought." He then turned his attention back to Juan.

"The slaves are deprived of personal freedom and compelled to perform a labor of services. They are held against their will from the time of purchase, capture, sale or even birth. They cannot refuse to work, cannot leave and do not receive compensation in return. Not much of a happy life the slaves have. Open warfare is what lead to the capture and purchase of slaves then sold for trade goods. Goods like swords, guns, whiskey, gold and that my friend is a God shame to my way of thinking." Juan finished his speech with disgust written over his seen profile by Alejandro.

"And this ladies and gentlemen brings us to the exit gate. You can pick up pamphlets which will take you much deeper into the history of Plantation Slave Day's in the information center. I hope you all enjoyed this tour and will leave a kind word behind in my behalf. Thank you for joining me and have a blessed rest of the day." Juan's words very kindly brought his presentation to an end as he pulled the carriage up bringing it to a stop in front of the unloading zone.

Chapter Ten

"Where are we going?" Trina asked Donald.

Donald turned to her and said "Just taking a drive."

"No really...I have to get back. You can just let me out here and I can catch a cab." She uttered her words trembling to him.

"I don't think so, I'll take you back." He said with hesitation between his words.

Silence fell between them. Trina didn't know what to do. She froze staring ahead with a blank trance exposed on her face.

"I will... all in good time." Donald said laughing out loudly.

She slowly turned her eyes to look upon him trying to not be noticed. He had a much derived look on his face.

"Think Trina, think." She told herself silently. "I should have known something was not right with him when he got loud with me at the diner. Oh God, what am I going to do? Better yet, what's he going to do?" She just kept running these horrific thoughts through her head. She was scared now but knew she had to try to talk her way out of the car. Trina drew in a long breath and said "Thank you but I really need to go. I can catch a cab from here; go ahead on your ride."

"Not so fast you pretty little thing. You didn't eat anything at the diner. I'm taking you somewhere that you will eat. Just relax, we'll be there shortly." He said without changing his hazy stare ahead of him.

"But...." She said before she was cut off by him.

"No buts about it. Now pretty one not another word. We'll be there soon." He angrily said.

Trina began to shake in terror. She was desperately searching for a way out of the car. It was moving too fast to jump out. She would surly die from that. He wasn't slowing down for anything so that was out of the question. She searched trying to keep a cool head on her shoulders.

"I could hit him in the head, knock him out, slide across the seat, grab the wheel apply the brakes and jump out quickly." She silently told herself and began looking around for something to hit him with. She impatiently twisted and turned in the seat desperately searching for something, anything that would work in her behalf. The only things visual to her was her bag and an ice scrapper lying in the floor.

"Relax." Donald said turning the car into a small dirt road.

Tears began to build in Trina's eyes as she watched him displaying no empathetic emotions what so ever. "Where are we? I demand to know." She said through her tears.

"You...my pretty little thing are in no position to demand anything." He said smiling from ear to ear.

Trina turned and looked straight ahead as the car pulled to the back side of a small cabin facing a scant stream of running water. The cabin was surrounded by large tree's and thicket briers. There was a path to the water's edge and the small dirt road that lead into the site. The rest of the area was nothing more than thicket briers.

"Here we are." Donald said as he turned the engine off and opened the door saying "Get out!"

Trina for once in her life did as she was told and quickly stood to the weeded ground outside the car. "What are we doing here? What do you want with me? Tell me what you're going to do with me? Please tell me something." She pleaded through tears and snubs of ample.

Donald took Trina by the arm and led her towards the cabin as he calmly replied "We're going to have dinner." And then smiled and whistled an annoying sound to her ears.

Alejandro arrived back at the hotel in a little bit better mood than when he left. He had enjoyed his day to himself and he too had come to terms with his feelings of Trina. He couldn't wait to find her. He wanted to feel her out and see how she would react to his being nice to her. He knew he wasn't her type but he had to release these feelings so he had decided to take his chances and test her.

"Hey, where have you been all day boy?" Max asked as Alejandro happily strolled through the lobby of the hotel.

"Ah, Max my boy; I've had a fine day. Thanks for your concern." Alejandro said and moved right on past him without stopping. He was headed for his hut and he was in a hurry.

Max grinned and said nothing as he knew Alejandro was realizing a little about himself and that was a good thing.

"You take a seat on the sofa while I prepare dinner." Donald told Trina pushing her down into a sitting position.

Trina looked around the small one room cabin. It was equipped with a modern refrigerator and cook stove. There was a single bed in the right back corner and the sofa she sat on was accompanied by one straight padded chair. A coffee table of oak wood stood in front of the little bit of furniture. Across from the kitchen area sat a small table with two wooden chairs. The floor was made of raw splintery wood of some kind. She wasn't sure what it was.

Donald moved about the cook stove as if he knew exactly what he was doing. He zipped back and forth from the refrigerator to the stove to the table. When the food was all prepared and on the table he took a single green candle from the cabinet and placed it in the center. Then stood back and admired his work before calling to her.

"Come on my pretty. It's all deliciously prepared for you." He almost seductively said as he walked towards Trina holding out his hand. Trina watched as he moved closer and closer to her. She was scared and didn't know what she was going to do. So she just sat and stared at him instead of doing anything.

"Right now I said!" He yelled glaring at her.

Trina jumped to her feet and the tears rolled hotter and thicker down her cheeks.

He took her by the hand and pulled her to the sink. "Wash your face and stop that idiotic bellow." He firmly told her while pumping water from the stream. Trina placed her small quivering hands under the pumped up water and cupped them together catching as much as she could hold. She bent over the sink and splashed the cold captured water on her face.

"That's good." He said handing her a towel to dry with. She took the towel and patted all around her eyes and cheeks until dry then laid it on the counter top.

Donald took her by the arm and led her to the table. He pulled one of the chairs out for her to sit and forced her down. Her arm was hurting where he had held so tightly squeezing it. She had to fight to hold back the tears. He pushed the chair and her up close to the table and then took a seat adjacent her.

"Now eat my pretty." He said with a smile and again began the annoying whistle.

Trina looked at the plate of food which sat before her. A steak that must have weighed a pound with loads of fried fat attached. Stewed Irish potatoes floating in butter and a salad drenched with grated cheese covered with dressing. A thick slice of toasted bread lay on a plate to the side. There was no way she could take one bite. The fat on the steak made her sick at her stomach just looking at it much less eating it.

"Eat!" He angrily belted out at her.

Tears grew thick and knots formed in the pit of her stomach as she slowly picked up the fork and knife laid out to the side of the plate. She sat there for moment with thoughts of using the knife to her advantage but how, how could she?

Donald very angrily reached and grabbed Trina by the wrist of the hand which held the knife. He shook her whole arm back and forth vigorously as he said "The knife if for cutting the steak only. Make sure you remember that little miss. Now eat." He then threw her hand in the direction of the plate of food.

Tears of horror ran down Trina's face as she scantly took small bites. Donald sat across the table and stared at her the whole time she ate. Each bite she took made the knot that sat in the pit of her stomach larger. The bigger it grew the closer she came to gagging. She fought with all her might to keep from it but couldn't hold it back any longer. She was sick and about to up chuck, so she jumped up and ran out the front door barely getting out before she lost all she had eaten.

Donald grabbed Trina by the arm and forcefully slung her back towards the cabin. "Damn it, you're going to eat that food and much more. Stop this ridiculous sick fraud and get back in there." He said.

Alejandro quickly showered and dressed himself in the best he owned. It was a pair of black tight fitting jeans and a black tank with black slip on shoes. He was comfortable and didn't look cheap or rich and that's the look he liked. So he was satisfied and headed out to look for Trina. The pub was a good place to start so he walked straight there. Once inside he scanned all around for her but she wasn't there. He quickly decided to wait her out because he knew she came there every evening before retiring for the night and he was sure to catch her by waiting. He quickly made his way through the small drunken crowd which loudly took up the center of the room. He chose the seat at the end of the bar where little light shown and pulled himself up on the stool.

"Give me a beer Vince. I don't care what kind." Alejandro said twisting making himself comfortable on the tall stool.

Vince reached into the cooler and without looking pulled a bottle out. He twisted the top off and sat it down on the bar in front of Alejandro.

"What's up with you?" He asked Alejandro puzzled and making swipes across the bar with a wet rag.

Alejandro shifted his weight and looked at Vince for a moment before checking the time on his watch.

"Has Trina been in here tonight yet?" He asked him with a puzzled look on his face.

"No, hadn't seen her." Vince quickly replied.

"It's already a quarter to ten. What time does she usually come in?" Alejandro asked him.

"That would be around nine. Sometimes it's a little before." Vince said after searching his memory.

"Does she ever miss coming here?" He eagerly asked Vince.

"No and she's never been this late either." He told Alejandro with concerned expressions.

"That's just my luck." He said staring at Vince with disappointment in his voice.

"Anything you want to share with the friendly bar keep?" Vince asked with a grin on his face.

Alejandro turned up the bottle of beer and downed it in one gulp. He sat the bottle down on the bar top as he turned the seat of the stool around.

"You know how it is with women...do you not?" He asked with a wink thrown towards Vince as he headed for the door.

"Yeah man, catch you later." Vince said picking up the empty beer bottle.

Alejandro walked across the hotel lobby slowly glancing in every direction hoping to catch a glance of Trina. He checked every nook and corner closely but no Trina. He didn't know where else to look so he just went back to his hut. "I'll catch her tomorrow." He told himself aloud as he undressed for bed.

CHAPTER ELEVEN

The night was dark and the big orange full moon was high throwing all kinds of shadows around the barely lightened cabin. Trina watched Donald as he took from a nearby closet a satin covered pillow and a fleece blanket.

"Since I'm going to have to keep an eye on you, I'll just move this reclining chair over by the bed. You can change now and get ready for it while I do that." Donald instructed Trina as he pushed the recliner towards the bed.

Her thoughts were that of "Thank God he's not going to get in the bed with me." They ran through her mind over and over before she made any kind of move.

"But, I don't..." She said with a shaky voice and got nothing more out before he interrupted her.

"Trina, you know damn well that closet hangs full of your things. You have night clothes as well. Now stop being such a bellow bag and get to changing." He sarcastically half way yelled at her. Trina slowly got up and walked to the closet and pulled the door open. There must have been at least fifty female outfits hanging in the center and shelves full on either end.

"I took it upon myself to rearrange your closet." He softly said and she quickly turned with a glare at him.

"Hurry up. Your night clothes are on the shelf to the left." He eagerly said as he spread the blanket across the reclining chair.

"You have a lot of eating to do tomorrow." He finished with a laugh out loud and then started whistling that horrific whistle she had heard on and off ever since they left the diner.

Trina turned and started searching through the clothing to find what would cover her most to change into. She selected a long sleeve floor length cotton gown. She looked around for a place to change. The only place there other than the one large room where he could see her was the closet itself. She glanced towards Donald and stepped into the closet pulling the door to as quietly as she could. She left a small crack for what little light there was to shine inside so she could see. She removed her top just about the same time the closet door slammed shut. It startled her into hysterics. "What are you doing? Let me out of here!" She yelled through her flowing tears and beating on the door at the same time.

"I knew you would go in there and now that I have you locked up I can get a good night sleep in the bed. Now shut up that yelling and settle down for the night or you'll make me have to gag you. You are where you are going to stay tonight!" He roughly belted out his words through the now locked closet door.

Trina beat her small fisted hands with all her might on the door yelling "Let me out of here! Please let me out!" She fell against the door with her face plastered against it hysterically crying and repeating over and over "Let me out!" as her body slid down the door crumbling to the floor.

Donald stood outside the door and listened as her voice slowly trembled and faded out. He then undressed himself and got into the small bed whispering in a low tone "I'll teach you Trina. I'll teach you."

Early morning sprung Alejandro eagerly from his bed. He was ready to face the most challenging endeavor he had met in some time. That challenge was Trina herself. To the best of his recollection she had been on the island for about three weeks and he wasn't sure of how much longer she would be. Several days had gone by without him even seeing her but that didn't stop him from thinking about her. He knew all that time he had some kind of feelings for her. He just didn't admit it to himself until now. He thought his sister's scornful approach to the subject jarred his heart a bit. He smiled and laughed aloud happily as he got himself dressed for his zestful day. He would first go to the hotel lobby where he would find Max and ask for the day off. He needed some uninterrupted time to throw his test words at Trina and had hopes that Max would understand and felt comfortable that he would.

Alejandro sung the calls of various birds. Birds he had heard in the small jungle area the trail had led him through many times. They were happy sounds he had never really paid any attention to. It was strange to him that he could sing them out as if they had always been a part of him. But he was happy today and nothing was going to worry him now. He was enthusiastically on a Trina mission.

"Hey, there you are Alejandro. I was just about to come looking for you. Joe called, she needs you to pick her up at the airport in a...." Max glanced down at his watch and slowly raised his head to finish what he was saying "an hour." He said as he arrived to where Alejandro was standing.

"It's only an hour?" Alejandro asked sighing deeply.

"Yeah and you better hurry. You have to go to the big airport up north of town.

The local port is still closed down. So you better get on the road. Don't worry about work, I'll get you covered for today. Now get going and say hello to Joe for me." Max spit his orders to Alejandro out like he was his father.

Alejandro turned and headed out the door scuffling under his breath as he exited it saying, "That sister of mine always chooses the right time."

Donald pulled the closet door open slowly peeking around the door. Trina sat in the back corner with a blanket wrapped around her entire body and covering her head. "It's time to get dressed now Trina, what are you doing in the floor of the closet. Come on get up from there we have to get going and your wasting day light," Donald pleadingly but firmly told her.

Trina didn't make a move. The tears started to roll off her cheeks and she very gently took the corner of the blanket whipping her eyes dry. Donald reached down grabbed the blanket and forcefully pulled it from around her body. He threw it to the side and turned to face her again.

"Get up and don't make me have to tell you again," he angrily said.

A vision of Uncle George, Jim, Jasper or even Alejandro's face passed through Trina's mind. "Where are you, any of you?" she whispered through her snubs as she lifted herself to her feet.

Donald stood holding on to the knob of the door as Trina slowly and cautiously stepped past him. "You need to get you some clothing Trina, we have to go into town and we are walking. You know that, what's wrong with you woman?" he ask sharply.

Trina turned her reddened eyes up to Donald's face and before she knew it she was screaming at him, "I am Trina, I don't know you and you don't know me, I am Trina." Of course her screaming made Donald furious. He vibrantly reached out and slapped her across the face leaving his finger prints in red. Trina screamed and grabbed to cover her eyes. Her left eye was hurting something fierce. His small finger had crossed her eyelid and it now felt like it was going to pop right out of her head. It stung and then burned and now was pouring water on top of her tears.

Donald reached into the closet and pulled out a white t-shirt and a pair of tan colored knee length shorts. He turned and threw the clothing at her and said," Now get them on, shut your ungracious mouth and hurry up about it."

Alejandro had decided to take the short cut into town and speed the jeep quickly down the dirt back road. Dust was flying every which way filling his eyes and hair full. He reached and took a snug fitting pair of sun glasses from above the visor and slipped them on. "That's better," he told himself aloud.

Around a sharp little curve he spotted a man walking down the side of the road ahead of him. He slowed the jeep as he approached the stranger. Once the jeep crept up close enough Alejandro saw it was Jasper and slowed the jeep to a stop beside him.

"Hey Jasper, You need a ride man?" Alejandro nicely offered.

Jasper turned and looked upon Alejandro as he pleasantly replied," No, I took the day off. I'm just going to spend it alone relaxing with all this glorious nature. I thank you for stopping and asking though."

"Did you hear that?" Alejandro quietly asks Jasper.

"What," Jasper ask.

"It sounded like a woman's scream," Alejandro turned his ear to the wind as he spoke.

Jasper laughing out loudly and replied," You probably heard one of them there big black cat's which roams this jungle."

"I don't know man, it was strange," Alejandro said with a worried look on his face.

"Ah, relax man. That kind of thing takes place all the time out here. You got to get out more," Jasper said as he continued to laugh aloud.

Alejandro turned his eyes to Jasper and said, "Yeah, if anybody would be right about them big cats, it would be you Jasper. If you're sure you don't want a ride I'll get going. That sister of mine gets upset when I'm late picking her up."

"No, I am sure. Appreciate it though. Have a good day and don't be late picking up your sister. See you back at the pub," Jasper said with a wave of his hand as he started walking ahead again.

Alejandro started up the jeep and headed up the road waving at Jasper as he left him behind.

Jasper slowed his pace to be sure not to miss one bird song or leaf rattle which surrounded the old dirt road. Dropping his chin to his chest he watched each of his boots as they stepped one then the other. It had only been a week since he had been on this road and he remembered the road to be a little more grown up than what it was now.

"I guess Alejandro has been using the road this week," he told himself aloud. Then a huge light turned on in his head. He remembered the old cabin which stood close to the water slue. Laughing aloud again Jasper scratched his head as he said," That old codger, his sister I bet. He's building that cabin up to try to impress Trina. I'm going to go see what he's done to it." Jasper reached into the top of his boot and pulled out a very long and sharp hunting knife and turned into the jungles surroundings. After taking six steps into the briers and vines which clung one to the other he began cutting a path towards the cabin.

"Will you come on and stop that god forsaken bawling," Donald speared at Trina as he drug her along behind him.

Trina's tears fell like heavy rain as the briars tore at the flesh on her lower legs. Blood trickled down and dripped into her shoe turning her white socks red. Donald's legs were much longer than hers and she had to practically run to keep up with him. His pulling and her running didn't rhyme and she kept falling to the ground. Her knees were starting to look like hamburger meat and she screamed out loudly with every step she took. Every time she screamed Donald's grip tightened around her small wrist and his tugs increased in power.

"What's wrong with you?" Trina asks taking all the air she could pull from her lungs.

Donald quickly turned and slapped her across the face as he expelled his demand, "Shut up." He then turned back to his mission and started whistling his awful tune again.

CHAPTER TWELVE

"Damn," Jasper said aloud when a brier caught his arm. "That damn thing cut deep," he whispered as he lowered his lips over top of the laceration to stop the bleeding.

The wind usually felt warm on Jasper's face as it whipped above the tree tops and into the openings the jungle allowed. Today it was not blowing and the jungle sounded of all the different species which inhibited its beauty. It was very peaceful and relaxing and Jasper loved visiting often. But this was a first time in awhile he had visited when the air was not circulating and it was hot.

"*Help*," Trina screamed as she tugged with all her might to get away from Donald. He yanked her arm so hard she thought it was going to break.

"Do you think screaming is going to do you any good," Donald ask her showing his anger.

Trina let out another painful scream as Donald yanked from her wrist even harder.

Jasper raised his head in a flash, his ears burned from the sound he had heard. "Alejandro was right, he probably did hear a woman's scream," he told himself in a low voice. Jasper slid the knife back inside his boot and lowered himself closer to the ground. Slipping through the vines and briar's making as little noise as possible he moved towards the horrific cry for help.

Donald gave Trina a hard jerk by her wrist as he scruffily said," Will you come on, if I have to keep pulling you along then I'm going to tie you to a tree and leave you. You would be helpless to all the wild animals until I returned."

Jasper raised his head above the thickened berry bush which he hid behind just enough to see over the top. What he saw was a big burly man pulling along a young woman with legs which looked like running streams of blood.

"Oh My God..." he excitingly said under his breath as he quietly ducked back behind the brier filled bush. "I got to get some help," he told himself quietly. "Think Jasper think, there's no time to go for help," he said with a scared look on his face. He ran his hand through his hair as he searched his mind for the answers he needed. The answers that poor girl needed.

He had his cell phone in his back pocket, but knew it wouldn't work from where he was, but he tried it anyway. No luck, it wouldn't work so he replaced it in his back pocket. He reached down and pulled his knife from his boot and twisted his body to where he could see once again. He patiently waited until the two were up ahead of him by a few feet. He then cut himself a small hole through the center of the bush and crawled through. On his feet again Jasper slipped quietly through the thickened jungle following the stranger whom was pulling along behind the young beaten down woman.

Trina's tears had come to a stop. She didn't want to be left tied to a tree. She wanted to make it into town. She thought it to be her only chances of getting away from this mean man so she was going to try her best to keep up and not look down at her knees.

Donald came to a sudden stop and turned as he told Trina, "Be quiet, I heard something." He stuck his ear into the air in search of any misplaced jungle sounds. Jasper quickly ducked behind a very large nearby tree hoping he was not seen. Donald stood for a long few minutes turning his ear east to west and north to south searching for the predator he believed he had heard.

Trina stood in silence relieved to be loose from Donald's tight grip to her aching wrist. Softly she ran her free hand around and around her blackened wrist. It hurt and it had begun to swell making it look like a water filled balloon. The pain was grave and it felt as though the freedom of Donald's grip made it escalate at a high rate of speed. Throbs sent burning lines to her elbow like a shooting star is shot through space.

She couldn't hold back any longer, she had to let it out even if it meant more pain. "Donald Dennison let me go; I won't tell anyone if you'll just let me go. My wrist," she managed to get out before he slapped her so hard she fell backwards into the eager awaiting berry bush which wanted its part of her too.

"Trina..." Jasper whispered asking himself.

"Oh my God, its Trina he has," Jasper's mind screamed at him. On that note he leaped from behind the tree and placed both feet on the ground slightly, but firmly spread apart. His eyes searched of Trina and spotted her in a nearby thorny bush. She was bloody all over so he couldn't tell the extent of her injuries. She didn't see him nor did the stranger who was now facing and listening in the opposite direction to Jasper.

Above his head on a low hanging limb in hiding lay what looked like a five foot serpent soaking up all the sun he could get. Jasper looked back at the stranger then to Trina who was now trying to get out of the bush and felt he had to move now. "Hey you," Jasper yelled as he reached for the serpent. The stranger turned with a quick jerk as Jasper pulled the serpent from the limb and threw it into the face of stranger. He then scuffled quickly across the dead wood, briers and vines which covered the ground beneath his feet.

Donald scuffled with the serpent and was just about to throw it to the side when Jasper leaped and landed on his back. They fought back and forth for what seemed like hours to Trina.

She drug herself up out of the berry bush with a glance towards the two of them and took off in the opposite direction.

After only a few feet she came to a quick halt. "That was Jasper," she told herself as she turned to go back grabbing a two foot limb which had fallen from a tree. Her knee's hurt so bad she could hardly walk but she had to help Jasper. So she tugged on dragging her legs behind.

The two men were rolling back and forth on the ground when she reached them. She drew the limb back over her shoulder and waited for the right moment to whack Donald in the head. Jasper rolled and Donald was on top. Trina spread her feet, raised her arms high in the air and flung forward with the limb making contact to Donald's back. The limb busted in half and flung to either side of the two men.

"Get out of here Trina, go now," Jasper repeatedly yelled at her.

The tears which fell from her eyes burned and made her vision blurry as she desperately searched of a better weapon not hearing anything Jasper was yelling at her. Jasper was on top again and Trina spotted laying close by the two, a big knife. She took two steps towards them and reached for the knife. Once she had it in her hand she stood and waited once more for the perfect moment to use it.

Donald reached out from beneath Jasper, and hit Trina in the ankle with his fist. She fell to the ground and quickly started scooting back on her butt pushing with her feet and pulling with her hands the best she could. Once she was back away from them far enough she got to her feet once again. She moved her position so she was behind the two men. She gripped the knife with both hands as tight as she could. Jasper's words pierced her ears with every effort he made, but she was not leaving him. She waited and then suddenly the two men rolled again, and Donald was on top. Trina positioned the knife blade in a downward angle, closed her eyes and leaped for Donald's back. The knife buried between his shoulder blades piercing his heart and his body fell limp atop of Jasper. Donald jerked and Jasper quickly pulled at him and worked his way out from under him.

"Trina, sweetheart you have to get up," Jasper said as he reached for her. Trina sat on her knees across Donald's upper legs. She stared with a blank mind. The tears stopped, the pain went away. She felt nothing at all. Jasper carefully placed his arms each under hers and lifted her to her feet. He picked her up and moved her away from Donald, sitting her gently back to the surface.

"You're safe Trina, your safe," his heart fully told her leaning down to look upon her eyes.

Trina said nothing she only stared in a far away daze.

"Alright baby girl, we have to get out of here," he told her.

He walked over to Donald, reached down and pulled the knife from his back, wiped it on his pant leg and placed it into its sheath inside his boot. He unbuttoned and removed his shirt and carefully placed it around Trina's shoulders. He then scoped her up into his arms and headed for the road toting her. Half way back through the thickets to the road Trina begin to scream and hit at Jasper. He stood her to her feet not letting go of her. "It's okay honey, its okay. Jasper's here and your safe now," he whispered as his own tears begin to build. He put his arms around her and pulled her close to him holding her tightly as he reassured her. For several long minutes the two of them stood in the safety of each others arms.

"Alright," Jasper said as he moved Trina back so he could see her. "We have to go Trina. Can you understand what I'm saying? We have to get you out of here. It's not much further to the road if we hurry and we are lucky we can catch Alejandro on his way back through," Jasper said in a rush heading Trina in the right direction.

"No, not Alejandro, I don't want to see him," Trina said through her sobs. Jasper wiped his brow and said, "Let's just get to the road and then we can decide, Alright Sweetheart," then started clearing the path.

Alejandro and Joe rode the first couple of miles in silence. When he went to turn on the old dirt road she didn't like it much.

"Why are you turning on this dirty road? Didn't you get enough dust in your eyes and hair on the way to pick me up? Let's stay on the highway, alright?" Joe finally started speaking.

Alejandro brought the jeep to a halt, put it in reverse and backed out onto the highway. "Alright Sis, just for you this time," he told Joe smiling innocently at her. "I ran into Jasper on the road on my way up here. He was a foot, just thought I'd check on him by going back the same way. I thought I heard something strange out there. But he's probably nowhere to be seen by now so it don't really matter," Alejandro told his sister as he pulled the jeep forward.

"So, how is old Jasper doing anyway?" Joe asks, smiling.

Alejandro turned to his sister and asks," Is it Jasper you really want to ask about or is it Vince?"

"Vince is doing great Alejandro. He is my beau and we have kept in contact. Unlike what I could say for you," Joe quickly snapped back at him.

Alejandro drew in a long breath and rolled his eyes in disgust at his sister.

"How is Trina, Alejandro? Why didn't she ride with you to pick me up? Why do you get so aggravated ever time I ask you about her? Have you told her how you feel? Has she left for home yet? What are you waiting on? It is not like it's not there on your face anyway. Everyone knows it but you and her. You two act like teenagers becoming interested in the opposite sex at the same time and afraid to even breathe around one another. You act like the couple which ordered a pizza and only ate one slice knowing both of you could eat the whole thing by yourself. I could go on and on with those kind of question's brother. But what good would it do, you don't listen. Not even to your own feelings." Joe angrily spoke her words throwing each one like a knife.

Alejandro laughed out loudly at Joe and pushed the gas pedal a little harder. The jeeps speed went up and the emotion's started to fly. "Yeah, that's right brother, laugh it off just like you always do. You just keep laughing while that girl goes home. Never to be seen again by you or this Island." Joe anxiously said while glaring at her brother.

"Alright...alright Joe, I'll talk to her. As soon as I can find her," Alejandro told her while reaching to offer comfort with a squeeze of her hand.

Joe surprised at Alejandro quickly asks," What do you mean as soon as you find her?"

"I started looking for her to talk to her yesterday. I was going to find her today. I was going to start out early this morning looking. But as soon as I got to the hotel, Max told me I had to come pick you up. I'll look some more when we get you settled back in at the hotel." he told her with a calming voice.

"That's just great. I am so happy to hear you have finally come to your senses. Now..., Vince has the afternoon off and we can help you look. Between the three of us we'll find her, how hard could it be on an Island? Don't worry we'll find her," Joe told Alejandro with rings of excitement flashing from her eyes.

"No, that's alright Sis, you have been gone for three or four days now hadn't you? Vince will be wanting that time alone with you. Don't worry I'll go looking for her I promise," he quickly replied and mashed the gas petal a little harder.

"Nonsense, we will help you. When we find her then we can all go to dinner and dancing and I will keep Vince on the dance floor so you can have time alone to talk. Or better yet, you can keep Trina on the dance floor and talk there," she anxiously told him.

Alejandro turned to look at his sister with a half grin on his face and said, " Your not going to take no for an answer are you Joe?"

"You got it brother," she replied smiling right back at him.

Alejandro waved his hand in the air at her and turned his attention to the road ahead.

CHAPTER THIRTEEN

Beads of sweat dripped from Jasper's nose as he whacked out the last bit of the path to the road. He pulled the vines and briers to the side so they wouldn't tear at Trina's skin anymore than they already had. Once the path was cleaned enough he went back through it a few feet to retrieve Trina.

Trina lay on the ground in front of a big tree. She looked so beaten down, worn out, in pain with oozing blood running from the lacerations on her legs. Tear's filled Jasper's eyes as he approached her. "Come on Trina, we've made it to the road," Jasper whispered as he lowered himself to the ground in front of her.

Trina moaned and turned bringing her arms around swinging at Jasper. "Get away from me," she screamed.

Jasper dodged and tried to catch her to pull her close to him as he said," No, Trina honey, it's okay, it's me Jasper." Trina continued to slap and scream at Jasper with intensity dying at a fast rate of speed. She had no energy and she drained herself dry quickly. Jasper laid his arm around her shoulder and pulled her to his chest. He lightly kissed her on the top of the head and said, "You're alright baby girl, Jasper's here."

"Where are we Tom? Are we lost?" Mattie asks with wide eyes.

Tom cleared his throat and said," Well Mama, I think we are headed for the hotel. The young fellow back at the car rental said this was a short cut."

"I think we are lost," she said leaning up in her seat.

He laughed out and said, "No, we'll be there soon Mama."

"Alright Tom, we'll see," she told him settling back for the scenic ride.

Jasper pulled his cell phone from his back pocket and popped it open. "Damn, still no service," he said aloud to himself.

"Trina sweetheart, I am going to walk out to the road and see if my phone will pick up. Just lay right here, I'll be right back," he told her as he ran his hand down her hair. Trina made no move as Jasper stood and turned. He made his way back across the beaten cut out path to the road. Once to the edge he looked around in the air for some sky way in hopes he could catch a signal to his phone. He walked out into the middle of the road which looked to be his best chance. He flipped open the phone just as Tom and Mattie's rented car come flying around the far curve. Jasper raised his eyes toward the sky and said," Thank you lord." He started waving his hands back and forth in the air from the middle of the road. He had hopes he could be seen through all the dust which now fogged the entire area.

"What was that sparkling I seen ahead Tom?" Mattie ask rising up curious.

"What sparkle," Tom ask.

Mattie drew a long breath raised her voice and said, "Slow down Tom. Stop! There's a man in the road." Tom threw on the brakes and brought the car to a halt just three foot from where Jasper was standing in the middle of the road. Jasper raced around the side of the car to the driver's window.

"Please Sir, I have an injured girl in the edge of the jungle there," he said pointing towards the path. "Can you please give us a ride to town?" he pleaded with the stranger.

"What happened to her?" Tom asks.

"It's a long story, I'll fill you in on the way, but she is hurt and needs to get to the hospital. Will you give us a ride?" Jasper continued to plead and now out of breath.

"For heaven's sakes Tom help the man, can't you see he's telling the truth?" Mattie said pushing on Tom's shoulder at the same time.

Jasper ducked down and peered at the lady sitting in the passenger's seat and said, "God bless you madam, Thank you!"

"I'll be right back; I just have to help her to the car. Stay right here, please," Jasper said as he moved backwards towards the path and waved his hand in the air towards the car.

"I'll help you young fellow," Tom said as he opened the car door.

Jasper quickly replied," Just open the back door, I'll be right back with her," and then disappeared into the jungle.

Tom opened the back door on the big Buick they had rented to use while on the Island. Mattie sit inside the car and watched the jungle where Jasper had entered holding her finger's on her lips anticipating his return with some poor little hurt girl.

"Do you think it's his daughter Tom?" Mattie worriedly asks. Tom walked up to the side of the front door where she sat in the car, reached through the window and squeezed her forearm.

"It's alright, Mattie. I think we're doing a good thing here," He softly whispered his words of love to her.

Jasper appeared at the head of the trail carrying Trina in his arms. Mattie sighed deeply and he headed for the back seat of the car. Tom rushed to the other side to help but Jasper had Trina and himself in the car by the time he got around there so he just got in also.

"Let's go back the way you were coming, it's the nearest hospital," Jasper told Tom.

Tom started the car and told him, "I'm not from here, so you'll have to tell me where to turn and such." "I will, let's just hurry and get her there," Jasper said as he gently stroked Trina's cheek.

Tom turned the car around and headed back the way he and Mattie had come. He did drive at a little faster speed than before.

Mattie turned herself around in the seat so she could see Jasper and Trina. "Oh, that poor girl, what happened to her?" she sympathetically asks Jasper.

Tom raised his eyes to the rear view mirror anticipating Jasper's answer to Mattie's question.

Jasper repositioned Trina's head on his shoulder and said," she was kidnapped and brought out into this jungle, I just happened to be here today. I thank God I was."

"Oh my goodness, it's alright honey, your in good hands now, we're going to take care of you," Mattie tearfully said as she reached and patted Trina on the back of the hand.

"Which way do we go?" ask Tom.

Jasper raised his head and looked around and then replied, "To the left." Tom turned the car in the direction Jasper had instructed.

Jasper placed a hand on Trina's cheek and gently held her head in place. "We're almost there baby girl," he whispered as he placed a peck on top of her head. Trina lay against Jaspers shoulder in silence. She only had a blank glaring stare in her eyes. Jasper was worried about her after all she's been through and no telling what all it had actually entailed or why. There were many questions running through his mind with no answers to achieve from Trina at this point.

"It's right up here on the right," Jasper told Tom.

"I see it, we'll be there in a jiffy," Tom replied turning the car into the drive.

Mattie turned around once again in her seat and said to Trina, "We're here sweetheart and everything is going to be alright now, just hang in there."

Tom pulled the car up in front of the double glass doors outside the emergency room of the local hospital. He got out and opened the back door. Jasper got out and carefully removed Trina. Holding her in his arms he walked for the doors.

Tom got back into the car and moved it into a parking space. He and Mattie got out and went in search of Jasper and Trina. Once inside the lobby of the emergency room they found Jasper sitting in a chair in one of the corners and moved to him.

"We're going to wait with you," Mattie said as she reached and placed a hand atop Jaspers shoulder.

"Oh, it's alright, you don't have to. Here let me pay you for all the trouble I already put you through," Jasper said reaching for his wallet.

"You'll do no such thing. We are concerned about that young girl in there too. No trouble, we'll wait." Tom took over speaking loud and clear.

Jasper raised his eyes to meet Tom's and said," I appreciate everything you've done. You can wait if you wish, but the law enforcement is on their way and when they get here I'll be tied up."

"I understand that young man, now you understand me, Mattie and I are Christian people and we care about what happens to that young lady. We didn't go this far to leave without any word as to her being alright. Now if I can do anything to help with the law, you just let me know," Tom replied to Jasper with firmness to his tone.

"As you like," Jasper said as he reached to shake Tom's hand.

"Let's take a seat," Tom told Mattie as he took her by the elbow.

"Jasper Long," the nurse called from a nearby doorway. Jasper got up and walked towards the nurse. "Right here," he said arriving in front of her.

"The doctor will see you now, follow me," she said turning back the way she came. Jasper stayed close behind dodging the busy gurneys and medical equipment being wheeled up and down the hallway.

"Dr Brian Jacob," she said as she pointed at the open door in front of him.

"Thank you, madam," he said as he entered.

The room was a small crowded office. There was little standing room and stacks of papers everywhere. The desk had two chairs sitting adjacent and a middle aged man sitting behind it looking at a file of some kind.

Jasper stepped forward with an outreached hand and said, "I'm Jasper Long, here with the young girl who came in a little bit ago?"

Dr Jacob stood and took Jasper hand in return of the greeting.

"Dr Jacob, Nice to meet you. I have a couple of questions I need to ask. Have a seat," he said returning to his seat as well. Jasper chooses the first seat closest to the door and sat down.

"How is she Doc?" he asked quickly and eagerly.

"She's in shock at the moment," he barely said before Jasper interrupted.

"Can I see her?" Jasper asks.

"At the moment she's being stitched up in places. I'll let you see her for a few minutes when we're done here and she's back to her room," he said understanding how Jasper was feeling.

"Agreed, how is she?" Jasper anxiously asks again.

"She has some lacerations on her knees quite deep, which required stitching. There are lots of bruises and scrapes. She's in shock; she's awake but not speaking. I think she will be fine in time, meaning once the shock has worn off. The stitches in the lacerations will be ready to remove in approximately ten days. Um...scaring...is a possibility since they are so deep. The biggest concern at the moment is the shock. I'll know more when I have had a chance to do further test. We will just have to wait and see on that one. Now I have some questions I need to ask," Doctor Jacob told Jasper.

"What happened to her?" the doc asks.

"It's my guess she was kidnapped from what I seen. She was being drug through the jungle over off Bard hill road by some man. One of the thickest jungles there is around here." Jasper said with his concern expressed in his tone.

"Kidnapped?" Doctor Jacob asks with a puzzled look on his face.

"I know this girl personally and I know she wouldn't have gone to that jungle with that man. I jumped him from behind. She got my knife and she stabbed him in the back. I brought her out of the jungle and here," Jasper spoke fast.

"Excuse me for a moment. I'm going to have to get my nurse to call the law on this one," Doctor Jacob said holding his hand up in the air towards Jasper.

"Don't bother," Jasper said.

"I already have, they are on their way here as we speak," he continued to say.

A knock lightly thumped on the door as it opened.

"There's an officer here to see you Doctor Jacob," the nurse said stepping back against the door so they could pass her by.

"Come in, come in, Doctor Brian Jacobs, I was just about to call you guys, "he said as he quickly stood up from his chair extending his hand in greetings.

"Thank you, sir. What's the situation you have here?" the estranged officer asks.

"Yes, well, this is Jasper Long. He brought a young girl in, mid twenties. He believes the girl was kidnapped and physically abused." Doctor Jacob said taking his seat.

"Have a seat officer," doc said extending his hand in a rotating motion towards the chair beside of Jasper.

The officer took a seat and turned to face Jasper.

"What's the story?" he asks looking straight at him.

"There's a man, he may be dead, I don't know. He's out a little ways from the cabin in the middle of the jungle off Bard hill road...."

"Wait a minute; you say he may be dead? Who is he?" the officer asks.

"Maybe, I don't know, he was stabbed in the back with my hunting knife. I heard her call him, Donald Dennison, when he was dragging her behind him," Jasper said as he pulled the knife from his boot.

"Alright, you'll have to come down town with me," the officer said as he stood and initiated a call into headquarters.

"Let me see her first," Jasper said as he stood from his seat. The officer stood and looked at Jasper for a minute and then said, "Alright, you can see her for just a minute while I get someone out on Bard hill road but I'm coming with you. If Doctor Jacobs here doesn't mind."

"I'll allow it for just a minute; she needs rest so no longer. Follow me," Doc said as he opened the door to the hallway.

Jasper followed along behind Doctor Jacobs and the officer behind Jasper. It was just a short distance down the hall before they arrived at the room Trina had been placed in. Jasper stepped inside and saw Trina lying there so innocent looking and pain stricken. Tears fell from his eyes as he approached her side. He gently ran his finger tips down the side of her battered face as he bent down close to her ear.

"Everything is going to be alright baby girl. You're going to be fine," he said holding back his tears. "I have to go take care of some important business and then I'll be right back here with you. The doc here's going to take good care of you while I'm away. I won't be gone long. You get to feeling better and just rest," he said as he softly kissed her forehead and gently squeezed her hand before turning to leave. Once out into the hall Jasper turned to the officer and ask," Can I give her uncle a call to let him know what's happened?"

"If I'm not looking I'll not see or know it," the officer replied feeling empathy.

"Thank you," Jasper said with a low tone.

He walked over a few feet for a little privacy and took his cell phone from his back pocket.

"How am I going to tell George this?" he ask himself aloud as he slightly shook his head scratching the side of it.

CHAPTER FOURTEEN

"There you are," Mattie said as she and Tom approached Jasper.

"How is the young lady?" Tom aggressively asks. He comes to a halt in front of Jasper looking him dead in the eyes. "We have not heard a thing since you left with the Doc. Is she going to be alright?" he asked.

"I'm sorry to you folks. She's going to be alright after a little rest. They have her sedated now. I appreciate all the help you've given us. Let me buy you two dinner one night while your here on vacation. Right now I have to go down the police station and answer some questions. What hotel are you all staying at? I can contact you in a day or two and make arrangements for dinner, "Jasper quickly replied emptying and refilling his lungs at the same time.

Tom looked at Mattie as she spoke up answering Jasper," Dinner is not necessary, glad to help. But we would appreciate being kept informed. We'll be at the Eternal Sunrise."

"Great, I work there as the trail guide. I'll catch you folks there. Again, thank you for all you've done." Jasper replied reaching to shake hands with Tom and then Mattie. "You'll have to excuse me now. I have to make this phone call and then go down to the police station. I'll see you in a couple of day's." he finished as he turned to walk away.

Jasper sat himself down on the edge of a seat in the corner of the hospital's front lobby. "Man, it's hot in here," he mumbled aloud. He opened up his flip top cell and searched for George's number. He decided calling George at his office the best choice as he pushed the call button. "Damn..it's busy." He aggravatingly said aloud closing his cell. His sigh was a long breath, swiping his finger tips across his sweat covered brow and sliding his tired body back into the seat leaning his head against the wall. "I'll try his office one more time then his home," he told himself as he sit back up straight once again flipping his phone open. Jasper pushed the redial and leaned back again.

"Hello," George's voice came on the other end.

Jasper sunk a deep breath and then said," Hey, George."

"Jasper, how are things going? Trina found a good man yet?" George quickly asks.

"Well, she is what I am calling about George. Listen to me before you go haywire. Just listen, alright?" Jasper said in hopes that George would not go crazy and not hear anything he was saying.

"What's wrong Jasper? What happened?" George anxiously asks.

Jasper sighed as he begins to tell what he knew of the situation. "Trina was captured by a man who kept her out in the jungle in a log cabin. Now I don't know what his intentions were for it. But I caught him dragging her through the jungle. She's got some cuts and bruises on her, but the Doc says she is going to be fine. But even worse..."

"I'm on my way." George said interrupting Jasper.

"George, listen to me." Jasper quickly responded and continued without giving him a chance to say anything back. "There is no need in your coming here. She is going to be alright. That's not all I have to tell you. Please listen to me. I don't have much time." Jasper said out of breath.

"Alright, alright Jasper just tell me," George frantically said.

"When I came upon them in the jungle, I followed them. I attacked him when I got the chance. My knife I keep in my boot came out on the ground. Trina got the knife and she stabbed the man. I don't know if he is going to live or not. But she is physically going to be fine. I don't know if she will even remember what happened. She's been hospitalized at Sunrise Memorial and she is sedated now for much needed rest. I have to go to the police station to give the information in which I know. I'll call you when there is a change of any kind, "Jasper told him and refilled his lungs afterwards.

"I'm coming on the next flight out and as soon as Trina can, I'm bringing her home," George said.

"I'll call you as soon as I'm finished at the law station. Don't do anything yet. Let me find out a little more about what's going to happen or has happened already. Okay George?" Jasper quickly asks.

"In the mean time I'll make preparations to fly out," George said.

"I can see there's no need in arguing with you. Alright then, I'll give you a call on your cell as soon as I know something more. I'll talk to you in a bit George." Jasper said finishing his conversation closing his phone.

The two officers were standing by the front entrance waiting for him. He hurried over to them and said," I am ready to go with you now."

"Well, you can just follow us over to the station if you like. Where is your car parked?" the closest officer ask.

"Oh, I don't have one here. I caught a ride with a little old couple here on vacation." Jasper replied.

"Alright, you can just ride over with us and catch a cab back when we are finished." said the second officer.

"I guess it wouldn't do me any good to ask if this could wait awhile, would it?" Jasper's words ask with a pleading tone.

The first officer straightened his stance as he said, "No, we really need to get this investigation underway. We have already waited longer than a normal amount of time."

"Alright, let's get it over with." Jasper replied following the out reached hand of the first officer towards the doorway.

Joe jumped out of the jeep in front of the hotel in a hurry to see Vince. It seemed like it had been a long time and she had missed his smiling face which accompanied his calming graciousness. "Give us an hour Alejandro and then pick Vince and me up here in front of the hotel. We will go find Trina and all will be well. Mark my words brother, you'll see." She told him as she headed for the front entrance.

"Alright sis, will do. But only if Vince agrees to it as well." He replied pulling the jeep into drive.

"Don't worry brother, he will." She said with a smile on her face.

Alejandro drove the jeep to the backside of the hotel and parked it. He got out and walked the trail to his hut. He took a seat and sprang back to his feet as fast as he sat telling himself aloud, "Why wait, I can check the area myself until time to pick them two up." He quickly walked the trail to the motor cross paths and asks if she was there. But he had no luck finding her. So he walked fifteen minutes across to the hot air balloon ride asking the same. Still, he had no luck. She wasn't there either. He took his hat off and briskly rubbed across his forehead asking himself silently," Where could she be?" He then remembered the Dolphins and how much she had enjoyed it. Maybe she would have gone for another time with them. It was a twenty minute walk from where he was and would make him late to pick Joe and Vince up but quickly decided he would just have to be late. After all he would rather find her by himself anyway so he took off walking in a high stepping hurry in hopes of finding Trina there. When he arrived at the front gate he questioned the teller of her presence. But he got no positive response.

"Are you sure she's not here? She's a kind of short feisty blonde, can you just check and make sure?" he pleadingly asks the lady behind the window.

"Sir, I'm sorry but I am sure. There are no blondes inside the park today." The lady told him with her face expressing her sympathy.

"Thank you, have a nice day," he said as he turned to walk away. Alejandro quietly strolled back towards the hotel slowly wondering with every step where Trina could be.

"Who is this Donald person anyway? Where did he come from?" Jasper asks the detective at the station.

"Just hold up there with your questions. I am the one with the questions for you." The detective quickly told him.

"Yeah, alright but I still have some of my own as well," Jasper replied firmly.

"As long as your questions pertain to you I have to answer them, otherwise I don't have to answer anything you ask." The officer replied.

"I do understand that, however I also feel like I deserve to know about the man whom I just had encounters with. And that little girl lying over there in the hospital has every right to know if she chooses to. She will be asking me, not you." He quickly replied staring the officer in the eye as he spoke. "I have told you every thing I know about what happened. She stabbed that man in self-defense. He dragged her through that jungle and has done no telling what else to her. I thank God I found her when I did or she might be dead now," Jasper continued not backing down. "I feel I need some answers to give her when she asks me. Does she need to obtain the assistance of an attorney?" he asks the detective just as firmly as he had begun to speak.

"Alright, off the record here. He escaped a mental institution over two years ago and is believed to be a serial killer of young pretty women. He captures them, feeds them forcing them to eat until they are no longer slim and then kills them. Finds another and starts the process over. It is believed he was abused as a child for being overweight and it warped him into passing the abuse onto women. It may have been his mother whom abused him. Which would explain why he chooses women?" The detective told Jasper as if he was questioning himself.

"Did she mention an annoying whistle he may have been doing?" he asks Jasper with a concerned expression.

"No, what does that have to do with it?" Jasper wanted to know.

"What it has to do with it, we have not been able to figure out. However it is the classic sign given by all women who have managed to escape from him. It is the only connection we have to link them all together. The ladies who have escaped him and I might add there has been very few, were so traumatized they can't remember what the man looked like or they don't agree on his looks. Long hair and beard, overweight, skinny and bald, glasses, no glasses, gold tooth to no teeth, we don't know. A whistle is all which is agreed on. The man might be a nut but at the same time he's smart," The detective replied.

"My God, now I really thank the big man for letting me find her before she was killed by that mad man." Jasper said as he stood. "If I am finished here, I would like to get back to her. I want to be there when she comes too." He said.

"Tell me how it is you came to be where she was and how you knew she was there at just the right time?" he asked Jasper.

"My day off, I always walk that road. It's usually peaceful. It's just my way of relaxing and I heard her scream more than once," Jasper replied.

"You won't be leaving town or anything will you," the detective asked.

"The only place I am going is back to that hospital to that girl's side. I promised I would take care of her and that's where I will be," Jasper quickly said as he stood.

"Yeah, we are finished for now, but keep your self available in case we have more questions. And when she is able, we will be questioning her as well." The detective told him.

"No problem. I for one would like to see the man back where he belongs." Jasper told him as he reached his hand out to shake the detectives before he headed back to the hospital.

"There might be a lot of folks who would like to say a thank you to you for taking this man off the street if he turns out to be who we think he is." The detective told Jasper.

"I only fought the man; Trina stabbed him and possibly killed him. From the looks of her she's lived some hell over the last few hours. She deserves all the credit and that's the way I would want it to be," Jasper said as he headed for the door and disappeared out it.

When Alejandro arrived back at his jeep he looked at his watch it was six fifteen. He thought," Joe's going to be mad, but oh well, its not like it would be the first time she's ever gotten mad at me." He got in and pulled the jeep around to the front of the hotel. Joe and Vince was nowhere in sight. He pulled the gears into first and turned the key off and started getting out. Just as he was about the reach the front door Joe exited with Vince behind her.

"Alejandro, have you been waiting long? We're running a few minutes late. I'm sorry, but we are ready now, so let's go find her." Joe said grabbing Vince's hand and heading towards the jeep.

Alejandro wiped his brow as he was thinking, "thank goodness they were late." He returned to the jeep anxious to continue searching for Trina. "Alright, where shall we start our search? Hello Vince, I appreciate the help you two are giving me. I tried to push it off but you know Joe she wouldn't take no for an answer." He said as he was starting up the motor.

"Glad to do it Alejandro. I know you would if the situation was in reverse. Why don't we start by searching all the activities the hotel offers?" Vince told him.

"I think that's a good idea," Joe eagerly added.

"Well, I have already searched the motor cross, the hot air balloon and the Dolphin Park with no luck at any of them." He sadly told the two.

"Okay, lets go search at the riding stables and if she's not there then lets search the beach cabana's," said Vince with Joe agreeing to everything he said.

Alejandro pulled the jeep out in silence and headed towards the head of the riding stables trail. He was hoping he would find Trina there. "You two wait here and I will run up there and check with Jasper. He would know if she is or has been here." Vince said upon the arrival of the trail.

"No, Jasper has the day off Vince. You'll have to ask Bernard or Bias," Alejandro replied.

"Alright, will do," Vince said as he exited the jeep.

"I'll get the jeep turned around while he is gone," Alejandro told Joe with a quick glance her way.

Joe smiled as she told Alejandro," It's going to be alright brother. We'll find her." She reached across and gave his knee a little squeeze of comfort.

Alejandro spoke under his breath saying to him self," I sure hope so."

Vince returned momentarily with news of no Trina present.

"Okay, let's go and check out the beach. Maybe she is just sunning in solitude somewhere down there." Joe told Alejandro.

"Alright," He replied pulling the jeep into gear. Once they arrived at the beach and were all out standing in the hot sand. Alejandro glared up and down the immediate front of them but saw no Trina.

"Okay, Joe you and Vince walk the beach towards town and I will walk it towards the jungle. We can meet back here once we have checked all the cabanas and open area's." he finally said after a few short moments of searching the present area.

"Alright, and don't worry Alejandro. We will find her. We will, listen to me. We will find her." Joe said seeing the worried expressions he was no longer trying to hide.

"Yes, we will buddy," Vince added to what Joe had to say.

"I hope so, I really hope so. Alright, let's just plan to meet back here at the jeep." Alejandro said as he headed down the beach towards the jungle.

Chapter Fifteen

The cab pulled up in front of the hospital. Jasper jumped out quickly pulling his wallet from his pocket to pay. He then hurried in to Trina's bedside. He didn't take the time to ask Doctor Jacobs if it was alright or not. He just went into the room and took her limp hand into his. "I am back baby girl; Old Jasper is here right by your side. I won't leave you again. It's all going to be okay, you're going to be okay. You just take your time and sleep as much as you need to. I'll be right here beside you." He told her close to her ear as he gently patted the back of her hand. Jasper looked around the room and spotted a straight chair against the wall. He walked over and picked it up carrying it back to the bedside. He took a seat and laid his head down on the side of the bed taking a hold to Trina's hand one more time. He closed his eyes and said a silent prayer in her behalf. He felt so tired but wasn't going to leave her for nothing.

After Jasper had sit next to her bedside for almost two hours in silence. The door opened and George stepped inside. "Jasper, how is she doing now and what has happened?" George asks rushing to Trina's side.

"She is still sleeping, I guess. I have been here with her for what must be at least two hours now and she has not moved a bit. I think Doctor Jacobs has her sedated." Jasper told him unsure of his answer.

"She looks awfully bad like she may be in some pain. Tell me what has happened Jasper," George demanded with tear's whaling up in his eyes.

"Why don't we step out into the lobby to talk George?" Jasper asks as he stands.

"Alright and I want to see that Doctor Jacobs too." He said as he leaned over and kissed Trina on the forehead.

Jasper headed towards the door with George behind him. He turned left and headed towards Doctor Jacob's office. "We would like to see Doctor Jacob's if we could Miss," Jasper told the lady outside his office.

She picked up the phone and called in to him and told him Jasper and some other man was there and would like to talk to him. She replaced the receiver carefully. "You may go on in," she told them looking at Jasper.

"Thank you," Jasper said as he headed for the door. Jasper entered and George followed close behind. Doctor Jacobs stood as the two men approached his desk. "Have a seat Jasper. What can I help you with?" he asks holding his hand out for a greeting shake.

"This is George, Trina's uncle. I think he has some questions for you." Jasper told him.

Doctor Jacobs turned his attention to George extending his hand. "It's nice to meet you George. Why don't you two fellows have a seat?" He said as he waved his hand towards the two chairs in front of his desk. Jasper and George took a seat.

"Jasper here has filled me in on what has happened to her but there is still one question I have." George spoke with a tremble to his tone.

"What's that?" the doc asks.

"Was she raped?" George asks, anxiously awaiting an answer.

Jasper turned his attention to Doctor Jacobs surprised he hadn't thought of that himself.

"No, there are no indications to confirm such activity." Doctor Jacobs replied. George deeply let out a sigh of relief as he leaned back in his chair.

"Do you have her sedated still?" Jasper asks him relieving the previous thoughts.

Doctor Jacobs leaned forward in his chair and said," No, I have not had her sedated at all. She has sedated herself. She is in a deep shock state when she arrived. There is nothing we can do but wait it out. She will wake when she is ready to wake. There is no guarantee's of how long that will be. But there is no indication's of any injury in which would make her be in a comatose state. It could be detrimental to force her to wake at this point. I'm sorry but in her best interest, we can only wait for her to decide it is time. I did test her for diabetes and it was negative. I can't find any head trauma that would be significant enough to keep her in a coma. No drugs, no alcohol and certainly not by hypothermia. It's possible she's experiencing a condition called Acute Stress Reaction which is characterized by a sense of dreamlike or unreal place of a specific traumatic event. All we can do is at this point is wait it out."

"So what you are saying is that we should not be trying to talk her into it?" George eagerly asks.

"You can talk to her, but I am afraid it won't do any good as long as she herself is not ready. She will hear you and all that you have to say but she may not comprehend it. With the horrific experience she has been through her state of being at the moment is not uncommon. There may be something you may say to her that will trigger her mind. But anything about what has happened could harm her more than do her good at this point." Doctor Jacobs replied with deep expressions of concern formed on his face.

"Alright, we won't speak to her of what has happened. Is it okay for us to sit at her side though?" Jasper quickly asks.

"I have no problem with that as long as you abide, and don't cause her more problems. No more than two at a time with her and all must understand to not talk to her of her ordeal. She's my patient and I won't have her sunken deeper than she already is." He replied firmly.

Jasper and George stood upon those words from Doctor Jacobs. "Don't worry Doc, we won't let that happen. You can count on it." George said as he turned towards the exit with Jasper behind him.

Meanwhile back at the beach, Joe and Vince returned to the jeep before Alejandro did. "Well...we beat him back." Joe said leaning against the jeep.

Vince stepped one foot to each side of Joe's and placed a hand to the jeep to each side of her upper shoulders. His face was only inches from hers. "I guess, that gives me time to kiss you then, don't it darling." He said with his eyes piercing into hers.

Joe smiled and puckered her lips. Vince started moving in closer and Joe ducked under his arm. She was starting to run across the sands of the beach. "Only...if you can catch me." She said over her shoulder not paying attention to where she was going. Vince turned and watched her just as she tripped over someone's freshly built sand castle. She fell to the wet sand that surrounds the castle. He quickly rushed to her rescue falling upon the top of her holding his weight up so he didn't smash her frail body. "You made it easy for me to catch you." He said as he lowered his lips to hers in a slow passionate kiss.

"Hey, what do you two assholes think your doing? Look what you have done to my castle. I'll whip the shit out of you both." A strange voice pierced the ears of the two playing in the sand.

Vince raised his head into the face of a mid-twenties boy with an angry look on his face. He drew a long hard breath and said to the young man," Do you want to take that butt of yours out of your mouth and put it back in your ass before I do it for you?" And then he stood extending his hand to Joe. She took his hand and he pulled her to her feet and then turned to the young man once again. "Destroying your fabulous bullshit castle was an accident. And for that we are sorry, but I won't have you talking that way to my girl or in front of her. I suggest you move on." Vince said wasting no breath with his instructions to the young man.

"If you two are finished with your display of manhood, I would like to get going now." Alejandro's frustrated voice came from behind. The young man quickly wandered off down the beach with no further words to exchange with Vince.

Vince turned his attention to Alejandro and asks, "No luck, huh?"

"We didn't have any luck either. Where shall we search now?" Joe asks Alejandro inquisitively not giving him time to answer Vince.

"Obviously she's not around here. It's getting late and starting to get dark out. Why don't you two just go ahead on and have a good evening. I think I will go back to the pub and have a drink and start fresh in the morning." Alejandro said with his head hung low. He thought maybe the two would leave him and he could pay a visit to Trina's room later catching her there.

"Alright, if that's what you want then we will have a drink with you." Joe replied quickly.

"No, that's okay. You two need some time alone. I don't want to take it all up." He replied as he turned in a heaving walk towards the jeep hoping they would get the hint he wanted to be alone. He didn't want to be rude. He knew his sister was just concerned. But he still didn't want to reveal his thoughts to her.

Joe looked up at Vince who knew what she was saying without speaking and he nodded his head in agreement. Joe turned her attention back to Alejandro and stepped it up to catch up with him.

"Nope, we are going to have a drink too. Like it or not, that's the way it is brother." She said as she caught up to him.

"Just get in the jeep, would you two?" Alejandro asks giving up his hopeless argument. Once they arrived back at the pub Alejandro went to the bar and ordered himself a beer. He took the bottle and a glass and found a table in the corner away from the crowd which now inhibited the enter pub. Vince and Joe followed closely behind. Joe didn't want to leave him alone. She was worried about her brother.

"So where do we start looking in the morning?" Joe asks as she takes a seat at the table.

Alejandro drew in a long deep breath filling his lungs before he quietly spoke. "I don't know for sure. I think I will try knocking on the door of her room early in the morning. Maybe I can catch her before she goes out anywhere." He told Joe as he slowly poured his beer into the tipped sideways glass he held.

"Hey, that's a good idea." Vince added to the conversation.

"Yes, it is, why don't you do it now?" Joe asks him.

"It's a bit late to do it now. I'll just wait until morning." Alejandro replied turning up his glass.

Joe turned to Vince and tipped her glass up downing the beer inside with one big gulp. "Bottoms up guys." She said with a half moon smile on her face. Vince smiled back at Joe and turned his glass up knowing what she was thinking. It was a funny sensation to him how he could just look at her and feel what her thoughts were. He was in love with her and he knew it.

Alejandro leaned back in his chair to where his butt was barely hanging on the seat. He stretched his legs out and yawned putting his hand over his mouth. He turned his glass up and downed the rest of the beer within. "Well, I think I'm going to turn in now," he said sitting the glass down on the table. He stood and smiled back at Joe before turning to leave.

"Alright brother, what time shall we meet in the morning and where?" she asks him quickly.

"From the way you two were acting out on the beach, my guess would be your place or Vince here place." He replied with a smirking grin. "But not too early though." He quickly added.

"Stop that brother, you know better than that." She embarrassingly replied.

"Yeah, okay, if you say so sis. So which is it?" he asks her still smiling.

"My place will be just fine," Vince quickly added throwing in his opinion while he had the chance to do so.

"Alright, will eight be alright with you?" Alejandro asks.

"Sure, that's fine." Vince replied.

"See you two in the morning then. Good night. Enjoy Sis." He said as he started walking away.

As soon as he disappeared into the crowd Joe turned to Vince. "Let's go." She said, quickly rising from her seat.

"Hold on Joe," Vince said reaching and taking hold to her wrist. "Don't you know Trina's door is where Alejandro is headed as we speak?" he asks her pulling her back towards her seat.

Joe took her seat and looked upon Vince with concern. She thought for a moment and then asks him, "Do you really think so?"

"Of course it is. Couldn't you see it in his face? He didn't want us tagging along. He wants to be alone with her when he finds her. And, I don't blame him. I know I would with you." He told her.

"Yeah, I guess you're probably right." She said relaxing a little more.

"Hey, I have some really good brandy at my place. Why don't we go there and have some. Relax ourselves and enjoy each other's company for awhile?" he asks Joe in hopes she would agree.

"I guess that would be alright. But I'm going with Alejandro tomorrow if he doesn't find her tonight." She told Vince with firmness to her tone.

Vince stood holding to Joe's hand and pulled her to her feet for the second time today. "Whatever you say sweetheart, whatever you say. But for the rest of the evening lets just get to know each other better." He said as he slipped his arms around her waist.

Joe looked up to Vince and replied," I'm all yours for the rest of the evening. Lead the way." Vince tightened his grip on Joe's hand as he led her through the crowd and out the door of the pub.

CHAPTER SIXTEEN

Jasper and George walked down the long hall of the hospital in silence. Each searching their thoughts of Trina and her well being! What was the best for her? What to do next? What to say to her to bring her out of this deep sleep she seem to be hiding in. George was the first to break the silence as they arrived at the front lobby. "Jasper," George said," lets take a seat over here for a few minutes and talk.

"Alright," Jasper replied as he moved towards the front row of seats next to the big outside window. The two gentlemen took a seat adjacent one another. The lobby was busy with small children running back and forth. There were parents, grandparents, brothers and sisters yelling at the young to sit and be quiet. But there wasn't much listening going on.

"Who is this man Jasper? What do you know about him? How did he come to be with my Trina?" George asks in a low voice.

"George, I don't know all the answers." Jasper said with a very frustrated tone.

"I wish I did." He continued to say with his tone expressing a feeling of helplessness.

"What did you find out when you went to the police station?" George ask wanting to know.

"The man's name is Donald. He escaped from a mental institution some time ago. They believe he was abused for being overweight in his younger years. Maybe by his mother and that's why they think he chooses young pretty women. He abuses them and then he kills them, or at least that is what they think."

George interrupted Jasper at that point. "Oh my God," he said.

"Yes, and I thank God I found her before it got that far." Jasper replied.

"So what are they planning to do with him?" George asks.

"I don't know. I don't even know if he is going to live or if he is even still alive." Jasper told him.

"What does that mean?" George inquired.

"Well George, I told you over the phone she stabbed him with my knife." Jasper said.

"I didn't hear that part. How did she manage to do that? How did she get your knife? Tell me what has happened Jasper." George anxiously questioned.

"I had the knife; it got knocked out of my hand. While I was wrestling around with him! She retrieved my knife and stabbed him in the back. She was still talking at that time, incoherently but talking. I lead her as far as I could and then carried her all the rest of the way out to the road. We caught a ride with a little old couple who are here for vacation. She was out of it by then. We brought her here." Jasper sadly told him about the events that had taken place.

"Where is he now?" George asks.

"He was brought here also. I don't know where he is, but he was just a couple of doors down from her. There were two guards outside the door." He replied looking towards the way he had seen the guards before.

"It's late, but I'm going to go and see what I can find out, anyway." George told Jasper as he was standing. Jasper stood and started walking towards the room he had seen Donald in before and George followed closely behind.

Alejandro tapped lightly on the door of Trina's room at the hotel. He knew it was late, but he had to speak to her. He just couldn't let it go any longer. He had to tell her how he was feeling. She might laugh in his face, but that was a chance he was going to have to take. He waited a few moments and then tapped again. No noise was coming from inside. He waited a few more minutes and then decided she was not there or she was already asleep one. So he left to return to his own hut telling her aloud without her presence, "I will be back early in the morning."

Alejandro took a seat in his big comfortable chair. He reached down under the end table and picked up his journal. He had been keeping it for some time, but never let anyone know about it. He thought they would think him girlish or something. So he kept it to himself. He had written all kinds of short stories and poem's. But never shared any of it, he felt it best just kept to himself. He took a pen from the drawer of the table and started writing with Trina in his mind and his heart. He had an entry for everyday and she seems to consume all the entries these days.

Joe sat leaned back on the big soft sofa Vince had in his hut. His hut was bigger than Alejandro's and had more furniture as well. Vince sat beside her with his arm across the back above her head. They each had a glass of red wine in their hand. They sipped in silence not knowing what to say to one another.

"Would you like to watch some television?" Vince finally broke the silence.

"If you don't mind, I would rather just sit here and relax sipping this great wine." She told him with a small smile curved to her pretty lips.

"I bet you are tired. Forgive me, I never gave a thought to the fact that you just returned from New York. By the way, you returned early. Why is that?" he ask her raising his eyebrows in wonder.

"I was sent there to make a deal for some zoo land animals to add another attraction here. But they didn't want to cooperate with a price that could even come close to negotiating. So I left. They will call and I will have to return. But it will be after they have had to think it over. "She said nodding her head as if she agreed with herself.

"Zoo land animals?" Vince repeated her words exactly adding them as a question.

"Yes, zoo land animals. For a petting zoo! Animals the vacationer's children can pet and feed. There is not much here for kids, you know." She told him looking into his eyes.

Vince held the stare for several moments before speaking. Joe was beautiful in more ways than one and he devoured that beauty as much as he could. "That was a good idea. Was it yours?" He finally asks her.

"Yes, it's one of them!" She replied.

"What else?" Vince asks interested in what she had to say.

"I would like to get a pool for swimming lessons. I think a skating rink with lessons would be good. And maybe a few amusement rides. Outside theaters, for puppet shows. You know have live shows to teach children how to have fun and get along with one another." She rattled her thoughts without stopping.

Vince listened in amusement to her excitement as she spoke. "You're a very beautiful woman Joe. You never seize to amaze me. Do you know that?" He asks her as he gently places his fingertips under her chin raising her face to peer into her loveliness.

"If you keep that kind of talk up your going to give me the big head. Did you know that Vince?" she replied trying to relieve the tension she was feeling while gazing deeply into his eyes. Joe felt weak against his tenderness and knew she had to do something or she would become putty before his gaze.

Alejandro laid his pen on the table top and stood from his big chair. He wanted to get an early start in the morning and thought it time he turned in for the night. He didn't want to let Trina escape him again. So he undressed and slipped into his big lonely bed with thoughts of her filling his mind, his heart and his deepened desires to hold her close. He twisted and turned until he was buried in the cover of his bed. In his mind the big pillow beside him represented Trina and his arms holding her tight. He thought of the fit she threw at the riding stables. With desire wrapping his heart he drifted off to dream land exhausted with a big smile on his face.

Alejandro shifted the big hat that covered his full head of hair. It was hot and he needed a beer to cool his insides. He had been out riding on the plains all day rustling cattle. So he headed his horse through the dirt streets of the little town his cattle drive had ended just outside of. His delivery was made and now he was going to relax and cool off a bit before heading back to his own town of residence. At the edge of town he dismounted his horse and took the reins leading his horse to the water trough in front of the blacksmiths shop. He carefully tied the reins and strolled inside wiping his brow.

"Man its hot today." He told the blacksmith from behind.

"Howdy stranger, it sure is hot. Names Jeb, what can I do for you," the blacksmith replied.

"I just come off a long cattle drive from Oklahoma. I tied my horse out by the water trough. I hope that's alright. Can you tell me where I can find a beer in this town?" Alejandro asks Jeb displaying his tired hotness.

"Well, yeah, the Hot Trail salon just downs the street a ways. Are you planning to stay awhile?" Jeb asks.

"Just long enough to cool off a bit before hitting the trail back home. Thank you, Jeb." He replied as he turned for the door.

"Just leave your horse right there young fellow. He'll be alright until you return for him." He told Alejandro as he exited the doorway.

Alejandro coughed and twisted to the opposite side in his bed. He put himself into a comfortable position and never woke completely up. He strolled down the wooden boarded sidewalk to the swinging door of the Hot Trail salon and entered walking up to the bar keeper and ordering himself a cold beer.

"Here you go cowboy," the bar keep said handing him a big mug full to the top. Alejandro took the mug in his hand and turned leaning back against the bar. He turned it up and took a big slug just as his eyes caught sight of the most beautiful woman he had ever seen in his life come to the head of the stairs leading to overnight rooms. He held his gaze upon her for a few moments and then turned to the bar keep.

"What's her name, "he asks?

"Who?" the bar keep replies.

"There at the head of the stairs, the pretty salon gal standing right there?" Alejandro asks with his eyes cut and pointing his little finger from the side of the mug.

"Oh, odd name that girl. Trina I believe it is," he said just as she took the first step down. On the second step she stumbled and tumbled to the bottom of the stairs. Alejandro sits straight up in the bed shaking his head awake from his dream. "Trina, she's hurt," he softly told himself aloud. Then jumped up putting his cloths on in a hurry!

Chapter Seventeen

Alejandro hurried outside his hut and got into the jeep driving up to the hotel. Got out and flew inside up the stairs to the door of Trina. He knocked very loudly and when he got no answer he went back down stairs to the desk demanding the key to her room. The desk clerk picked up the phone and called Max refusing to hand over the key. It was just a few moments before Max arrived at Alejandro's side. "What's going on Alejandro? It's three o'clock in the morning." he asks half asleep.

"Max, Joe, Vince and I spent the entire last evening looking for Trina. We couldn't find her anywhere. So we gave up for the night, went home and went to bed." He said before Max interrupted.

"And that's where we should all still be boy." Max said scratching the side of his head.

"No, Max, listen to me. I had this dream that woke me; it was like she was calling to me. She's hurt and I have to get into that room to help her. You have to give me that key." Alejandro anxiously said.

"I can't do that Alejandro. What if you open that door and she is in bed sleeping. Then we have broken policies and face a possible law suit." Max firmly replied.

"Then I'll take full responsibility for it, but I have to get into that room Max." Alejandro said displaying aggravation.

Max turned and walked a short distance away running his hand through his hair. He thought for a couple of minutes and then returned in front of Alejandro. "Your not going to take no for an answer are you boy?" he asks him.

"No, I'm not Max. I feel there is something wrong. I'm going to check that room one way or another. I know I am not wrong Max. She may not be in that room, but she is hurt somewhere. And I have to check it out." he replied firmly.

"Well, I guess I can write it up as an inspection of the room. But I'll have to have a reasonable excuse for it." Max said shaking his head back and forth.

"How about, missing guest? That sounds like reason enough," Alejandro replied.

Max walked around the counter and took the key from its hanger. He turned to him and said, "Come on boy." Half way up the stairs they meet up with Joe and Vince on their way down.

"Alejandro, where are you two going?" Joe asks.

"Not now Joe. I'm going to check Trina's room. To see if she came in last night." He told her without stopping. Joe turned and started to follow him. Vince reached out and took hold of her hand pulling her back. "Wait Joe, I have an idea," he said.

"What?" she quickly asks.

"One night in the pub, Alejandro and I was talking when Jasper came in and took a seat at the bar there where we were. He got a phone call from someone. The conversation was about Trina. So Jasper knows something about that girl that we don't. Maybe he knows where she is. I know its late, or early morning but let's go find Jasper and find out. We don't have to tell Alejandro just in case he doesn't know anything. It would just save him more heartache." Vince told Joe with hopeful excitement of his idea written all over his face. "Good idea," Joe replied following Vince down the stairs. Max and Alejandro continued up the stairs and they each went their separate ways.

Jasper caught up to George and passed him walking up to the room where Donald had been placed when brought in. The curtains were open and the bed was empty. There were no guards standing outside the door. Jasper turned to George and said, "Well, this is it. He was put in this room when he was brought in."

"Not here now, looks like," George replied.

Doctor Jacobs was coming down the hall and Jasper stepped in front of him. "Where is he at?" he ask him.

"Jasper, I'm sorry, he passed on, early this morning," he said with a concerned look on his face.

Jasper drew a long breath and put his hand over his mouth rubbing up and down, then mumbled, "Thank you." He turned to George and just stood there staring at him.

"If it's any consolation to you, I think there was a reward out for his where bouts," Dr Jacobs added.

"Thank you again," George said.

Jasper walked over to a small nearby waiting area that was vacant and took a seat. He placed his elbows on his knees and hung his head. He rubbed his hand back and forth over his chin. His whiskers were getting long and itching. He hadn't left the hospital since he returned from the police station.

George stood in front of him and said," Come on Jasper, lets go check on Trina and then you go get yourself a bath, shave and take a nap. You're tired and I'll be right here. I'm not going anywhere. I'll call you if anything changes. But you need a bath and some rest for now. You can come back when it gets daylight."

Jasper once again stood and said, "I am fine George, I don't want to leave. I promised her I would stay with her."

"I am here Jasper. I think she would understand. And I know she wouldn't want you wearing yourself out like this," he firmly said as he turned and started walking towards her room.

"Let's just check on her first," Jasper said following along behind. They entered her room and Trina still laid the same as she was when they had left. She still appeared to be sleeping. She hadn't as much as moved a hand.

"Alright, I'll take a seat right here by her side and I'll stay put. Now you go and get cleaned up and get yourself some rest. We will be here when you get back. Take your time and get plenty of rest Jasper," George said as he moved the chair to Trina's bedside.

"I am alright George, I promised her," Jasper said.

"We are going to have to take turns Jasper. I'm not a young man and neither are you. You go first, I'll stay and when you get back I'll go," George said.

"Alright then George, I could use a bath at least," he replied running his hand through his hair.

"And some sleep," George said.

"Alright, I won't be long," Jasper said as he leaned and kissed Trina on the forehead.

Max unlocked the door to Trina's room and Alejandro hurried through the door. He went straight to the bedroom. The bed was still made. No Trina in sight. He quickly checked the rest of the large penthouse. Still no Trina in sight or any signs of her have being there in awhile. "See Max, she's not here and hadn't been here. Something is wrong. I feel it in the pit of my stomach," Alejandro worriedly said.

"Relax boy, she probably just stayed in town last night. You don't know. Don't invent things that might not be true. That won't help you any. Now come on and let's get out of here," Max said pointing towards the door. Alejandro followed Max out the door closing it firmly behind. He hurried down the stairs and said over his shoulder," I'm going to find her Max so I won't be working later today." And he flew on down the stairs not giving Max a chance to say anything more.

"How about we go to a diner and have some breakfast before we start looking for Jasper?" Vince asks Joe.

"That sounds good to me. It is kind of early still. That will give him time to wake and get to work. We can catch him there," she replied with a smile.

"Consider it done then," he said reaching across the car for her hand continuing to drive towards town.

"It's a quarter to six. Do you know any place with good food that's open at this time?" she asks him.

"Yes, I do, it's about five minutes up the road beside the hospital," he replied with a satisfying grin on his face.

"Great, because I am starving to death now, I don't think we ever did eat anything last night. Those drinks we had almost done me in." she said squeezing his hand tightly.

"Jasper arrives at work early. This little place is quick with their service so we'll have time to eat and be waiting on him when he gets there," Vince said pulling the car into a parking spot.

"Vince, look, there is Jasper right there. He came out of the hospital. Let's catch him," she said jumping out of the car yelling. Vince pulled the car into park and shut down the motor. He got out and followed Joe towards Jasper.

"Hey Jasper, Jasper…" She yelled loudly. Jasper turned into the face of Joe with Vince coming up strongly behind her.

"Joe, Vince…how are you two and what are you doing up so early?" he asks.

"We were just going to breakfast. Why don't you join us? It's my treat of course. I would like to talk to you for a few minutes if I could," Vince took over the conversation before Joe gave it away.

"What is it Vince, I'm really in a hurry," Jasper said repositioning his stance.

"You look tired and like you need some coffee," Joe spoke up saying as she took Jasper by the arm pulling him towards the diner.

I've got to get cleaned up. I don't have a lot of time and I'm not fit to go into the diner," Jasper replied.

"You are fine, come on some coffee at least won't hurt you," she said continuing to pull him towards the little restaurant. Vince opened the door and held it while Joe and Jasper entered then he followed them inside. They took a booth in the corner and ordered coffee while they looked over the menu.

Jasper sat staring out the window towards the hospital while he sipped his coffee not saying a word.

Joe looked up from the menu at him and then Vince. She was the first one to speak. "I'll have the country ham and eggs," she said laying the menu down on the table.

"I'll have the same," Vince replied turning to Jasper. "Are you sure you won't have some food Jasper," he asks him.

"Thank you but I am sure. What's this all about Vince?" he quickly asks.

"I'll get right to the point. Do you remember back when you was in the pub at the bar sitting beside Alejandro and you got that phone call about Trina?" Vince asks taking in a deep breath.

"We can't find her," Joe quickly added and Vince gave her a, be quite look. Jasper glanced at Joe before turning back to Vince.

"Yes, as a matter of fact I do," he replied not offering anything more to the subject.

"Good, then you have to know that I am sure you know more about her than you are telling. Alejandro is in love with her and he is about to go crazy looking for her. He wants to tell her how he feels. He has been looking for a couple of days now. Do you know where she is?" Vince finished off with the big question wasting no time getting to it.

Jasper peered out the window towards the hospital again before he spoke. Trina telling him she didn't want Alejandro to see her like she was run through his mind. He turned back to Vince and looked at him for a few moments before he stood. "I'm sorry, I can't help you two," he said.

"Please Jasper, if you know something tell us. My brother is in terrible shape. He loves that girl so much its tearing him apart that he can't find her. Please tell us," Joe pleaded with sad eyes.

Jasper again peered out the window towards the hospital for a moment and then replied," I really can't help you. I am sorry. But thank you for the coffee." He then turned to walk away.

Vince reached out and grabbed him by the arm and asks," What's her last name? Can you at least tell us that much? We can go back to the hotel and get that information but it would save some time if you could just tell us."

Jasper knew that was true so he looked Vince straight into the eyes and softly said," Wright," then he turned and walked out of the diner.

Joe reached across the table and took hold to his hand and said," Well that didn't help us much.

"Ah, but it did Joe, a lot more than you are realizing. Eat up, we've got a lead to follow," he said and began to eat his breakfast. Joe did the same speaking no further words putting all her trust in Vince.

Chapter Eighteen

Alejandro walked the beach in deep thought. He was beside himself with wonder of where to start looking for Trina. He kept asking himself over and over where she could possibly be. Why did he have such a pitiful feeling deep inside?

The moon was still high and shinning full. He sat down in the sand and leaned backwards propping on his hands. He watched and thought as it slowly started disappearing being replaced with the rise of the sun. It was the only time of the day that the air was cool on the beach. He had goose bumps risen and wasn't sure if they were from the cool air or from the not knowing what was going on with Trina or where she was. He began writing her name over and over in the sand with his finger tip thinking about where he should go from there. Feeling depressed, lost and alone he raised his eyes to the rising sun and ask God to lead him to Trina. And he once again found himself walking the beach searching for her with no understanding of the nauseated feelings he store inside.

Vince and Joe finished their breakfast and stepped outside the diner. He took her hand as he turned to face her. "Joe, did you notice Jasper kept looking out the window every time we ask him about Trina?" he asks looking into her eyes.

"Well, no I didn't, why? What are you thinking?" Joe quickly asks.

Vince ran his fingers across his mouth concerned as he started to speak and said," He looked towards that hospital every time he peered out that window."

"Oh no…you don't think! Oh my God Vince, could it be?" Joe eagerly replied turning her eyes towards the building.

"There's one way to find out, come on," he said, leading the way. They crossed the street in a hurry and entered the front doors into the lobby of the hospital. Vince looked around for the information desk.

Joe said pointing, "There it is, come on Vince." They walked up and he bent down peering through the window but nobody was there. He looked at his watch reading half past seven.

"It's too early. The sign says they open up at eight. We'll have to hang out until then, its only thirty more minutes," he told her.

"Yes and maybe they'll get here a little earlier than that too. Lets take a seat right here," she said pointing towards some chairs straight across from the desk.

"We can watch for Jasper to come in too and follow him if he does," Vince said.

"That's a good idea," Joe replied walking towards the seats. "I hope when someone does get here they'll tell us what we want to know. I am going to say whatever I have to get the information. If Trina is here I'll find out."

They had been sitting in the seats about fifteen minutes when the lights came on in the small office of the information center and the window opened up. Vince jumped up and walked swiftly to the window. He bent and stuck his head almost all the way through it.

"Good morning." He said loudly.

The lady inside turned quickly as if he had scared her.

"Oh, sorry about that, I didn't mean to startle you," he said apologizing.

"I just am not used to such early callers. I didn't expect anyone and before coffee," she replied.

"Again I am sorry, but I am in a hurry here, if you could please see fit to helping me out a little early this morning," he told her turning on his charm.

"What can I do for you," the clerk asks him walking towards the window.

"Trina...ah," he hesitated and turned towards Joe. "What did Jasper say her last name was," he asks Joe.

She pushed him aside and leaned down into the window. "Trina Wright, what is her room number," Joe asks the clerk.

Vince and Joe both were leaned into the window by then. The clerk looked from one to the other and said," You two seem to be insistent, but you're going to have to give me a few minutes to get my computer up and running." She said sitting down in her chair in front of it.

"We understand," Vince replied quickly.

The clerk pushed the button turning the computer on and waited for it to load. She turned to them while it was and began to talk again. "So, is this person someone special to you two?" she asks them curiously.

"To my brother she is. We have been looking for her for what seems likes days. My bother is in love with her and he needs to tell her but we haven't been able to find her as of yet. We're hoping we have found her, and she is okay. I'm sure you understand the importance," Joe replied with a pleading tone.

"Is your brother young?" she asks her.

"He's in his twenties, and stubborn when it comes to love. And now that he has finally realized he is in love, he can't find her," Joe said.

Vince watched and listened to the two ladies carry on as if he wasn't even there. "Excuse me," he said. "The computer is loaded now," he continued pointing towards it.

"Ah, it is, isn't it," the clerk replied still looking towards it. "What was her name again," she asks.

"Trina Wright," Vince eagerly replied.

She typed her name into the search bar of the patients list. Before hitting the enter key she turned the screen so it was visible to only her. Trina's name popped up under the secured rooms list. The clerk's face grimaced.

"What is it?" Vince quickly asks, noticing the change of her face.

"I have no information to give you," she said.

"I saw your expression change. She is here isn't she," he asks firmly.

"I'm sorry, I can't give out that information," she once again told them.

"Then turn that screen back around and turn your back," he eagerly said.

The clerk looked from Vince to Joe back and forth for a moment. Then she turned to the computer screen one more time before speaking.

Looking back at Vince she said, "Excuse me for a moment please." She got up and left the desk walking across the room to the other side keeping her back turned. Vince reached through the window and turned the screen just enough for him to see it. "There it is right there, room three forty-two. Come on Joe," he said grabbing her hand and heading down the hall in a hurry.

"What room are we looking for?" she asks out of breath.

"Three forty two," Vince replied.

"There it is on the right," she said hurrying ahead of him.

"There's a sign on the door that says we have to report to the nursing station before entering," she told him turning to face him.

"That's because it is listed as a secure room," he replied stepping past her and pushing the door open.

George raised his head and peered towards the sound of the door coming open. "Who are you? And how did you get in here?" he ask them as they entered the room.

"Trina is a friend of ours. Who are you?" Vince replied approaching the bed.

"This here is my niece," George said standing.

"We met her at the hotel where she has been staying. What happened to her?" Joe broke in asking.

"Young lady, this is a secure room. There's not supposed to be anybody else in here. I could have you two thrown out if I had a mind to," George said turning towards her.

"Yes sir, I understand that but we have been looking for her for several days now. You see, it's my brother. He is in love with her and he needs to tell her so. That's why we have been looking for her," Joe pleadingly replied to George.

George scratched the side of his head and said, "Your brother huh?"

"Yes sir," replied Vince protecting Joe.

"And just who is your brother?" George asks.

"His name is Alejandro and he met Trina at the hotel also. He works there. She is in love with him too but they both have been denying it to themselves. He has realized it now and needs to tell her. But we couldn't find her. We saw Jasper leave here and took a chance on finding her here," Joe said almost in tears.

Vince put an arm around Joe and pulled her close to his side. The door opened and all three turned towards the door just as Jasper walked in. "Vince, Joe what are you two doing here?" Jasper asks them.

"You know these two?" George quickly responded to Jasper's entered greeting.

"Yeah, I know them," he told George.

"I think you know the answer to that question," Vince quickly replied.

"Let's step out to the lobby and talk," Jasper said opening the door. All three followed Jasper out into the lobby. They took seats in the corner where they could talk without being disturbed by people walking back and forth.

Jasper raised his head and turned his attention towards Joe and Vince while George became attentive to what Jasper was going to say. "Well, it's like this. You can't tell Alejandro where she is," he managed to say before Joe spoke up.

"And just why not?" Joe aggressively asks wanting to know.

"The last thing she said to me just before she went out like she is now was she didn't want him to see her like that. I promised her and I intend to keep that promise. That's why not," Jasper said.

"You promised her Jasper, we didn't. You don't know what Alejandro is going through with worry of her. You can't be blamed if we tell him. We found her and you didn't tell us or show us where she was," Vince eagerly added. Jasper bowed and propped his elbow on his knee placing his palm on his forehead holding his head up.

"What happened to her anyway?" Joe asks with a soft tone of sympathy in her voice.

"Now you two just wait a minute. If she doesn't want this Alejandro boy to see her then he's not going to see her," George said ignoring Joe's question reaching over and patting Jasper on the shoulder.

"You are her uncle, right?" Vince asks.

"That's right I am," George replied firmly.

"Then you have to understand this boy is in love with her and she is with him too. He could be a great help to her right now in her time of need. Why would you want to stand in the way of what she is in need of?" Vince asks almost too loudly.

"Ah, hello, what happened to her?" Joe squeezes in her question one more time.

"Or maybe you are just thinking of what he is in need of," George replied.

"No sir, I am thinking of what they both are in need of," Vince quickly comes back with.

Jasper sighed deeply and raised his head looking at George. "It's true George. She is in love with him. She told me about it. The last time I talked with her before this she said she was thinking on returning home early to avoid him because he had someone else. I didn't know who she was talking about. I have thought about it and I do now. She also asks me to keep her informed on how he was doing," Jasper said running his hand through his hair.

"Who, who does he have," Joe asks quickly.

"Well Joe, I believe it was you she saw him with. Does she know you Joe?" Jasper asks her.

"Not directly I don't guess. I have seen her and she has seen me but we have not directly talked or been formally introduced, No I guess she don't," Joe said placing her hand over her mouth as she walked over to the window. "All of this is partly my fault," she sadly whispered peering out. Joe stood quietly not paying attention to the three men behind her hashing back and forth. She still didn't know what had happened to Trina. All she could think about now was Alejandro and how she had been part of the reason his heart was aching.

Chapter Nineteen

Alejandro walked back and forth over the sandy beach. People had started gathering and it was filling up fast. Everything was beginning to enclose around him. All he wanted was to find Trina and tell her how much he had fallen in love with her over her stay. He knew it was a short time and he didn't understand it himself but felt this was something he had to do.

"Hey, are you working today?" a voice came from over Alejandro's shoulder. He turned into clear air until he looked down into face of a small child who appeared to be about six or seven years old. She was a cute little girl with a big grin on her face.

He knelt down and said," No, not today but I'll answer your question you have."

"You look like a big man who can out swim all the sharks that are out there. I want to learn how to do that. Can you teach me?" she replied still pointing towards the water.

He smiled and seated himself once again on the sand in front of the little girl. "What's your name?" he asks her.

"Emmy, really its Emily but I like Emmy better. What's yours?" she asks him back.

"Well Emmy, mine is Alejandro. Can you say that?" he asks her still grinning.

"Nope…, but I'll just call you Big Al. I can remember that." She said taking a seat in the sand as well.

"Big Al it is for you and Emmy it is for me. Where is your Mommy and Daddy Emmy?" he asks her pushing her hair back out of her eyes. The little girl pointed her finger towards the sky and said," Up there with God in heaven. Their waiting for me to come up there too and I'm going to go one of these days."

Alejandro lost his grin and felt a stabbing pain in his heart for the child as she continued to talk.

"I live with a bunch of other kids while I'm waiting to find someone to live with. Miss Jane brought us to the beach today so we could swim. But I can't swim well enough. I'm scared of the sharks and that's why I want you to teach me how to swim faster than them. Can you, huh…please Big Al?" she asks him in a pleading tone.

"Wait a minute now, what happened to your parents?" he asks her tenderly.

Emmy dropped her head and stared at the sand in front of her for several minutes while Alejandro waited for her response in anticipation. She raised her eyes full of tears and softly said," A car wreck."

Then she jumped up and grabbed his hand pulling at him saying," Come on Big Al show me how to swim fast."

"Emmy…Emmy… where are you?" a voice came calling from down the beach.

Alejandro and Emmy both turned towards the voice as a middle aged lady approached them. "Right here Miss Jane," Emmy replied loudly and then turned to Alejandro. "That's Miss Jane, she's looking for me," she told him.

"Emmy, you shouldn't take off like that. I was worried about you. Go back over with the other children now," she told her turning her towards the other kids by the shoulder.

"But Miss Jane, Big Al here is going to teach me how to swim fast. Isn't that right Big Al," she told her.

Alejandro reached over and rubbed Emmy on top of the head and said," Maybe you better do what Miss Jane here says for now Emmy. Big Al will be around and see you again soon. I promise…"

"Remember you said you promise me Big Al," she replied pleading with her tone.

"I will," Alejandro said with a smile.

Emmy ran off across the beach towards the other kids. Alejandro turned to Miss Jane whom was just about to walk off.

"What happened to her parents?" he asks her.

"They were both killed in a car accident almost a year ago. Emmy doesn't talk about it. She still has not released. She's awaiting adoptive parents and until then she is with my husband and I in our home. We house several children in the same situation as Emmy. All awaiting homes," She told him.

"I would like to visit her if that's alright with you. Maybe I will teach her how to swim faster than the sharks," Alejandro said.

"Are you a married man Mister?" she asks with a concerned expression easy to see.

"Alejandro is my name and please…you are free to use it. I work here at the hotel. Married, no, but I am working on it," he said still watching Emmy across the beach.

"I see, and what makes you think I should allow you to visit Emmy?" Mrs. Jane asks him.

"Madame, I saw into that little girls eye's when she told me her parents were in heaven waiting for her to come. I saw inside her eyes when she told me they left her in a car wreck, and I saw in her eyes when she expressed her fear of swimming because she couldn't swim faster than the sharks. You have no fears to express. I am an honest man and I can't turn my back on that little girl. Please understand I am a trust worthy man. I would like to at the least be a big brother to her," he replied firmly staring her in the eyes and not turning away.

"She told you all that?" Ms Jane asks him surprised.

"Yes she did and I feel I could help her as much as she could help me," he replied.

"Just how could a small child like Emmy help you?" she asks him quickly.

"She could take my mind off of my not being able to find the woman I am in love with. I have been looking for her for several days now. I feel I have reached a limit and Emmy can help me to think straight again," he said with no hesitation.

"Well, Alejandro, I don't allow the children to swim right away. They eat first and then build sand castles for at least an hour before allowed in the water. Maybe you could join us in our picnic and I can get to know you a little better before making a decision.

But of course you would have to meet with my husband as well for a final decision," she told him with her invitation.

"I would be more than pleased to join you and the children. Thank you for this opportunity," he said holding his hand out towards the kids. Alejandro followed the lady back over to where the children were anxiously waiting.

"Are you going to eat with us?" Emmy excitedly asks him.

"It would seem so," he told her with a big smile on his face.

"Oh… goody, we're going to have fried chicken and potato salad," she said jumping up and down.

"Sounds delicious to me," he told her taking her hand.

"Well, we have to wait until Miss Jane calls us first," she said.

"Miss Jane…Miss Jane, big Al and me are going right over here and scoop some sand up with our feet for my sand castle I'm going to build. When you call us to eat we will come right back. Is that alright with you?" she very excitedly asks.

"Okay Emmy, just so long as I can see you. Don't go any further away," she replied with a pleased smile at Emmy's reactions to Alejandro. She hadn't seen Emmy smile like she was now since she's been inside her home. Maybe Alejandro was right, just maybe he would be good for Emmy.

"Okay, come on big Al," she said grabbing his hand. Alejandro followed Emmy's lead across the beach to a close by area where the sand seems to be layered deeply.

"Pull your shoe's off big Al," she said slipping her tiny feet out of her own.

"Alright," he told her sliding his big feet out of his slippers.

"This is the way to do it," Emmy told him turning her foot sideways and shoveling the sand into a small pile. Alejandro watched the child as she ran back and forth grabbing at the sand with her feet and pulling it into a small pile a little bit at a time.

"Well come on big Al, help me get it. I'm going to build the biggest castle on the beach," she told him out of breath. Alejandro smiled and began pulling sand with his feet to Emmy's pile. It made him feel like a child again. He got so involved that he forgot about his problem's with Trina and devoted all of his attention to sweet little Emmy. And until she decided to start asking questions he was feeling care free.

"Are you married big Al," Emmy asks him looking up at what seems like miles to her into his face.

Alejandro's thoughts went right straight back to Trina instantly with that question. He turned his eyes to Emmy and said, "No... I am not."

"Why not, your old enough to be, aren't you?" she very quickly asks him!

"Yeah, I guess I am," he said not adding anything extra for the curious little girl.

"Don't you have a girlfriend you could marry?" she continued to question.

"Emmy, why are you asking me all these questions about being married?" he asks her kneeling down beside her.

"I'm sorry, I just was wondering is all," she said with a downward curve around her mouth.

"And why was you wondering?" he asks her lying his hand on her shoulder.

"I don't know because you're nice. I thought you might be," she said still displaying a grimace on her face.

"Are you sure that's all there is to it?" he asks her giving a little squeeze to her shoulder.

"We better get some more sand," she said turning and running back a ways to start gathering again.

Alejandro stood and watched the little girl wondering what her real thoughts were.

"Emmy...Emmy, come on now, its time to eat," Mrs. Jane called out.

"Okay, we're coming Mrs. Jane," she yelled back. "Come on big Al, the food is ready to eat. Then we can build my castle," she said running up and grabbing him by the hand.

Alejandro followed behind Emmy to the tables where the other children had already gathered around and were sitting. "Come over here big Al. You can sit beside me," she said patting the bench beside her.

"That's okay Emmy, you just go ahead. I'm going to stand," he told her back.

"Okay," she replied reaching for her drink.

Alejandro wondered around the tables watching the children as they ate the meal Mrs. Jane had prepared for them. "Won't you eat a bite?" Mrs. Jane asks him from behind.

He turned and said," It's alright, maybe I will after the children get finished. Would that be alright with you?"

"Well of course but there are plenty of food," she told him with a wrinkle of curiosity to her forehead.

Alejandro peered into Mrs. Jane's face and finally cocked a small smile saying," Alright, maybe I'll take a chicken leg then."

"That's better. I'll get it for you," she said returning to the table and retrieving a paper plate, then put two big fat legs of chicken on the plate and a large helping of potato salad then grabbed a paper towel with a plastic fork and returned to his side handing it to him. He took the plate without any words said. The children continued to eat their meal in a hurry wanting to get to the castle building and then swimming.

Alejandro turned towards the ocean and peered out across the waters. It took his mind back to Trina because she came from across those waters. He questioned himself over and over as to where she could be. And why she hadn't returned to her room last night. He didn't know where to look. He had been all over the island and had no luck. At that moment an idea hit him. He thought about how upset she had gotten that night in the pub. The last time he saw her float up those stairs. A burning idea filled his mind that maybe she had gone back home in a rush without taking her things. She was pretty upset, upset enough to do just that he thought.

"I'll go check at the airport," he told himself out loud.

"What are you going to the airport for big Al?" Emmy ask with her head leaned back as far as she could get it looking up at him.

Alejandro looked down at her and smiled saying," Nothing Emmy, nothing that concerns you my little friend."

"Are you going somewhere?" she asks him ignoring his words.

"I will have to be going soon," he said taking her hand leading the way to the sand pile they had pulled up before the meal.

Emmy walked along steady asking him, "Where are you going?"

"I'm not going anywhere until we get that castle built. Then I have to go to work," he said.

"But you told me you wasn't working today," she replied.

Alejandro stopped and peered down at the little girl for a moment and then said," Yes, I guess I did, didn't I."

"Yeah, you did," she said.

"Well, I have some things I have to get done on my day off too," he told her running his hand across the shinny shimmer of her sun soaking blonde hair.

"Maybe Mrs. Jane will let me come with you then," she excitedly said.

"No, I don't think so Emmy," he quickly said.

"Why?" she asks him without a hesitation.

"Well, you and Mrs. Jane just met me and you don't know me well enough for Mrs. Jane to let you go off with me. That's why," he told her.

"We can ask her and see can't we?" she asks pleadingly.

"You can ask her but I'm sure she'll say no," he told her.

"Mrs. Jane…. Mrs. Jane, can I go with big Al when we finish building the sand castle? He'll bring me home in a little bit," she yelled out loudly.

Mrs. Jane raised her head and instantly said," No you may not Emmy."

"See, I told you," Alejandro said.

"Why?" she asks with a frown.

Mrs. Jane had approached them by that time. "Emmy, you nor I know this man that well yet. And Mr. Jack has to meet him first too," she told her.

"But Mr. Jack will like big Al just like you Mrs. Jane," she said.

"Still the same we will wait and let Mr. Jack decide that on his own. Now you can build your castle and there will be no more talk about leaving with Al here," she told her.

Emmy knew it was time to stop questioning Mrs. Jane on that note. So she fell to the sand and began packing her pail with the moist sand.

"May I speak with you please, over here?" Mrs. Jane said to Alejandro pointing towards the tables. He followed her to the table where she started questioning him," What was that all about? Did you ask her if she wanted to go with you? What made you think I would allow such a thing and how could you put her up to asking?" she rolled her questions one right behind the other quickly.

"Hold on a minute, I didn't ask her. It was all her idea on her own. She asks me if she could ask you. I told her you would say no and why you would. Don't bury me before you have the facts of the situation Mrs." He said frustrated.

"I'm sorry; it just took me by surprise that's all. I should have given you the chance to explain," she told him.

"It's alright, I understand your concern," he replied with a comforting smile.

"Why don't you let me give you our number? You can call in the next day or two and make arrangements to come by and see her and meet my husband. I don't know why but Emmy seems to have taken to you and that's more than I have seen out of her since she has been with us. I can't deny her what seems to make her happy at the moment. Maybe after a few visits at the house we will allow you to take her for ice cream or something," she told him.

"Fair enough," Alejandro said holding out his hand.

"Big Al, come on now, I started without you," Emmy called across the beach.

Alejandro returned to where Emmy was working hard on the castle. He knelt down so he could talk to her. "You're doing a good job without me Emmy. It looks good so far. I have to be going now. I told Mrs. Jane I would call and make arrangements to come by the house and visit with you in the next day or two. Then we'll think about them swimming lessons," he gently told her not wanting to upset her that he was leaving.

Emmy's eyes got as big as half dollars," Really, you told her that?" she asks him.

"Yes, I did and I promise you I will do it," he said.

"Well, alright big Al, I'll be waiting on you at the house then," she said jumping up and throwing herself around his neck.

Alejandro hugged little Emmy tight and whispered in her ear," I promise Emmy. I promise."

CHAPTER TWENTY

After Joe and Vince had left the hospital they returned to Joe's apartment to freshen up a bit. Vince fell asleep on the couch while Joe was showering. She had thrown a blanket over him when she returned finding him asleep. She took a seat in the recliner across the room and fallen asleep herself. She was lost in her thoughts of her brother's aching heart and how she was responsible for it. If she hadn't been in the pub that night then Trina would never have seen her and her bother together and gotten the wrong idea about them. She woke to a tender kiss on her forehead by Vince's soft full lips. Peering into his eyes she smiled a small cock of a grin.

"Good evening baby," he said holding his hand out.

"What time is it," she quickly asks him jumping up.

"Its late afternoon, we both fell asleep. I guess we were more tired than we thought," he replied.

Joe stretched once she was on her feet. While wiping her brow she walked to the window that faced the front of the hotel and peered out without saying a word.

"What's wrong Joe?" he asks coming up to her back and sliding his arms around her waist.

"Did you hear what Jasper said about my being the girl Trina saw Alejandro with?" she asks him almost in tears.

"Hey now Joe, stop that. You're blaming yourself for something that's not your fault. It's not your responsibility to see to it that those two understand one another or communicate," he said turning her to face him at the same time.

"But…" she said before he interrupted her.

"No buts about it Joe, Trina jumped on that before she knew the facts and Alejandro didn't bother with telling her so it's their fault only, not yours. I won't have you blaming your self for their own faults. Their grown and their acting like kids," he quickly blurted not giving her a chance to say anything more.

"It's just that it tears me up to think I'm the one who had caused his pain. He's been through so much already and it's a big step for him to even consider a relationship. I fussed at him about it on the way to the airport. I care and I can't stand the fact that it was I who she saw him with even if it was the wrong idea," she told him looking up into his eyes with a tear rolling down her cheek. Vince ran the backside of his fingers over the tear wiping it away and hugged her tightly.

"Oh baby, don't you see, it's not your fault. Alejandro is a grown man. It didn't have to be that way from the start. He could have told her. You know and so do I that he had to have seen the hurt in her eyes that same day. Just as you and I did. He could have went for her then and told her everything. Instead he chose to ignore her. She jumped to conclusions and he ignored her. What kind of time bomb do you think that built? It wasn't your fault," he said squeezing her tight in his arms and running his hand up and down her back.

Joe sobbed into Vince's chest and then stepped back peering up at him. "I'm so sorry Vince. I know your right and I'm just being a blubbering idiot," she said.

"Nonsense Joe, you just love your brother that much, and you want to protect him. But you have to let him live his own life. Especially his love life," he told her bending and kissing her forehead again.

She squeezed her little arms around Vince as tight as she could and once again peered up at him saying," I love you Vince."

Vince picked her up to peer back into her eyes at equal level replying," I love you Joanna."

"How did you get to be such an expert in love?" she asks him.

"I'm not an expert. I'm a side stander peering in, and seeing what love has blinded," he replied to her.

"Oh my God, I just realized something," she said.

"What did you realize Joe?" Vince asks knowing darn well what she was about to say.

"We just told each other we love one another for the first time. And I don't know about you but it came from me without a second thought," she said.

"Yes Joe, we did and I know I have loved you for a very long time. Will you marry me now?" he asks her, feeling it was the right time to do so.

The question took Joe by surprise. She stepped back and cleared her head before speaking.

"It's alright if you want to think about it Joe. I understand but you know that I have no second thought about wanting to marry you either. I love you more than words can say," he said.

"Yes...Oh yes... I will marry you," she replied practically running to his arms and diving into them. He picked her up and slung her around in a circle and sat her back down again. He bent and kissed her hard and long for she had made him the happiest man on the island.

"Vince, can we just order dinner in tonight and stay here. We can figure out what were going to do about Alejandro and Trina and start out fresh in the morning. Is that alright with you?" she asks him.

"Sounds great to me," he said just before kissing her again.

"You set up that table over there and I will order dinner. And Vince don't forget the candle," she said turning for the phone while pointing at a table in the corner.

"Anything you want Joe. I'll put a hundred candles if you want them," he replied smiling hugely. He turned and moved to the table Joe had pointed to. He was floating on his own cloud and he was untouchable.

Alejandro had spent the rest of the afternoon just wondering around the island with his eyes open hoping for a glimpse of Trina. But he didn't see her anywhere. When he had grown tired and lost all hope, he had returned to his place and fell into his soft chair for comfort. With his head leaned back and his eyes closed he let his mind travel over all the places he had been looking. He had even searched the places that he knew she had really enjoyed. But nothing and no place had given him promise! He was tired and his feet hurt from all the walking he had done. Yet his mind wouldn't let him slow down. His heart wouldn't let him slow down. He had to find this woman who had captured his long lost emotions for love.

"Where were Joe and Vince all day?" he asks himself aloud. He raised his head from the back of his chair and rubbed across his forehead wondering why his sister hadn't been around pushing at him. Then he got worried about her. It wasn't like her to not try to push at him. He looked up at the clock on the wall. It was a quarter to seven. He leaned forward searching for his shoes he had kicked off earlier. He thought he would just go and check on her. He was hungry anyway and he could grab himself a bite to eat while he was out.

Alejandro reached down into his pocket for the jeep keys and pulled out the piece of paper that Mrs. Jane had written her address and phone number on. Peering down at it he realized it was only two blocks from the property line of the hotel. He knew exactly where it was. He had seen those kids outside playing there before and thought it must have been a day care of some kind. "Hmmm…I'll just pop by for a few minutes and surprise Emmy. I'll meet the husband while I'm at it," he told himself aloud.

He picked up a teddy bear he had kept for a few years. He had bought it for the last woman he had tried having a relationship with, but never got to give it to her before she dumped him. So he would just take it to Emmy. He thought it would be a big surprise for her and she might like that. With the teddy bear under his arm and keys in hand he headed out the door one more time for the day.

Alejandro pulled into the driveway in hopes that Mrs. Jane wouldn't be upset because he had told her he would call first and make arrangements to visit. But he thought it a better surprise for Emmy if he didn't and hopefully Mr. Jack and Mrs. Jane would understand. A tall middle aged muscled up man walked around the corner of the house just as Alejandro opened the door to the jeep. He stepped out and shut it behind him forgetting to retrieve the teddy bear.

"Afternoon Sir," Alejandro said.

"Afternoon young man, what can I do for you?" the tall man asks him.

"My name is Alejandro. I met your wife and little Emmy today at the beach," he replied before the man spoke.

"Jack Spear," the man replied holding out his hand. Alejandro reached and took hold of Mr. Spear's hand in a firm shake.

"I know, I told Mrs. Jane that I would call before I came by, but I wanted to surprise Emmy with a teddy bear. I don't have long to stay. I hope you understand," he told him.

"Yes…Jane told me about you. I would like to know just why you found such an interest in Emmy. She's a fragile little girl with not much to say. And I won't have any emotional trauma put on her," Jack wasted no time telling him.

"Not at all Sir, I wish I could tell you why but I can't I don't know myself. Just from what little bit Emmy told me she made my heart go out to her. I didn't and don't feel I could turn my back on her," Alejandro quickly replied.

"Jane said Emmy told you a little bit more than what she has even thought about bringing up here. She lost her parents both at the same time and she emotionally shut down. She hadn't spoken about it at all. I do find it interesting that she would open up even a little bit to a stranger like you. I'll allow you to visit with her here and we'll go from there," Jack told him.

"That's fair enough for me but I want you to understand I intend on being like a big brother to that little girl. I'll eventually want to take her for ice cream or something, but I understand your concern and when you say it's alright then and only then will I do it," Alejandro told Jack as he was opening the door to the jeep back up. "May I see her now? I want to give her this teddy bear," he said reaching inside the jeep to retrieve it.

"You wait on the porch and I'll go inside and bring her out there," Jack told him heading for the front door.

"Yes sir, that will be fine," Alejandro said following behind to the big porch. He took a seat in a white wicker rocking chair a couple of feet from the front door. He placed the teddy bear behind his back and waited for little Emmy to surprise her with it.

"What are we going to do Mr. Jack?" Emmy was asking as the two exited the doorway onto the porch.

Emmy had her back to Alejandro, so she didn't see him when she came out. "See me for a minute," Alejandro said from behind her.

Emmy turned at the voice from her back and when she saw him she smiled hugely and ran jumping up on his lap throwing her arms around his neck saying," Big Al, you did come. Just like you said you would. You came you really came."

Jack stood back and watched Emmy's reaction in total amazement. It was just like Jane had told him. Emmy hadn't shown any interest in anything since she had been with them. And this reaction to this man just might be a God send into that little girl's life. How could he deny her a big brother?

"Yes I did Emmy, I promised you, but I can only stay a few minutes," he said hugging her back.

"Why...you can stay a long time, its ok isn't it Mr. Jack?" Emmy asks turning to peer at him.

"Well it won't be long until all little girls bed time Emmy. And big Al here, as you call him has already said he couldn't stay long," Jack replied just as Jane was coming out the door to join them.

"Hello Alejandro," Jane said from her husband's side.

"Hello Mrs. Jane, I won't be here long and I told your husband I hoped you understood why I didn't call before I came," he replied turning his attention back to the little girl sitting on his lap.

"Why did you come?" Emmy asks him quickly.

Alejandro pulled the teddy bear from his back saying," To bring you this Emmy. It's a special sleeping teddy bear. He will listen to all your fears. He'll keep you warm all night long and his name is little Al. He needed a good home with a sweet little girl instead of a big old man like me."

Emmy took hold of the big soft cuddly bear and squeezed tightly. "Oh thank you big Al thank you. I'll never let him go. And I'll take care of him just like he's going to me. I love him, I really, really do," she said with emotion pouring through her tearing eyes.

Emmy turned her attention to Jack and Jane standing across the porch. "Look at what big Al brought me. Aren't he pretty?" she asks them.

"Yes, Emmy he is ISN'T he," Mrs. Jane replies almost tearing herself.

"I'm sorry Mrs. Jane, next time I will say isn't," Emmy replied holding tightly and hugging her new friend, little Al.

"Alright, well I have to go now Emmy," Alejandro said picking her up and sitting her feet down on the porch.

"But you just got here," Emmy replied.

"Yes, but it's your bedtime and I have to go find my sister now," he said patting the top of her head.

"You have a sister?" Emmy asks him puzzled.

"I do and maybe someday you can meet her too," he said grinning.

"I would like that too," Emmy said reaching with one arm to hug him bye. Alejandro reached down and picked her and little Al up giving them both a big bear hug.

"I'll be coming back soon Emmy. Now you and little Al better get to bed so you can dream nice dreams and be all rested for the daylight to come," he said returning her feet to the porch. Emmy disappeared inside with little Al held tightly in her grip.

"Thank you for understanding and allowing me to see her," Alejandro told Jack and Jane.

"You are very welcome, and may return anytime you want to without calling first," Jack replied holding out his hand once again.

Alejandro took Jack's hand in a friendly shake saying," Thank you again and it was very nice meeting you. Take care."

"Will do and it was nice to meet you as well. Be safe and have a good night," Jack said taking his wife by the elbow and turning her towards the door.

Alejandro returned to his jeep and headed back to the hotel.

"Now, he had to hurry so he wouldn't be late to his sisters for dinner. He rushed to get into the jeep and then drove away feeling good about his visit with Emmy.

CHAPTER TWENTY-ONE

"What's taking them so long with the dinner, I wonder?" Joe said walking over to the desk to call and find out.

"Well Joe, we only ordered the kitchen. It's going to take a little bit of time. Come here and sit beside me and let's talk a bit about what were going to do with the information we've learned," Vince said still smiling hugely.

Joe took a seat beside Vince on the couch and turned to face him. "What are you thinking?" she asks him concerned.

"Are we going to tell Alejandro where Trina is at or not? What do we do, how do we tell him and what do we say?" his words flew out one behind the other quickly.

"I'm not going to ask you to tell him. I will in my own good time. I know it's going to upset him but it would upset him even more if he found out we knew and didn't tell him. So when the time is right after dinner this evening I will tell him and that will keep you in the clear. I think Jasper would better understand it if I was the one instead of you since I am his sister," Joe replied firmly.

"You're probably right but I'm not concerned about Jasper getting upset. After all he practically told just by looking out that window at the diner. But I'll abide your wishes," he said.

Joe leaned in and gave Vince a kiss on the cheek just as a knock came rapping at the door. "Our food is finally here," she said jumping up to get the door.

Joe opened the door into the face of Alejandro. "Alejandro, it's about time you got here.

"I'm fine Alejandro but thank you for your concern," she said.

"Well… are you going to let me in or what?" he asks her with a grin.

"Oh… yes of course, come on in," she said stepping to the side.

"Hey Vince what's going on?" Alejandro asks spotting Vince sitting on the couch.

"House rent and grocery bill Alejandro. What's up with you?" he asks in return with a chuckle.

"Same old thing the pile just keeps getting bigger is all," he said taking a seat in the chair across from Vince.

"Where have you been Alejandro?" Joe asks returning to the couch beside Vince.

"I spent most of the day on the beach. I looked a little while for Trina but I spent most of the day with a little orphan girl I met on the beach," he said proudly smiling.

"An orphan girl…" Joe repeated, confused.

"Yes, her name is Emily but she likes to be called Emmy. She stays at that house a couple of blocks from the hotel that I always thought was a day care," he told them still grinning.

"I'm shocked Alejandro. How did that come to be?" she asks him leaning forward propping her chin on her fist.

"We can talk about that later. I'm starving, what do you two say about getting a bite to eat with me?" he asks changing the subject.

"We've ordered room service already. You're more than welcome to join us here. Joe ordered the kitchen so there will be plenty of food," Vince said laughing out loud.

"Alright if that's ok with you sis I'd be happy to stay," he said.

"Of course it's alright with me. Beside's I have some news to tell you," she said.

Alejandro leaned up asking," What news is that Joe?"

"Vince has ask me to marry him and I have accepted," she said laying a hand on the knee of Vince.

"Well…congratulations is in order I see. I wish the two of you years of happiness together. You couldn't have made a better choice Vince but look out for that temper of hers," he said laughing out.

"Oh…I know all about that temper," Vince replied joining in with the laugh.

"You two stop that. It's all supposed to be happy moments," she said.

"It is Joe, it is. Don't you see us laughing?" Alejandro said even though it brought Trina back into his mind. He was trying to avoid it and just be happy for his sister. He got up from his chair walking over and leaning with a kiss to his sister's forehead and shake to Vince's hand just as a rap came at the door.

"Our food is here," Joe said jumping up to return to the door once again.

"Good, I'll get another set up for the table and we can all sit down and enjoy," Vince said heading for the kitchenette.

Joe opened the door and Blas wheeled a rather large cart into the room covered in silver bowels with lids.

"Where would you like the food Joe?" he asks her peering up at Alejandro.

"Well, looks like she did order the kitchen. That's my sister," Alejandro said smiling at Blas.

"Then we shall all eat well tonight," Joe said pointing towards the table Vince had set up.

Blas pushed the cart over beside the table and began to sit the dishes of food over on it.

"Why don't you just leave the cart Blas? I'll bring it down later," Vince said.

"Looks like that might be a good idea," Blas replied turning to leave.

Joe followed him to the door slipping a tip of twenty bucks into his hand.

"That's not necessary Joe. You all are my friends. And I didn't mind wheeling it up for you," he said handing the money back to her.

"Non sense, take it," Joe said.

"May as well take it Blas otherwise you'll have to deal with her," Alejandro said still grinning.

Blas smiled in return and turned to Joe saying," Thank you Ms. Joe. He then left the room pulling the door to behind him.

"Let's see what all we have here," Vince said trying to arrange the bowels for easy access.

"Lets do, I'm starving. Come on brother take a seat," Joe said pulling a chair out from the table.

They all sit down and began dipping roast, steak, potatoes and vegetables into their plates with crescent rolls and butter on the side.

"Wow sis, you must have been hungry when you ordered all this. What's for desert if there is any room left for it?" Alejandro asks her.

"Like you wouldn't know its strawberry shortcake of course," she said grinning.

"Of course, I should have known," he replied laughing out loud.

Vince was busy eating his roast by the time Joe had her plate fixed with a spoon of everything there was there.

"So Alejandro, tell us about this little orphan girl you spent the day with," Vince managed to say between bites.

"I met the little thing on the beach," he said smiling.

"Really, and what were you doing on the beach this morning?" Joe asks.

"I had just been sitting there watching the sunrise and thinking," Alejandro said.

"So how did the girl come into play?" Joe asks him.

"She came up to me and ask me if I was working and wanted to know if I could teach her how swim faster than the sharks," he said laughing out loud.

"Faster than the sharks, wow, how old is she," Vince asks.

"I never did ask but I suspect six or seven years old," he replied.

"Did you teach her how to swim so fast?" Joe asks him.

"No, we talked, had lunch and scooped sand for her to build a castle with. I went by the house before I came over here and took her a teddy bear. I'm going to be her big brother," he told them with a pleased grin.

"That's very sweet of you brother. I didn't know you had it in you. How did she get your attention like that?" Joe eagerly and curiously asks her brother.

"You know, I don't know. There's something about her that I just can't quite put my finger on. But I was drawn to her and according to the foster parents of the home she opened up more to me than she has done since she has been with them. I'm just not sure what it is," he said with a look of curiosity on his face.

"Well, everything happens for a reason brother. You just remember that and it will all work out for the good," Joe said.

"Okay sister mom, I got you. Now when's the big day?" Alejandro asks looking at Vince who was still busy cutting at the roast.

"You're asking me?" Vince asks.

"Yeah, I guess I did," he replied grinning.

"If it's left up to me I would say today," Vince replied glowing inside his eyes.

"I'm happy for you two I really am. I just wish...," Alejandro started saying and then cut him self off to silence.

Joe looked across the table at Vince and found him looking back at her. "What do you two say we finish up here and watch a movie or something?" Vince quickly took the conversation elsewhere.

Alejandro laid his fork down and said," I thank you two for the meal but I believe I'll just go on back to my place now."

"You will do nothing of the sorts. You're going to finish your meal and have desert," Joe blurted out quickly.

"I appreciate it sis but I seem to have lost my appetite," he replied.

"You can't and won't do a thing by mal nourishing you. Now you eat your meal and we will figure things out together," she said.

Alejandro sits peering at his sister for a few moments before speaking again. "You're so much like Mom was. It's not even funny," he said, reaching and patting the back of her hand.

"Then I guess you better listen to what I say, huh?" she quickly asks.

"Yeah, I guess so," he replied picking up his fork again.

"Why don't you tell me about your plans with the little orphan girl?" Joe asks him.

"What do you mean?" he asks her.

"Like what are you going to do? Are you just planning to visit her at the house? Are you going to take her places? What are you going to do with her? Things like that, you know," she asks him.

"Well, after a few visits at the house I plan to take her for ice cream and go from there," he told her.

"What do the foster parents think about that?" she asks him trying to keep him talking about the little girl and his mind off Trina.

"Mr. and Mrs. Spear or Jack and Jane, very nice couple and formative I might add. However it was their idea for the few visits at the house first so they can analyze me and make sure I'm real and honest," he said.

"Makes sense," Vince said.

"She wants to meet you too Joe, because you're my sister," he said with a chuckle.

"Who the lady parent or the little girl?" she asks him quickly.

"Little Emmy," Alejandro said.

"If she means this much to you brother I would be happy to meet her," she told him.

"She does Joe, she does," Alejandro said and returned his attention to the food on his plate.

"Well, I don't know about you two but I'm ready to check out that strawberry shortcake," Vince said.

"You're already ready Vince?" Joe asks.

"Yes, I have been eating instead of talking. I was hungry," he replied.

Joe chuckled a little bit reaching for a plate of the desert to hand to Vince.

"I'm about to give up," Alejandro said finishing up his plate of food and retrieving some of the desert for him self.

"What are you giving up on?" Vince asks seeing Joe busy getting some desert for her self.

"Trina," Alejandro said.

Vince looked at Joe wondering when she was going to tell him what they had found out just as Joe dropped her fork.

"Careful sis, you'll break the plate like that," Alejandro said smiling a fake smile.

Joe picked up her fork and began eating the cake without a word to say. Vince just sat looking at her in wonder. Finally she laid her fork down and turned to Alejandro.

"I'm done are you two finished?" she asks them both peering at him.

"I'm done," Vince replies.

"So am I," Alejandro said.

"Then let's get comfortable in the living room. I have something to tell you brother," she said standing from her chair. Alejandro and Vince followed Joe to the living room and both took comfortable seats in anticipation of Joe's next words.

"What is it sis?" Alejandro asks being the first to speak.

"Promise me you will at least sit here and talk to me for a few minutes after I tell you what I have to say," she said.

Alejandro leaned forward expressing deep concern on his face knowing it had to be something she was worried about telling him.

"Alright, I promise," he said.

Joe turned to Vince sitting beside her and held her hand out for him to hold for support. Once he had a firm grip she turned back to Alejandro.

"Vince and I found Trina today," she said.

"What...and you're just now telling me," Alejandro said rather loudly.

"Brother you have to listen to me. I didn't know how to tell you. Once I tell you everything you'll understand why I didn't," she said.

"Tell me and don't leave anything out. Where is she? Why have I not been able to find her? Did you talk to her? Is she avoiding me?" he excitedly asks one question behind the other not giving her time to answer one.

"Slow down man, take it easy. Give her a chance to explain to you," Vince said jumping to Joe's defense.

"I'm sorry sis, I'm sure you have a good reason. It's just that I been looking for her for what seems like eternity and you knew that too," he said rubbing across his forehead.

"I know brother and believe me if it had been different circumstances I wouldn't have hesitated to tell you," she said.

"What do you mean different circumstances?" he asks sure she was going to tell him Trina wanted nothing to do with him.

Tears began to whale in Joe's eyes. The thought of telling him she saw her but was unable to talk to her because of her condition. And what little she knew of what has happened to Trina was almost more than she could bear. But she knew she had to for his sake.

"Don't cry Joe, its ok, just tell me," Alejandro said reaching and taking her free hand into his with a little squeeze of comfort. Joe released both their hands and stood turning her back to them. She crossed her arms in a self hug.

"Just tell me Joe," Alejandro said.

"Ok...okay... she's in the hospital," she blurted out through her falling tears.

Her blurt shocked Alejandro and he fell backwards into the chair with his mind going crazy in wonder. "The hospital...why is she there and what hospital? Is she alright?" he stuttered asking.

"I don't know. She hasn't spoken since she's been there. They don't know why she hasn't. It's just been like she's sleeping. Jasper's worried, I know that," she said before he interrupted.

"Jasper... What's he got to do with it?" he asks quickly.

"I don't know that either, but apparently Jasper knew about her before she came here. There is another man there that says he is her uncle and Jasper already knew him before he got here," she said.

"Okay, what happened to her?" Alejandro asks.

"I think I can partly answer that one Joe, "Vince spoke up taking some of the pressure off Joe.

"It looks like she was kidnapped and held for some unknown crazy reason by a man whom had escaped the mental institution. Jasper found them in the jungle and jumped the man. Trina stabbed and killed him and she's been the way she is now ever since," Vince said.

Alejandro vigorously rubbed his hand up and down the right side of his face. "How badly is she physically hurt?" he finally manages to ask.

"She has some cuts and bruises, but according to Jasper the concern is her not waking up. They don't know why she doesn't, they can't find a medical reason for it," Vince told him.

"Where is she? What hospital?" Alejandro sadly asks as he stands from his chair.

Joe replied, "She's at the local one, Sunrise Memorial!" Knowing he's going to go.

"Alright, I'm out of here. And sis, I understand," he said turning for the door.

"Alejandro wait, we'll go with you," she said.

"No, I have to do this alone sis," he said opening the door.

Joe started towards him just as he pulled the door to behind him. She opened the door and stepped out into the hallway but he was already out of sight. Vince took her by the hand and led her back inside closing and locking the door behind them.

CHAPTER TWENTY-TWO

Alejandro entered the front door of the hospital to find Jasper sitting asleep in the lobby. He went over to him tapping him on the shoulder. Jasper opened his eyes and focused on his face for a moment before sitting up straight. "Alejandro, I knew it was just a matter of time before you showed up. Especially after Joe and Vince this morning," he told him as he wiped across his eyes.

"Where is she Jasper?" he eagerly asks.

"She's resting," he said.

"Apparently that's been going on for a few days now. Why didn't you tell me?" he asks him angrily.

Jasper drew a long breath and got himself ready for the inevitable. "That would be because she asks me to not let you see her. She didn't want you to see her in the shape she's in," he firmly said.

"That's not fair. She doesn't know how I feel about her," Alejandro rapidly replied.

"How do you feel about her young man?" a voice Alejandro didn't recognize came from behind him.

"I'm in love with her. I care deeply about her well being. Nobody could care any more than I do," he said turning into the face of George.

"I take it you are this Alejandro I keep hearing about," George said.

"Yes I am and who might you be?" he asks in return.

"Alejandro, this is Trina's Uncle George, George, meet Alejandro," Jasper interrupted to say.

Alejandro straightened and held his hand out saying," I heard you were here. It's nice to meet you. I wish it could have been under different circumstances. I beg your forgiveness it's just that I'm very upset that nobody told me about Trina's occurrences."

"Let's sit down boy and have a little talk," George said after shaking Alejandro's trembling hand.

"Very well sir," he said taking a seat adjacent Jasper.

"I'm not going to attempt to tell you how Trina feels about you. That's not my place. However my concern lies only in her and her well being. Jasper said she didn't want you to see her so I have no choice but to abide by her wishes. I'm not going to let you see her. But I will tell you this much. The doc says she's going to be alright and as soon as she wakes I'm taking her home," George wasted no time or effort telling him.

"I understand your concern sir, but she doesn't know how I feel about her. She doesn't know that I'm in love with her. If I hadn't been so stubborn and told her before maybe this wouldn't have happened. Please, I have to have the chance to tell her," he pleadingly replied.

"George, why don't we let him see her for just a minute and then Alejandro you have to go on home and give us a chance to talk about it. You can come back in the morning and we'll give you our decision," Jasper says sitting up to the edge of his seat.

George turned to Jasper seeing his sincerity letting his faith take control and said, "Alright Jasper, if you think it's alright I trust in you."

"Don't give us no hassle Alejandro, none or you won't see her again. Do you understand?" Jasper said as he was standing.

Alejandro stood and studied Jasper's face for a moment and then said," Alright Jasper have it your way but know this, I will be back come daybreak."

"I figured as much Alejandro. Okay, fair enough, follow me," he told him waving his hand in the air.

Alejandro followed them to Trina's room. He stood outside the door and took a deep breath preparing for what he might see on the other side. After a moment he pushed the door partly open and turned to George and Jasper asking them," Can I have a minute alone with her please?"

George looked at Jasper just as he nodded and replied, "Okay, but we'll be right her outside the door."

"Thank you," he said and pushed on the door stepping inside and letting it close behind him.

"Jasper, are you sure about this," George asks him.

"Yes George, I'm sure," he replied.

Alejandro raised his eyes slowly to a vision of pure beauty terrorized beyond his comprehension. Trina was so beautiful he just didn't know how anybody could want to hurt her. She lay there black and blue with stitched cuts that were reddened inches around them and motionless. Tears filled his eyes as he approached her bedside taking her hand into his.

"Oh baby, I'm so sorry I wasn't there for you to stop this from happening. Please forgive me. I love you Trina and I always will. You have to know that, I have to let you know that. Wake up so I can tell you; show you… just how much I do," he said as his tears began to drip from his chin and run down her up held arm.

He gently kissed the back of her hand repeatedly smearing his tears that encircled his lips across her limpness. Taking a deep breath he bent and kissed her forehead softly. He ran his free hand through her hair pushing it backwards from her closed eyes. He then places the back side of her hand to his tear covered cheek and holds it tenderly tight whispering," I love you Trina, come back to me. Give me the chance to show you. I'll protect you and care for you like no other." And then he stood in solitude just holding and caressing her hand to his cheek.

After standing there for what seemed like seconds the door opened and Jasper said," Alejandro, come on man, it's time now. She needs rest."

"Yeah, okay Jasper," he replied without turning around.

Alejandro softly kissed the back of Trina's hand. Then he bent down over her to whisper in her ear. "I'll be back come morning my sweet baby. Tonight you rest and think about waking up. Tomorrow I'll tell you again how much I love you and every day there after until you hear me. Rest now Trina, just rest and think. I love you my dear baby Trina. I love you."

He slowly backed towards the door and the tears rolled from his eyes even harder knowing he had to leave her again. But George and Jasper was giving him no choice and he would be back come daybreak with full force of staying. He backed on out the door keeping his eyes on her as long as there was sight. Once outside and the door had closed in his face. He reached up and wiped his tears from his cheeks before turning to Jasper and George.

"I'll be back come daybreak just like I said," he told them without looking at them and swept on past them. Jasper reached out and patted him on the back as he past him by without saying a word. But Alejandro just kept going. When he arrived back at his cabana his tears still had not let up. He threw his keys on the table beside his chair and fell backwards into it. His mind was going crazy thinking about Trina and the shape she was in from some mad man. Not to even give a thought as to what was going to happen to her when she did wake because she had killed the man. There were so many possibilities that it was endless thoughts consuming his mind. The only thing he was sure of was that he loved her and he would be beside her from now on as long as she would let him be. He tilted his head backwards and closed his eyes for a moment and then picked up his pad of paper and pen and began writing thinking about Trina.

Back at the hospital George asks Jasper, "Why did you let him see her after she had told you not to?"

"George, I know she didn't want him to see her in the shape she's in. But it's been days now and she's made no attempt to waken. The doctor can't find a reason for it. And I happen to know she loves Alejandro as much as he loves her. I took a chance on him being the question she would have to answer," Jasper told him walking back towards the lobby.

"What does that mean?" George asks.

"It means he could be our only hope and when it's all said and done she just might not forgive us if we didn't let him in. I know how she feels about him," he said.

"Does she really love him?" George continues asking questions.

"Yes she does a whole lot. She talked to me about it and I gave her warning to him because he himself has been morning of love lost for a very long time," Jasper strongly replied.

"Alright, it's settled then. We allow him to see her come daybreak. I'm going to sit with her for awhile. Why don't you try to get some sleep? Go on home for awhile, I'll be here," George said.

"No, I'll just wait here in the lobby. It won't be long until daybreak and Alejandro will be back like he said," Jasper told him.

"Alright, have it your way. I'm going to sit with Trina," George said as he headed back towards the room.

Alejandro woke with his pad of paper lying on his chest still in his chair. He sat up straight and peered at the clock. It was almost seven in the morning. The sun would be all the way up soon so he jumped up and laid his pad on the seat of the chair and went to jump into the shower. When he finished he got dressed and returned to the table beside his chair to retrieve his keys. His eyes fixed on the pad of paper where he had been writing. He quickly pulled the top sheet off folded and stuck it in his shirt pocket and headed out the door. He got out into the jeep and turned the key and nothing happened. The battery was dead. He had forgotten to turn the headlights off the previous night.

He slapped the steering wheel asking his self, "Damn...how could I have forgotten?" With nothing to do but hook the battery up to the charger he got out of the jeep and retrieved it as quickly as he could. It was going to take another two hours to charge so he thought he would just walk the couple of blocks it was over to see Emmy while it charged. Maybe that would make the time go by faster. It was already almost eight in the morning. But he wasn't sure if it would be alright with the Spears or if they would even be out of bed yet. He knocked on the door anyway.

Jack opened the door and asking, "Alejandro, your kind of early today don't you think?"

"Yes sir. I apologize for it. I forgot to turn the headlights off on my jeep last night so my battery is dead this morning. I put it on the charger and thought I would walk over and visit Emmy while it charged. When it's done I'm off to the hospital. I'm not sure how long I'll be there so I thought I better tell her it might be a few days before I can see her again. I hope that's alright with you and the Mrs.," he quickly told him.

"Well, it's a little early but under the circumstances I guess it's alright this time. Why are you going to be at the hospital for awhile?" Jack asks curiously just as Emmy entered the doorway.

"Big Al, you're early. Are you going to have breakfast with me and little Al?" she asks him through the screened door.

"I didn't come for breakfast Emmy," he said in return.

"It's okay isn't it Mr. Jack?" Emmy eagerly said looking up at him.

"Emmy he said he couldn't. Run get washed up and let me talk to Al for a minute or two. Hurry up now," Jack told her patting her on the back.

"Okay Mr. Jack. I'll be right back big Al," she said as she turned and hurried away from the door.

Jack stepped out on the porch and offered a seat to Alejandro.

"Now, why are you going to be at the hospital for a few days?" he asks him again.

"It's a long story so to keep it short, just let me say the girl I plan to marry is in there and I'm going to be there when she wakes up," he told him.

"I'm sorry to hear that. I hope she gets well soon. What's wrong with her?" he asks concerned.

Emmy busted out the door again just as Jack had finished what he was saying. She ran over and jumped up on Alejandro's lap.

"Why are you up so early big Al? We're not going to the beach today. Mrs. Jane has some shopping to do and we're going to stay here and play with Mr. Jack until she gets back," she told him grinning huge.

"Emmy I just came by to tell you it was going to be a few days before I could come by and visit with you again. I didn't want you to worry about me or think I wasn't coming back," he told her.

"Why not...where are you going?" she asks him quickly.

"Emmy, it's none of our business where he is going. That's not a nice question to ask," Jack told her.

"It's alright Mr. Spear I don't mind," Alejandro said turning his attention back to Emmy.

"Emmy do you remember when we talked about my getting married?" he asks her.

"Yep sure do big Al. Are you getting married now?" she asks him.

"No, but the girl I'm trying to marry is sick and in the local hospital so I'm going to stay with her for a few days," he told her.

Emmy turned her attention to Jack again and said, "Mr. Jack can I pick a flower to send to big Al's girlfriend? It might make her smile and feel better."

"Yes Emmy you may," Jack replied smiling at her sweetness.

"Can I pick her one of them big pretty roses?" she asks him.

"Yes you can, but be careful of the thorns," he told her still smiling.

"Will you take it to her big Al and tell her I sent it to her?" she asks Alejandro who was just about to shed a tear at Emmy's innocence.

"I sure will Emmy. I'll be happy to do it for you," he told her holding to her arm while she climbed down off his lap.

When she was safely footed on the porch she turned to run down the steps calling behind her," I might pick two of them Mr. Jack." Jack laughed out loud along with Alejandro.

"She's something else, that little girl," Alejandro said wiping across his eyes.

"She is a special one alright. It's good to see her smiling. She hasn't done much of that," he said still watching her.

Alejandro felt the care Mr. Spear had inside his heart for Emmy and knew he felt it for all the kids. He was a good caring man that was easy to see.

Emmy returned to the porch with two white roses formed with huge petals. The sweetness poured the aroma to the air. "Here we are big Al, now make sure you tell... what's her name? You forgot to tell me her name big Al," she said with a twist to her cute little mouth.

"Trina is her name Emmy and I'll be sure and tell her Emmy sent them. I better get going now. You behave like a good little girl for Mr. Jack while Mrs. Jane is shopping," he told her.

"I will big Al and you come back as soon as you can. You can bring Trina with you too. It's alright isn't it Mr. Jack," she said handing the roses to Alejandro.

"Yes Emmy it will be alright. Now you go eat your breakfast Mrs. Jane has prepared," he told her standing from his chair.

"Okay I'm going," she said and disappeared inside.

Alejandro turned to Mr. Spear and said," Thank you again for understanding." And he reached to shake hands.

"Not a problem and I hope all goes well with Trina. Come back when you can," he said shaking hands before disappearing inside.

CHAPTER TWENTY-THREE

Alejandro arrived at the hospital at approximately nine a.m. to find Jasper and George sitting in the lobby.

"You're a bit later than I expected," Jasper said as he approached them.

"Yes, I know, but I forgot to turn my headlights off on the jeep when I got home so the battery was dead this morning. I had to charge it before I could come," he told him.

"Oh, sorry to hear it, is it alright now?" George asks him.

"Yeah, I just had to charge it up. How is she this morning?" Alejandro asks.

"The same," Jasper answered.

"Did you two have time to talk?" he asks Jasper and George looking back and forth between them.

"Yes we did and we decided to let you see her," George said.

"Thank you, I'm glad you did but I have to tell you I wasn't going to give up if you said no," Alejandro replied.

"Jasper knew that and now I do," George said.

"That's some pretty flowers you got there," Jasper said.

"Yes they are. Emmy a little girl from the orphanage home around the corner from the hotel sent them to Trina," he said.

"Oh really, I didn't know Trina visited the home," Jasper said.

"She didn't, I do," Alejandro said. George smiled hugely at the thought. It was definitely a plus for Alejandro in his book.

187

"Okay, well I'm going to take them in to her now," he said turning towards the room.

"Hold on Alejandro," Jasper said.

"Why," he asks quickly.

"Their in there changing her bed and cleaning her up a little bit right now. That's why we're out here. They'll let us know when their finished," Jasper told him.

"Yeah young fellow, come have a seat with us," George said.

Alejandro took a seat across from George watching him. "Tell me something about her," he asks him almost pleading.

"What would you like to know," George asks.

"What's her life like back home?" he asks him not taking his eyes off of him.

"Well, she works at my firm as a journalist. She's quite good at it too. One of the best I might add and not because she's my niece. Because it's true," he said.

"Has she ever been married?" Alejandro asks.

"No, she came close one time but the fellow turned out to be a dog and tore her heart right out of her chest. She lost her parents just before he done it too so she had a double whammy put on her all at one time. She closed her self off after that from everyone. She buried herself in her work and didn't give another a chance. She loves riding horses and doing anything that presents a challenge to her. She's a unique young woman with a lot to offer the right young man," George continued without even realizing he was telling Alejandro a lot about Trina.

"I hope to be that young man you speak of. I think I should tell you I plan to ask her to marry me as soon as it's possible. She may say no but I still plan to ask her," he told George without blinking an eye.

"I believe you. You don't have to tell me twice," he said.

"Not only do I care sir, I'm in love with her. I want to be the man taking care of her, protecting her and making her happy for the rest of her life," Alejandro said with expressions of love written all over his face.

"All done," the nurse called from the hallway.

"Thank you," Jasper called back as he stood. "We can go back in now," he told George and Alejandro.

Alejandro stepped off into the gift shop to buy a vase for the flowers Emmy had sent before he entered the room. Once inside he spotted a huge helium balloon in the shape of a heart that said I love you on it. He couldn't pass it up so he bought it too and then headed for the room. He sat the vase with the two big white roses on the table at the foot of the bed and tied the balloon to the head of the bed so she could see them when she woke.

"That's a big balloon," Jasper said.

"Yes it is and I don't think she'll have any problem seeing it when she wakes," Alejandro said.

"I think you might be right," George quickly added.

"George how about we go get us some breakfast and let these two have some time alone?" Jasper asks him.

George turned to Jasper and saw the meaning in his face before asking anything and said, "Alright that sounds good to me. Can we bring you something back boy?"

"No, thank you," Alejandro said, "I'm just going to sit here with Trina and talk with her."

"Alright, we'll be back in a bit," Jasper said as he was pushing the door open.

"We're going to have to let him have some time alone with her," Jasper told George once they were in the hallway.

"I understand what your saying and I agree," George said.

The two wondered on out the front door gibbering back and forth while Alejandro moved a chair in close to Trina's bedside.

"You know Trina, I'm going to stay right here until you wake up and tell me to leave," he said taking her little hand into his and laying his head down on the bed beside her. When Alejandro woke he glanced at the clock on the wall across the room from where the bed was. It had been two hours since he first laid his head down there.

Jasper and George was not back or at least they weren't in the room. He first thought he would just peek out and see if they were sitting in the lobby but quickly changed his mind. He wanted all the time he could have alone with Trina. He turned his attention back to her and realized he wasn't holding her hand anymore. In fact her hand was lying on her chest. She had to have moved it while he was sleeping. So he reached up and took hold to it again and when he did she flinched pulling it back again. He quickly stood and bent down over her calling her name over and over again,"Trina…Trina…baby, are you waking. Trina wake up sweetheart…wake up. It's me Alejandro, I'm here and I'm not leaving you. Trina…Trina."

She turned her head in the opposite direction of his close face and moved no more. Nor did she speak.

"You're a sassy woman Trina and if you think turning away from me is going to tell me you want me to leave, well, you better think again," he said walking around to the other side of the bed.

"I've looked for you for days going out of my head with worry. Afraid you had returned home and I would never get the chance to tell you how I fell in love with you. And when I found out you were here my heart flip flopped in my chest with a pain so great nothing and nobody was going to keep me away. Not Jasper, not your uncle George, not nobody," he continued talking as if she was listening to him.

"The day at the Dolphin Park, I was there watching you from a distance. You were so beautiful and had those dolphins eating out of your hand like they were little babies. Not to mention the handsome pool guide. I was jealous; I wanted to be that pool guide or one of those dolphins. I would have taken the place of anything or anyone just to be next to you," he just kept right on talking and telling off on himself.

Trina pulled her hand lose and turn over in the bed without ever even opening her eyes. Alejandro was so excited it didn't even dawn on him that these were first signs of physical life Trina had shown since she had been at the hospital. So he made no attempt to call for the doctor, but just kept right on talking.

"Hell girl, I was even at the riding stables and I know you made a fuss over the horse you rode. I know blackball ran away with you. Jasper had to lead him by the reins beside of his horse," he said and then stopped long enough to draw in a deep breath.

"And what about that bus tour. You stuck your gorgeous legs out in the isle blocking the walkway to everyone. And you made fuss about people having to get around them. You couldn't wait to bust me out once you realized I was on that bus. Why did you do that? I know why you did that. You did it to get my attention and you done a fine job of it too," he said taking hold to her hand one more time.

Alejandro gently laid her hand down on the bed beside her long enough to pull his chair up to the head where he could look her in the face as he talked to her. Then he took hold to her hand once again.

"Here's the best one of all Trina and the most far away from the truth one. What about the pub when you fell into my back and then hit the floor landing on your butt. Why did you fall into my back? Why was you sitting or standing to my back? Who did you think the girl was that I was talking with? You know the one I was making plans with for the following morning. I know what you thought and I knew what you thought but I was too stubborn to straighten it out when I had the chance. I'm really sorry for that. I should have done it then. But the girl was my sister and I was making plans to take her to the airport the next morning. That's where we were headed when you watched us from inside the hotel as we got into the jeep and drove off. Yeah, I knew that too. You see Trina I was a lot more observant than you thought I was or have been. You ticked my clock the first day I saw you.

And you really ticked it when I brought you that drink out on the beach catching you with your hand down your top. Wow girl, you can't know what that did to me," he said drawing at another deep breath.

On that note Trina pulled her hands lose from him one more time and turned back over in the bed placing her back to him again. "Are we going to just keep playing this walk around the bed thing? You're not going to get rid of me like that. I told you I'm not leaving until you tell me to. And by the way that means verbally," he said getting up and walking around the bed again.

Once he was positioned on the other side with her hand in his he continued talking. "What about the little scene you pulled with Blas in your hotel room. Putting on that pretty skin showing dress and ordering a drink right at five o clock knowing it was his time to getting off work. Did you think getting him into your room would make me jealous or what?" he asks getting ready to retrieve his chair again.

The door opened just as he arrived to the side of the bed and Doctor. Jacobs walked in. "Good Morning Trina," he said walking up the adjacent bed side of Alejandro.

"Young man," he said nodding his head while looking at Alejandro.

"You must be Doctor. Jacobs," Alejandro said.

"Yes, I am. And who might you be?" he asks him.

"I'm Alejandro, Trina's worst nightmare. Meaning the man that's going to harass her until she agrees to marry me," he said.

"My congratulations then, just in case I miss it," Doctor. Jacobs said continuing his evaluation of Trina's lungs.

"Thank you," Alejandro said.

"Everything sounds good Trina. We're just waiting for you now. It's all up to you as to what happens. Everything else will heal in time. I'll check back with you later," Doctor. Jacobs said as he turned and headed out the door.

"Okay Trina. It's just after lunch and I'm starved. I'm going to have a bite to eat. You think about everything I have told you while I'm gone. I'll be back in an hour or so.

It's all up to you," he said as he bent and kissed her on the forehead before leaving the room. Once he reached the lobby he found Jasper, George, Joe and Vince sitting and talking. They all four looked up as he rounded the corner.

"Is everything alright," Jasper asks him as he approaches them.

"Yes, Doctor. Jacobs just left and said everything looked good that it's all up to her now. I'm starving and I'm going to have a bite to eat now. Anybody want to join me? "Alejandro asks them all.

"We will," Joe said getting up from her seat followed by Vince. She was surprised that Alejandro was leaving Trina like this. She didn't understand but had every intention of doing so.

"I think I'll just hang out here and pop in on Trina from time to time. Go ahead and get yourself a hot meal," Jasper said kicking back in his chair.

"Yeah, I think I'll stay here too but thank you for the invite," George said.

"We shall return in an hour or so," Alejandro said as he turned and headed for the front door. Once outside the hospital he walked across the street walking in long steps. Joe and Vince followed behind.

"I have one stop to make then we can go get that bite to eat," he told them.

"Alright, it's not a problem," Vince replied taking Joe by the hand leading her down the street behind Alejandro.

Alejandro walked about three blocks before he exited the street into a jewelry shop.

"What's he doing?" Joe asks Vince remaining on the street waiting for him.

"I have no idea Joe but he seems to know. And he seems to be a bit happier than he was when he left the hotel yesterday evening. Let's just go along with him," he told her gripping her hand tightly.

Alejandro returned and said," Now let's go eat. Got any idea's on where?"

"We could go to the little diner across from the hospital. We had breakfast the other day there and the food was tasty," Joe eagerly replied.

"Sounds good to me," Vince said.

"Yep, I too, lead the way sis," Alejandro said smiling. The three headed off down the street on foot once again with Joe leading the way this time. Vince was at her side and Alejandro right behind bearing a strange vibrant grin on his face.

CHAPTER TWENTY-FOUR

"How's everyone's brunch?" Joe gave in asking Vince and Alejandro. She had to break the silence she couldn't stand anymore.

"Mine is delicious," Vince quickly replied.

"How about yours brother?" she asks.

"How about my what, sis?" he asks raising his eyes to meet hers.

"Your brunch how is your brunch? Where is your mind? What's going through your head? Why do you have such a smirking grin on your face? What's going on Alejandro?" she quickly asks one question right behind the other without giving him a chance to answer any of them.

Alejandro sat in silence for a moment smiling at his sister's curiosity eating at her. He knew how protective she tried to be of him. She was like an old mother hen and he didn't believe she thought he was grown at all. So he very carefully thought before speaking. "Lunch, brunch or whatever you want to call it is great sis. I was thinking," he managed to get out before she interrupted him.

"Oh no, what were you thinking?" she asks.

"I don't want to go back to the hospital too quick. So I was thinking how about you two coming with me and meeting Emmy?" he asks her.

"You are acting really strange brother. I would have thought it would have taken a bulldozer to drag you away from that hospital. What's up with that?" she quickly asks him.

"Nothing, I said my piece there. The doctor says she's going to be alright. I told Trina my thoughts for the most part. She needs time to think and I intend to give it to her. I just thought maybe you and Vince could come with me to meet Emmy while I wait just for a little while. She wants to meet my sister and I told her I would try," he said finishing up the last bite of his meal between words.

Joe peered over at Vince before speaking. She wasn't sure what to think. She knew Trina wasn't awake and hadn't been since she arrived at the hospital. She was concerned that her brother was snapping at the lose ends, grasping for straws that wasn't there to get a hold on. "How do you know she heard what your piece was?" she finally asks him.

"Oh, she heard me. I know she did. I can feel it and then there was the fact that she kept turning away from me. I'm sure she heard. Now how about it are you two going to come with me or not?" he asks still smirking a grin.

"Sure, we'll come with you Alejandro," Vince spoke up answering.

Joe turned to Vince and before she could speak he was winking at her and offering his hand of comfort. She took his hand and his gentle squeeze told her everything was alright. "Alright brother, I believe in you so let's go meet Emmy," she said as she was standing from her chair.

"Wonderful and I will drive. But first let me take care of this ticket. Brunch as you called it is on me," he said speaking over his shoulder walking towards the counter.

"Something is really strange about his actions Vince. There's such a big change in him from what he was just yesterday," she told him.

"Yes Joe there is but don't lose your faith in him. He's a grown man and you have to believe he knows what he's doing. Just support him. It's all you can do right now. He'll love you for that even if everything he's doing turns out to be wrong," Vince told her putting his hand to her back and leading her towards the exit.

Alejandro arrived at the exit door about the same time Joe and Vince did. He opened the door and stood back allowing them both to pass through before him.

"Thank you for brunch Alejandro. Next time it's on me," Vince said.

"It's my pleasure, future brother in law! The jeep is just across the street there," he replied still wearing that smirking grin and pointing in the direction he had parked in.

"I'm glad to see your happy today. I don't understand but I'm happy for it," Joe told her brother walking beside him.

"Why, thank you sis. And I do believe your going to love Emmy right away. Just as I did," he said picking up his pace a bit.

"You know how I am about children so your probably right brother," she said.

"Vince? How are you going to deal with my sister as your wife?" he asks him laughing out loud.

"One day at a time for the rest of our lives," Vince replied.

"You mister have a strong will. She can be a tough one at times. You have all my best luck wishes," he said chuckling.

Joe slightly popped Alejandro on the shoulder and said," Lay off brother. Are you trying to run him off or what?" She finished asking as they arrived at the jeep.

Alejandro opened the door pointing inside and saying," Get in sis." Joe climbed into the front seat and Vince got into the back. Alejandro walked around and got into the driver seat, started up the jeep and headed it out of town towards the Spears place.

Trina tossed and turned with her eyes half open not wanting anyone to know she had awakened. Everything Alejandro had said to her earlier kept running back and forth across and then front to back of her mind. How could she have been so stupid to let herself be so obvious to him and how could he have hidden and watched her from a distance. He saw and knew everything. Everything Alejandro had said to her consumed her mind and she didn't even give a second thought as to why she was lying here in this hospital bed with all these cuts, scrapes and bruises decorating her body. Nor did it even cross her mind that Jasper might be worried about her. She flipped over on her back just as she heard the door start opening. She quickly closed her eyes and lay still. She wasn't ready to talk yet. She had a little thinking to do first. So she quickly decided she would pretend she was sleeping until whoever it was coming in had left. After all it could be Alejandro again. He had said he would be back.

"Well George, looks like sleeping beauty is still sleeping," Jasper said as he walked up beside the bed.

George, Uncle George is here? Could it be my Uncle George Jasper is talking to? Trina silently asks her self.

"Looks that way," George said as he bent and gentle kissed her forehead.

"Oh my God, it is my uncle George. How long have I been here," she asks her self silently again.

Jasper took Trina's hand into his and softly patted the back of it. "We are going to be here when she wakes George. Don't worry she will when she's ready to. She's been through quite a traumatic experience. One she doesn't even realize and she'll need some questions answered when she does wake. She just needs rest, that's all. Let's go have some lunch. Alejandro will be back soon," he told George.

"Alright Jasper lets do that," George said.

"Trina honey, Uncle George is here and I love you. Just keep that in your mind wherever you are," he said turning towards the door behind Jasper.

Trina barely opened one eye so she could see her Uncle George. She couldn't believe he was there. He had been her only inspirations in life since she had lost her parents and she felt really bad about not speaking to him. But if she did then everyone would know she had awakened. Including Alejandro and she weren't ready for that yet. She knew her Uncle George would understand once she explained to him. The two men quietly slipped on out the door leaving her alone once more. She looked all around the room and saw the white roses in the vase next to the bed along with the huge balloon hanging over her head. The words I love you in big white letters on the balloon brought tears to her eyes. Her Uncle George was special. But the roses had no card attached and she could tell they were fresh cut and didn't come from a florist. The petals were huge and the flowers reaped of a sweet aroma. They were beautiful roses and she wondered who set them there. "No doubt, it has to be Alejandro," she told herself aloud with a little tone of frustration. She lay back fixing her head comfortably on her pillow and let her mind start to roam over everything he had said to her earlier. Her frustrations began to grow even heavier because he had been following her all that time with her having no knowledge of it. He had deceived her.

"Where was he when that man had me?" she anxiously asks herself. "That man, what man? Oh my God, I remember now. How did I get here?" she asks aloud just as the door creaks open and a voice comes through.

"We brought you," Mattie said smiling at seeing Trina was awake. Trina turned her eyes towards Mattie and Tom in confusion.

"Who are you," she asks her.

"This is my husband Tom and I'm Mattie. We're here on the island for vacation. We were driving the shortcut when Jasper flagged us down for our help to get you here," Mattie replied.

"I suppose I should say thank you then. But I don't remember that," Trina said with wrinkles to her forehead as if she was growing even more confused.

"Well, the important thing is that you got here and you are alright," Tom spoke up saying.

"Yes, that's all that's important dear," Mattie followed with.

"Did you see Jasper and my Uncle George outside the door there anywhere?" Trina quickly asks realizing these two were the first two to know she was awake.

"No, we didn't. We saw the room Jasper went into a couple of days back when we were here and took a chance it was still yours today," Tom said.

"I don't know how to thank you with anything other than words at this point. I'll make it up to you for all your help. But for now I'm really tired and I need to rest," she quickly told them pulling the cover up around her neck.

"We understand, and you don't owe us anything. We're just glad you're alright. But we'll come back later this afternoon after you have had some rest and check on you again. Is there anything we can bring you? Like a book, magazine, clothing or maybe just some food of some kind?" Mattie quickly asks her.

"No thank you, I'm fine. I appreciate your coming by. Be safe with your stay here on the island and I hope your vacation turns out to be a very nice one for you," she told them hoping they would go on and get out of the hospital before Jasper and George returned.

"Okay dear, we will see you later this evening then," Mattie said patting Trina's hand.

"Yes we shall see you later today," Tom added as he took Mattie by the elbow turning her for the door.

"Thank you again," Trina said as they exited the door.

"That was a close one," she told herself pushing the cover back down some. She repositioned herself slightly and closed her eyes forgetting about the man, Tom and Maggie and Jasper and Uncle George. Alejandro consumed all of her thoughts as she fell asleep.

"Big Al you came back," Emmy said running towards the jeep as Alejandro pulled up the drive. He quickly stopped the jeep and jumped out grabbing Emmy picking her up. Joe and Vince got out and walked around to where he stood with Emmy in his arms just as Alejandro started to speak. "Emmy, don't you ever do that again," he said.

"Do what big Al," she asks puzzled.

"Run up the jeep that way," he said.

"But big Al, I knew it was you. Mr. Jack and Mrs. Jane always tell me to stay away from people I don't know in cars and stuff. But I knew it was you big Al," she said.

"Yes Emmy, you knew it was me but the jeep had not stopped. It was still moving and that's dangerous. Don't you ever do it again? Wait until I have completely stopped. You scared me. Okay, is it a deal?" Alejandro asks her firmly.

"Alright big Al, it's a deal. Who are she and him?" Emmy quickly asks.

"Who are they? Not who is, Emmy," Alejandro corrected her.

"Who are they? Did I say it right that time big Al?" Emmy quickly asks.

"Yes you did and this is my sister Joanna and her finance Vince. I brought them to meet you like I told you I would," he replied.

"Let me down big Al," she anxiously told him.

Emmy walked up in front of Joe and stuck her little hand out to her. "I'm glad to get to meet you Joanna, big Al's sister," she said holding her hand out for Joe to take into hers in a shake.

Joe bent over taking Emmy's little hand and gently shook it saying, "It's my pleasure Emmy. And I'm happy to meet you."

She pulled her hand from Joe's smiling and walked up in front of Vince asking," What's finance?"

"It means I'm going to be Joe's husband soon," Vince replied grinning from ear to ear.

Emmy turned to Alejandro asking," Is that what you are to your girlfriend that's in the hospital big Al?"

"Maybe I will be someday Emmy, maybe…someday. Where is Mr. Jack?" he quickly asks changing the subject.

"Mrs. Jane came back from shopping and Mr. Jack's in the house helping her unpack everything. Do you want me to go get him?" she eagerly asks.

"Yes Emmy, we'll wait by the porch," Alejandro replied.

"Okay, I'll be back," she said turning and running towards the house. Just before she got to the porch she suddenly stopped and turned around yelling," Oh, big Al, if you wondered. I put little Al down for a nap. He was tired." Then she took off again.

"Alright Emmy, that was a good thing," Alejandro said laughing out loud as she disappeared inside.

"I can see why you fell in love with that little girl brother," Joe said patting him on the shoulder.

"She's something else Joe," he replied.

"Why is she in a foster home?" Vince asks him.

"She lost both her parents at the same time is all I know," Alejandro told him.

"You don't know how or anything?" Joe asks concerned.

"I think it was a car wreck but I'm not sure. She don't talk about it and Mrs. Jane said it was a miracle that she told me that much," Alejandro said just as the front door to the house opened.

Mrs. Jane and then Mr. Jack both stepped out onto the porch.

"Joanna? Is that you?" Mrs. Jane quickly asks.

"Jane…yes it's me. I had no idea you were who my brother was speaking of," Joe replied.

"Honey, this is Joanna the girl I told you about who helped me in the Middle East to get the home for the children set up. This is my husband Jack," Jane said with a huge smile radiating from her face. She then rushed off the porch throwing her arms around Joe's neck with a big hug. "I'm so happy to see you again," she told her.

"Likewise on my part. This is my fiancé Vince and you already know my brother Alejandro. It's very nice to meet you Jack. I heard a lot about you," Joe replied hugging Jane back.

"Please, won't you all come in for a cup of tea or something?" Jane asks.

"No thank you, we don't have the time. I thought I was bringing my sister over to meet you all. But I can see I'm too late for that. Anyway we only had a minute and I wanted her to meet Emmy. We have to get back to the hospital," Alejandro told her.

"Yes, Jack told me about your girlfriend. I'm very sorry to hear about it. How is she?" Jane quickly asks.

"She's still sleeping, but seems to be doing alright. Thank you for asking," he replied.

"Mrs. Jane can I go with big Al to see his girlfriend?" Emmy interrupted to ask.

"Emmy...sweetheart, not now," Mrs. Jane told her.

Emmy frowned and turned to Alejandro asking," Did you give her those roses I sent by you big Al?" Alejandro reached down and picked Emmy up again saying," Yes Emmy, I gave them to her. I stopped at the hospital gift shop and bought a pretty pink vase and put them in it and sat it beside her bed so they'll be the first thing she see's when she wakes up."

Emmy smiled real big saying," Oh thank you big Al, thank you."

Joe seeing the bond that had formed between her brother and the little girl was over whelming to her. She wanted to help him out so she walked over beside where he was holding Emmy and said," Maybe this afternoon if you're a good girl today, Mr. Jack and Mrs. Jane will let me come and pick you up and take you to see big Al's girlfriend for a few minutes Emmy."

"Oh, would you Mr. Jack, would you?" Emmy excitedly asks him.

"Well, I don't know Emmy," he replied running his finger across his upper lip. "I promise I'll be a good girl today Mrs. Jane. I promise I will," Emmy quickly said.

"Okay, only if you're a good girl though Emmy," she replied smiling knowing Emmy would be safe with Joanna.

"Good, and we'll take you to dinner too Emmy," Alejandro told her giving her a tight hug and then returning her to her feet on the ground.

"Alright go on in the house now and get ready for lunch Emmy," Jane told her.

"Alright, I'll be ready big Al's sister when you get here," Emmy said as she scurried up the steps to the house.

"Okay sweetie, I'll come around five if that's okay with Mrs. Jane and Mr. Jack," Joe told her.

"Is that okay?" Emmy asks before going through the door of the house.

"That will be fine," Mr. Jack replied and Emmy disappeared into the house.

Joe walked back over beside Jane and whispered to her, "Thank you, It means a lot to my brother. She's a real inspiration to him. I really appreciate it."

"Well, we better get going," Alejandro said.

"It was very great meeting you nice people," Vince said as he approached Jack with his hand out.

Jack reached and took Vince's hand saying," It was nice to meet you all as well." Then he took Alejandro's hand giving him a farewell shake as well.

Jack and Jane stood and watched as Alejandro, Joe and Vince returned and got into the jeep backing out of the drive. "I see something good with Emmy and Alejandro," Jack told Jane.

"Yes, so do I and I don't think it's a bad thing," Jane said with happy tears forming inside her heart.

Chapter Twenty-Five

Once the three had returned to the hospital they found Jasper and George again sitting in the lobby.

"Anything happen while we were gone?" Alejandro quickly asks thinking of all he had said to Trina before he had left.

"No not a thing," Jasper replied leaning forward on his seat.

"Brother, I think Vince and I will go for a little while. We'll be back this afternoon with Emmy," Joe told him reaching for his arm.

"Okay Joe. I'll be out here in the lobby when you get back with her," he said nodding his head at the same time.

"Take it easy Alejandro. And we'll be back. See you Jasper and George," Vince said as he followed Joe towards the front door.

Vince and Joe disappeared out the front door and Alejandro turned to Jasper and George and said," I'm going to go sit with her now. Why don't you two go catch yourself a nap? I'll be here and I'll call if you're needed for anything or if anything changes."

Jasper turned to George and said, "Why don't we take him up on it and go to my place. There are some things we need to discuss anyway. We can do it there and we don't have to be gone too long either. I'm sure Alejandro will call if anything changes or if we are needed."

"I hate to leave her," George said.

"It will be fine. I'll see to it that she's taken care of," Alejandro anxiously said.

"I know you will boy, but—" George managed to say before Jasper interrupted.

"No buts about it George, if Alejandro says he'll see to it, he will. So come on and let's get out of here for a little while. Trina will be safe with him," Jasper said comforting George.

"Alright Jasper, you know I trust in your decisions," George replied as he stood from his seat.

"Oh, by the way, Joe is going to bring Emmy by this afternoon. We're going to take her to dinner around five thirty," Alejandro told the men.

"Who's Emmy?" George quickly asks.

"Don't worry; she's a little foster child only six or seven years old. I'm like her big brother," Alejandro told him proud of himself.

"Oh, okay then. We'll be back by then for sure won't we Jasper?" he asks with a puzzled look on his face.

"Of course, we can be back by then for sure," Jasper quickly replied.

"Alright, you two go ahead on and I'll see you in a little bit," Alejandro said as he headed for Trina's room. He eased the door slightly open and peeked inside. Trina was lying on her back with her eyes closed pulling the sheet up around her neck. When she heard the creek of the door Alejandro pushed a little further open she let her body instantly become motionless. He walked up beside the bed to the side she had her face turned to. He bent down and kissed her forehead before speaking.

"Oh Trina, I'm back now. Tell me have you thought about everything yet? Have you realized anything at all? I know you can hear what I'm saying to you. You see I have realized something. You're a stubborn beautiful woman along with many more things but you don't have me fooled," he rattled away his words as if she was staring him right in the eyes.

It was hot inside the room to Alejandro so he decided to unbutton a couple of the top buttons on his shirt. When he ran his hands over his chest he felt the paper he had stuck in his pocket when he had left his place. He had forgotten about it being there. He pulled it out and opened it up remembering what it said. He grabbed the chair and took it to Trina's side taking a seat. She still had not opened her eyes or spoken a word as bad as she wanted to. She remained strong at will and kept silent.

Alejandro leaned forward in the chair and began to whisper to her. "Every now and then I write my feelings down in different forms. I don't let anyone see what I write. But I'm going to read this one to you Trina because it's about you, my feelings and what I would like to see happen. So here goes and it's the only time I will do this so if you don't listen then you will never know," he told her with hopes it would make her start talking to him. Alejandro leaned up getting comfortable close to her face and he began to read the poem he had written and fallen asleep with in his arms at his cabana. "Okay here it is,

TRINA

Your eyes are blue pools-
The windows of your soul!
Reflecting your beauty-
Which makes you whole
When you don't have a smile-
Then neither do I.
Awaken for me-
So we can give our love a try.
Where you are makes me feel-
We're miles apart.
But I rest your beautiful smile-
Inside my heart!
The day I met you-
My love came to be!
I'm sitting and waiting-

For you to awaken for me!
You're in my prayers-
You're in there every day.
And inside my heart-
Is where you'll always stay.
I want to see your lips-
Spread from ear to ear.
Melting my heart-
And taking away all my fear!
Come back to me-
And my love for you will show.
I will protect you-
Always holding you so!
The time has come-
It has always been near.
When all that's happened-
Has become clear!
Now open your eyes-
So I can see to your soul.
And I'll tell you how-
You made me gain control.
You showed me love-
And you showed me life.
My dream now is-
For you to become my wife!
This is my story-
You must know it's true.
And the reflection of my soul-
Says I love you.

That's it and it's the way I feel. It's all up to you now," he told her wiping tears from his eyes as he spoke. He refolded the piece of paper and stuck it back into his shirt pocket before standing and pushing the chair back. He didn't even look down at her he just turned walked to the window and stood peering out of it thinking what else there was he could do.

Trina felt the tears roll down her cheek. What Alejandro had just read to her was the most beautiful thing she had ever heard. It was the most beautiful words anyone had ever said to her. She fought to remain silent and control her tears, but Alejandro was too hard to ignore. He had told her he loved her and now she wanted and needed to tell him the same. She could speak now because she didn't feel like she had to be afraid anymore. For some weird reason he made her feel there was no reason to be afraid of a relationship. She was going to accept she felt love for this man and open her heart to him.

She whispered softly saying," Yes."

Alejandro swiftly turned and practically ran to her side. Her eyes were still closed but he could see the tears streaming. "You spoke, you said yes. Yes to what Trina? What does yes mean?" he asks her anxiously.

Trina swallowed the big lump in her throat before she spoke again. This time Alejandro was right there in her face. "Yes Alejandro, I'll be your wife," she softly said.

Now it was Alejandro who had the lumps in the throat. He stood wiping his eyes and swallowing hard. He reached in his pants pocket and pulled a little black case out. He opened it and laid it before her eyes. "Open your eyes Trina and see," he told her.

She lay for a moment before she slowly opened her eyes to the golden diamond ring he held before her face. Her tears really started rolling then. "It's beautiful," was all she could say.

He removed the ring and laid the case to the side. He took her hand and slid it onto her finger saying," You'll be my bride and let me love you, take care of you, protect you from harms way and be by your side for eternity to come." His words brought her tears on even stronger and he gathered her into his arms holding her tightly while she cried his chest full of the best feeling he had ever in his life felt. It was her tears. Trina's tears and they were happy tears. She had accepted his proposal of marriage. How could he ask for anything more?

The two remained silent laying and leaning into each others arms for quite sometime before letting go. When they did let go of one another they peered straight into each others eyes for the very first time. His brown eyes turned dark and milky encircled by a darker ring and poured his love into hers. Her blue eyes were full of watered starlit sparkles of love beaming into his. For the first time it wasn't dreadfulness or mislead hatred they felt. It was pure love for one another. Love nobody or nothing could get between ever again.

Alejandro was the first to speak asking, "Let's get married, today…here at the hospital. We can do it right here in your room. Or if you're strong enough we can do it in the chapel here. What do you say?"

"You are delusional and I am hallucinating. I am in a hospital bed for God's sake. This isn't really happening. It's not real and you're deceitful," she excitedly replied with puzzled wrinkles formed on her forehead and a raised tone to her voice.

"No you are not. And no I am not. It's very real. Here I'll pinch you so you can feel I am real and really here talking to you," he said raising his voice trying to keep it pleasant at the same time. Then he reached out and gently pinched her upper arm in a place where he saw no bruising, cuts or scrapes.

Trina jerked her arm away from him and scooted down in the bed pulling the cover over her head almost yelling, "Will someone wake me up. This can't be happening."

Alejandro reached and took hold of the sheet pulling it down from over her face. He bent and gently kissed her forehead. "You are so beautiful when you think you're getting your way. How could I ever not love you?" he asks her remaining bent down over her.

"Why does this kind of thing always have to happen to me?" she asks not really aiming at him.

"Stop being so spicy and realize that you love me as much as I do you so we can get on with this marriage. I'm sure I can find you a pink gown to wear," he said with a little chuckle to follow.

Trina quickly sat up in bed growling her voice as she said, "You are impossible."

"And you love me," he quickly replied.

She blew her breath out with a squeaking noise straight at him knowing he was telling the truth. She pulled herself up into a sitting position leaving a space open on the end of the mattress. Laying her arms across her chest she very softly said," Yes I do."

"Then let's do it. I can go down and talk to director and get permission to use the Chapel here," he told her sitting down on the bed at her feet.

"I don't know...I just don't know," she said almost in tears.

"Oh come on Trina. You're tough. What is it? Are you already married or what?" he quickly asks her on a whim.

"No I am not," she replied getting aggravated again.

"I don't understand then. You love me, I know you do. I love you I already told you that. I gave you a ring and I don't take that lightly. You were just as deceitful as I was. We're like two peas in a pod. It will be a wedding of a different kind. I'll get me some P.J.s to wear if that will make you happy. I'll do anything for you. Just tell me what you want," he pleadingly spoke clearly.

"Okay...okay already. I'll do it but only if I can have the time to speak with my uncle George first and not be rushed. And I mean alone. I have some explaining to do to him. His opinion is important to me believe it or not," she told him expressing concern of her feelings.

"That's not a problem. I have to take Emmy to dinner anyway. It's already four and she'll be here around five. I can go and get everything we need and be ready by this afternoon," he told her standing from the bed.

"Who's Emmy?" she quickly asks.

"Oh…she's the little girl that gave you those white roses there. She sent them by me. She's a foster child that I play big brother to. My sister is bringing her up here because she wanted to see you and I told her I would take her to dinner. I'll let her help me get the arrangements made. She'll love that. When we are finished then I'll bring her in to meet you. You can do your talking to George while I'm gone doing these things," he said with a huge smile spread across his face.

Trina smiled up at Alejandro and said, "I didn't know you had it in you. What a sweet thing to be a big brother to a foster child."

"There are a lot of things you don't know about me, but the most important thing to know right now is that I love you more than life itself," he replied taking hold to her hand gently squeezing it.

"I look forward to meeting her. I'm sure she loves you kind of like I do. Except on a brother bases," she said squeezing his hand in return.

"She's some little girl and you are going to love her too," he said.

"I'm sure I will," she softly replied.

"I'll go and start by getting permission to use the chapel here then. Do you want me to send George in now?" he asks her just as a knock came on the door and it pushed opened. Alejandro turned into the face of Doctor Jacobs and his nurse.

"Well young lady how long have you been sitting up now?" he asks Trina walking up to her side removing his stethoscope from around his neck.

"Who are you?" she quickly asks without answering.

"Oh, I'm Doctor Jacobs. I've been seeing to you since you've been here. How are you feeling now?" he quickly asks her as he is placing his scope to her chest.

"I feel fine. I'm a little sore but otherwise fine," she told him.

"Well you certainly look fine and sound fine. But just the same my nurse here will take a little blood for a few test to make sure and then I'll get back to you. Take it easy and don't you over do it until after we make sure you're fine," he told her.

"I won't but I'm getting out of this bed," she told him.

"That's great news and I'll bet you're hungry too. Am I right?" he asks her.

"Yes you would be correct in assuming that," she replied.

"We'll get you some dinner ordered then. I'll be back to see you once I have the results of your test. It's good to see you awake," he said across his shoulder as he was turning to leave the room.

"Alejandro?" Trina called out.

"Yes baby, what is it?" he asks her.

"Nobody but you, Tom, Mattie and the doctor knows I'm awake, so be gentle with Uncle George when you tell him. I'm worried about not letting him know it," she sadly said.

"Don't worry Trina, I'll take care of it and I love you," he said and bent to her lips planting a soft gentle kiss.

"I love you too," Trina said laying back on her pillow as Alejandro went out the door. Now she would silently wait for her Uncle George!

CHAPTER TWENTY-SIX

Alejandro found George and Jasper sitting in the lobby as usual. Same place as before. He quickly explained that Trina was awake and talking and that she wanted to see George alone for a few minutes. George jumped up from his seat and headed towards her room. Alejandro stopped him asking," I have proposed to Trina. She has accepted and if it's possible we'll be married this afternoon in the chapel. I would like to know if we will have your blessing sir."

"Young man I trust in Trina and if she accepted then yes you will have my blessing," George told Alejandro holding his hand out for a shake.

"Thank you sir I know it will mean a lot to her. And by the way take it easy on her. You'll see what I mean when you talk to her," he told George turning to Jasper. George gave Alejandro a puzzled look and then scurried on off with no more words spoken.

"Well Jasper would you like to join me in a visit to the director's office? I'm going to find out if it's alright to hold a wedding in the chapel here," Alejandro asks him.

"Do you think you can pull this off this fast?" Jasper asks as he is standing to join Alejandro in his quest.

"I always said if you really want something bad enough you can pull it off with a little work. And I really want this Jasper. I really do," Alejandro said heading down the hall.

"Well then, let's see what we can do about it. I'm willing to help in anyway I can," Jasper replied with a pleased smile spreading across his face.

"Thank you, we do appreciate it," Alejandro replied.

"Look at you talking for the both of you like your already married," Jasper said as they arrived at the door of the office.

"Emotionally, we are," Alejandro replied as he first knocked and then pushed the door open.

Inside sitting behind a huge desk was a rather large man in a suit and tie talking on the phone. He held up one finger as if he was asking them to wait for one minute. Alejandro looking the man in his eyes nodded his head in acceptance of the wait. After a couple of moments the man hung the phone up and stood up holding his hand out. "I'm Mr. Holcomb, John Holcomb the hospitals director. What can I do for you gentlemen?" he asks after introducing himself.

"I'm Alejandro Azure and this is Jasper Long. I've come to ask permission to use the hospital chapel for a quiet wedding this afternoon say around eight if that's possible," Alejandro told the big man.

"I don't think that's possible Mr. Azure. We don't let folks come in off the street like that. The chapel is for family members of their loved one's who are here sick in the hospital. I can't recall a wedding ever taken place there. That's quite a different experience of our chapel," he told him.

"I do understand your point sir however; the lady I plan to marry is here in the hospital sick. Ms. Trina Wright is her name. We would greatly appreciate the use of the chapel just long enough to hold the ceremony if you can see your way fit to allow it," he told him.

"Why don't you two fellows have a seat?" he said directing his hand towards the two chairs sitting in front of his desk. Alejandro and Jasper each took a seat at the same time Mr. Holcomb returned seated into his. He propped his elbow on the arm of the chair. Placed his finger on his top lip and ran it back and forth across wrinkling his forehead between his eyebrows as if he were in deep thought.

"We'll only be in there long enough for the ceremony and then we'll be out," Alejandro told him breaking his concentration.

"Well, I guess it would be alright providing it's not in use by a family in need. That's a first and must be, and I'm assuming here that her doctor has given his permission for this occurrence with his patient," he told Alejandro.

"Doctor Jacobs examined her just a few minutes ago and said everything was looking great," Alejandro quickly replied.

"All right then, as long as you're out, as soon as I do's have been said," Mr. Holcomb told him as he stood from his chair once again holding his hand out.

"Thank you for your cooperation in the matter. We do appreciate your kindness," Alejandro said taking his hand in a shake.

"You are very welcome and congratulations. May you two live a long and prosper life together," he told him reaching to shake Jasper's hand as well.

"I'm sure we shall sir," Alejandro said as he pulled open the door to the hallway. Alejandro and Jasper arrived back at the lobby just as Vince, Joe and Emmy entered the front door.

Emmy carried in her hand three more of the huge petal white roses and six smaller red colored ones with the stems wrapped in a wet paper towel. She was dressed in a gorgeous white chiffon dress that fell right at her knees. Her fine silk blond hair was pulled back on both sides and pinned with cute little purple colored rose barrettes. She was adorable.

"Big Al, there you are," Emmy said running to his side.

"Emmy say hello to Jasper one of my friends," Alejandro told her.

"Hello Jasper big Al's friend," she said looking up at him.

"I brought your girlfriend some more roses," she said turning her attention back to Alejandro and holding up the flowers.

Alejandro took the flowers from Emmy's hand and said," Their very pretty Emmy, thank you.

We'll take them to her a little bit later. She's busy at the moment and we have to go have dinner. Remember I promised you."

"Alright big Al and yes I remember see I got all dressed up," she said as she held her arms outward from her body and taking hold to each side of the bottom of her dress.

"And you look beautiful too," he told her smiling widely.

"I picked it all out by myself. I did a good job didn't I big Al?" she asks him grinning from ear to ear.

"Yes you did Emmy. Why don't you sit right here in this chair while I talk to Joe for a minute and then we'll go have dinner," he told her picking her up and sitting her in it.

"Okay big Al I'll be right here," she told him. Jasper sits down beside Emmy knowing what Alejandro was going to tell his sister. So he thought he would just strike up a conversation with the little girl and keep her occupied while Alejandro told Joe all about what was going on.

"What time do I have to have Emmy back home?" he asks Joe.

"Jack and Jane are going to pick her up here at the hospital around seven or so," she told him.

"Good, that will be a help," Alejandro said.

"Why?" Joe wanted to know.

"Because sis your dream is coming true. I'm getting married this evening around eight if I can get Emmy fed and find a preacher in time," he excitedly told his sister who threw herself around his neck and began to sob.

"Has Trina been released? Has she awakened? What's going on Alejandro?" Vince took over with the questions he knew Joe would want answers to.

"She has and I have ask her to marry me and she has accepted. We will be married here in the chapel this evening if I can get all the arrangements made in time. So I need to take Emmy to eat because I promised her I would. Then I need to go and buy Trina a pretty white silk gown and rob set.

And I suppose make some phone calls to find a preacher or someone whom can marry us," he said as he took Joe by the shoulders removing her from around his neck.

"I'm so happy for you brother. I really am. Vince and I will go to dinner with you and Emmy if that's alright," Joe said wiping the tears from her cheeks.

"Sure it's alright but we need to get going now," he said as he turned to walk back to where Emmy and Jasper was sitting.

"Are we ready to go see your girlfriend now big Al," Emmy asks him as he walked up.

"No, not now Emmy we're going to go to dinner first and then we will. Why don't you leave the flowers here with Jasper until we get back unless of course he would like to join us," Alejandro said.

Emmy turned to Jasper and ask him," Are you going to go eat with me and big Al?"

"No Emmy, I think I will just stay here and watch over these pretty flowers until you get back," Jasper told her patting her on the top of the head.

Emmy turned back to Alejandro and said, "He's not going he's going to watch my flowers until we get back big Al."

"Alright Emmy, come on and lets go. Are you hungry I know I sure am starving? Vince and Joe are going to go with us though," he told her reaching for her little hand.

Emmy put her small hand to the side of her mouth and whispered, "That's alright big Al I like them."

Alejandro laughed out loud and said," Come on sweetheart, let's go eat." He took her hand and led the way towards the door.

"We will be back by seven o'clock Jasper," Alejandro called over his shoulder.

"I'll be here. Enjoy your dinner date," Jasper replied to Alejandro's call.

Outside the hospital Alejandro lead the way to the jeep. He picked Emmy up and put her in the back seat buckling her seat belt around her. Joe got into the back with Emmy and Vince in the front with Alejandro. He drove to a nearby restaurant that had no dress code but was known for a nice casual look. The food and atmosphere was good and it didn't have a cheap appearance. The four was seated at a table beside the window. Alejandro spotted a store across the street which looked like it might have some fine choices of clothing. After ordering their food he said," When we get finished eating I need to go over there to that store." And he pointed in the direction through the window.

"Why are we going over there big Al," Emmy quickly asks.

"I need to buy Madam. Trina a new sleeping outfit Emmy and maybe myself too," he told her.

"Why are you doing that big Al?" she continues to question him.

"Because Emmy Madam Trina and I are getting married this evening and she needs a new set to wear," he told her.

Emmy's eyes got as big as half dollars. She began to clap her hands together and smile huge enough that all of her little white teeth sparkled. And then she got a confused look on her face. "But big Al, Madam Trina is in the hospital still isn't she?" she quickly asks him.

"Yes and we are getting married there. That's why she needs a new sleeping outfit and me too Emmy," he told her.

"Oh now I understand it. Can I pick it out for her big Al? Can I please?" she asks pleading.

"I don't know Emmy. That's a big decision for such a little girl to make," he told her.

Emmy dropped her head for a moment and then quickly raised it back up saying," Big Al my mommy had some real pretty things like that. I remember what they looked like and I'll pick out one that's just as pretty as my mommies was I promise."

Alejandro's heart leaped knowing it took a lot of courage for Emmy to say those words. "I'll let you help me Emmy. How about that?" he asks her fighting back tears of his own.

Joe on the other hand couldn't hold hers back. She let them flow reaching over and taking Emmy's little hand into hers saying," And I'll help too Emmy."

"Madam. Joanna is you and Mr. Vince going to get married at the hospital too? If you are we can pick out some for ya'll too. Isn't that so big Al," she asks excitedly.

Alejandro smiled from ear to ear and said, "Yes we can Emmy. How about it you two? Do you want to have a double ceremony? I think it's a great idea Emmy has there. And I know Trina won't mind at all."

"And so do I," Vince quickly spoke up answering peering in anticipation of what Joe was going to say.

"Yeah, come on Madam. Joanna it will be fun," Emmy said smiling hugely at her.

"Oh I don't know," Joe said.

"Come on sis its going to happen anyway someday why not now. It will be great to share the same anniversary. Look at it this way you two will always have someone to celebrate it with," Alejandro said.

Joe sit for several minutes with her hands cupped over her mouth and tears rolling down her cheeks. "Why not," she finally said. "It just might be fun after all Emmy."

"Oh boy I get to help pick out two sleeping outfits then," Emmy said grinning and clapping her little hands together.

Vince jumped up from the table saying," Come on lets hurry up before she changes her mind Alejandro."

Alejandro laughed out loud and dropped some cash on the table to cover their meal.

"Let's go Emmy," he said. "We have a lot to do and a short time to do it in."

"I'm ready big Al. Let's go," Emmy quickly replied.

Across the street they all practically ran into the store and to the lingerie section. Alejandro and Emmy picked out a long floor length white satin with spaghetti straps gown that came with a satin lined lacey cover up for Trina. He told the store clerk to box it up and find one like it or close to it for little Emmy. Then he set out to find himself some PJs of white satin. Joe and Vince had gone their own way in search of their attire in agreement with Alejandro that it would be sleep wear. When they were all finished shopping with their purchases boxed up they headed back to the hospital. Emmy was the first one through the door carrying her little package. She was now in search of the roses she had left for Jasper to watch over. Then she would be all set. Alejandro was right behind her right on her heels. He was surprised to see that Jack and Jane had already arrived to pick Emmy up. It wasn't quite seven yet.

"Mrs. Jane. Make a guess what," Emmy squealed out a little too loud.

Jane stood putting her finger across her lips with shish sound towards Emmy.

"What is it Emmy and don't be too loud. This is a hospital with sick people. They need their rest. Now what is it?" she asks her again just as Emmy comes to a sudden halt in front of her.

"Big Al bought me a package. I mean he bought me what's in this package. And he and his girlfriend are getting married. I get to watch them too," she said with eager excitement shinning deep inside her blue eyes.

"That was very sweet of Mr. Azure. Did you thank him?" she quickly asks her.

"Yes I thanked him and I got to help pick out her marriage outfit. I got one in my package kind of like it too. Are you and Mr. Jack going to watch them too?" she asks barely taking time to breath in any air at all.

"Well I don't know Emmy. When are they getting married?" she asks grabbing hold to her shoulder to slow her jumping up and down.

"Right now and so is Mr. Vince and Madam. Joanna. Right here at the hospital. It's going to be a lot of fun," Emmy told her still jumping up and down.

Jack and Jane both turned their eyes towards Alejandro at the same time. "Is this true Alejandro?" Jack asks.

"It sure is and I would appreciate it if you would allow Emmy to be a part of it. And you remember Vince here. He's going to need a best man Jack. I'm sure he would appreciate it if you could do that for him," he said to Jack turning to Vince.

"Yes, that's correct and Joe is going to need a best woman to stand with her Jane. What about it? Are you two up for it?" Vince asks.

Jack turned to Jane and ask," What do you think honey?"

"I'd love to if Joanna wants me to," Jane replied smiling.

Jack nodded his head at Vince and said, "We would love to help you out."

"That's just great and don't worry about cloths. I'll buy your outfits to wear. Let's go to the gift shop here and see if they have them," Vince said turning to Joe.

"Joe? Jack and Jane have decided they will stand with us as our best man and woman. Isn't that great? I'm going to the gift shop to purchase their outfits for them. Do you want to come along too?" he asks her.

"Wait a minute," Alejandro said. "Hold on one second Vince." Vince and Joe turned to Alejandro and watched as he walked towards Jasper and a little older couple they didn't know.

"Hey Jasper," Alejandro said.

"Oh hey Alejandro I have good news. Tom here is a preacher and can marry you two. I already ask him for you. I hope you don't mind," Jasper said.

"Not at all, thank you that's great to hear. One more worry off my mind and off the list of to do's. But I wanted to ask you if you would stand with me as my best man and be willing to wear silk PJs?" Alejandro asks smiling hugely.

"I would be happy to," Jasper said.

"Good because I already bought the P.J.s for you. I just knew you would say yes," he told him handing him a package.

He then turned to Trina's uncle George and handed him a package saying," And this one is for you. So you can give the brides away."

"You have it all figured out don't you boy? But who's going to stand with my Trina?" George asks as he takes the package from Alejandro's hand.

Mattie spoke up and said," Me, let me stand with that beautiful dear. I want to help her too."

"I'm afraid I don't know you madam," Alejandro said.

"Oh this is Mattie, Tom's wife. The couple that helped me to get Trina here to the hospital! They gave us the ride," Jasper quickly told him taking up the slack.

"Then by all mean's we would love to have you help her out again Mattie," Alejandro said.

"Oh this is so exciting," Mattie told Tom grabbing his elbow.

"Mattie would you and Tom wear sleepwear for this?" Alejandro asks her.

"I don't know about that," Tom spoke up saying.

"Oh stop it Tom. Of course we will. We'll do whatever we can to help out," Mattie said.

"Can you go with my sister to the gift shop to get them? My treat of course," he asks her.

"Sure we can. Come on Tom," Mattie said with her facing glowing as if it was she getting married all over again.

"Alright follow me please," Alejandro said.

He walked over to where Vince and Joe were standing and asks Joe," Will you see to it that these two get sleepwear as well?"

"Alright brother I will. Let's go," Joe replied.

Alejandro handed Joe a wade of bills and told her, "Their outfits is my treat." Joe took the money from him and headed towards the gift shop with Vince, Mattie, Tom, Jane and Jack following behind. Alejandro walked back over to where Jasper and George had taken seats beside Emmy.

"Did everything go alright George while I was gone? Did you talk to Trina?" he asks him.

"Don't worry boy, everything is ok," he said with a big smile.

Alejandro let out a deep sigh of relief and turned to Emmy. "Emmy you have your flowers ready to go meet Madam. Trina?" he asks her.

"Right here big Al. Let's go," she said jumping up.

"Here let me carry your package for you," he said taking it from her little arms.

"Alright but be careful with it big Al," she said turning lose. Alejandro laughed out and laid his hand to Emmy's back guiding her towards Trina's room. He pushed the door open allowing Emmy to step inside first. Once in he walked up to Trina's bedside bending and kissing her softly on the forehead.

"Emmy this is Trina. Trina this is Emmy," he said holding his hand out towards the little girl standing next to him.

"I'm very pleased to meet you Emmy," Trina said.

Emmy stood in amazement for a moment and then she turned to Alejandro and said," She has yellow hair just like me big Al."

Alejandro laughed out loud saying,"Yes Emmy she sure does."

"Oh these are for you Madam. Trina," she said stretching the flowers upward toward the bed.

"Why thank you Emmy. There very pretty just like you are. Don't you think so big Al," she said taking the flowers from Emmy and raising them to her nose grinning.

"Yes they are," he said snarling at Trina for making fun of what Emmy calls him.

"Big Al let me help him pick out your outfit to wear when ya'll get married today," Emmy told her.

"He did? Well wasn't that sweet of him?" she asks her still grinning hugely.

"Yeah and I got one too. Big Al said I could carry your ring and throw the flowers for you step on too," she said and then she began to frown.

"What's wrong Emmy," Trina quickly asks her.

"Big Al forgot to get the flowers," she said pouching her lips out.

"Come up here and sit beside me Emmy. Help her up big Al," she said as she patted the bed beside her.

Alejandro picked Emmy up and sat her down on the bed beside Trina.

"Now Emmy sweetheart don't worry about the flowers because we have some very pretty white and red roses right here," she told her taking her little hand into hers.

"Oh yeah, that's right it's the ones I picked for you anyway," she said and began to smile again.

"Yes and they are beautiful too," she told her smiling back.

"We can pin one on everybody. Big Al and you and Mr. Vince and Madam. Joanna and all the rest too," Emmy anxiously said.

"We sure can Emmy," Trina said adoring her.

"Mr. Vince and Madam. Joanna are getting married too," she continued to tell her.

Trina turned her eyes to Alejandro who was obviously admiring Emmy to a great extent. "Yes, I hope you don't mind but I told them we could have a double ceremony here in the chapel. Everyone bought sleepwear to wear too. And Mattie has agreed to be your best woman. I hope that's alright too," he told Trina with only a glimpse her way.

"Well big Al, it seems as if you have taken care of everything," she said with her eyes starting to light up.

"Do you want to see my outfit, Madam. Trina?" Emmy asks her.

"Yes I do and I want to see mine too," she said.

"Show her big Al," Emmy quickly replied. Alejandro first pulled Emmy's out of her little box and held it up for Trina to see. And then he pulled hers out holding it up. Tears filled her eyes as she admired beautiful white flowing silk and lace yardage of what was soon to be her wedding dress. She hugged Emmy up close to her and they both peered in silence with big teary smiles on their face. Alejandro glanced at his watch. The time had flown by and he had to get everything in order.

"Okay Emmy we have to go let Madam. Trina dress now. We have to get everything ready," he told her as he returned her feet to the floor.

"One question before you two go? Who is Mattie?" Trina asks even though she thought it was the lady of the older couple that had visited her earlier. She just wanted to make sure.

"Mattie and her husband Tom who will be the one performing the ceremonies are the couple who brought you to the hospital," Alejandro told her.

"Oh, I see. Well that's great then. Can you ask her to come in and give me a hand? And tell your sister she can join us here as well, okay?" she asks him.

"That I will do and I know Mattie will be happy to do it. Joe will too for that matter. We'll need this too," he said as he bent and swiped a kiss across her forehead taking her hand and removing the ring he had placed on her finger earlier.

"Alright," she said.

"Oh and Trina, I would like us to have some words of our own in the ceremony too. Would that be alright with you?" he asks her as he grabs the flowers from the night stand. He laid back the two biggest petal white roses there was for Trina and Mattie.

"Yes it will be fine. Now go and get Mattie and give us a little bit then send Emmy back in. We'll all need to be together when the ceremony gets close to starting time," she said brushing her hand in the air towards the door.

"Emmy you make big Al behave himself for me," she told her as she and Alejandro arrived at the exit door.

"I will Madam. Trina. I'll be back too," she said as the door closed behind them.

CHAPTER TWENTY-SEVEN

When Mattie arrived in Trina's room she was already dressed in her outfit. She was a lovely older lady and just as sweet as the smell of Emmy's roses. "Hello Dear, I can see you are feeling much better," Mattie said as she approached Trina who was standing in front of the mirror.

"Hi, how do I look?" Trina asks as Mattie walks up behind her and peers over her shoulder into the mirror as well.

"You are lovely my dear. You look like the spring flower blooming in July instead of May," she pleasantly said smiling as she spoke.

"You're too kind Mrs...Oh I'm sorry I don't know your last name. I'm afraid I have forgotten if I ever did know it," Trina said as she turned to face Mattie.

"Hill dear, my last name is Hill and it's quite alright. You're not expected to remember things like my last name on your wedding day," Mattie told her still grinning like there was no tomorrow.

A knock came at the door and it slowly opened. Trina and Mattie turned the direction just as Joe walked in carrying her package.

"Hi, I'm Joanna Azure, Alejandro's sister. He told me you said it was alright to join you and Mattie here," she told Trina as she continued to walk up to her.

"Oh yes of course it is. I understand you and Vince will be celebrating a double ceremony with your brother and me," Trina quickly replied.

"Yes we are and I do hope you don't mind. It was my brother's idea. He said you wouldn't mind. And he can be pretty persuasive sometimes. Anyway you look great. Alejandro really loves you and I am so happy the two of you have suppressed your differences and come to wedding terms. Congratulations my soon to be sister-in-law," Joanna nervously rattled almost continuously.

"Well, thank you and congratulations to you as well. Now you better hurry up and get dressed. We don't want to be late for our own weddings," Trina told her smiling.

"No we don't. Oh and Alejandro said to remind you two to put your roses on your shoulder like a corsage. He gave me this one. Do you have safety pins in here?" Joanna asks her.

"No, I don't, so now what are we going to do," she said aloud not directing her question at anyone.

"Don't fear Dear. I'll just run out and get some real quick and be back in a flash," Mattie said as she hurriedly headed for the door. Mattie hit the lobby walking so fast it was as if she was running nearly. Out the front door and across the street she flew. Not once did she stop to think of how she was dressed. The cars in the street come to sudden halts. Horns started blowing. People started yelling out their windows and the folks on foot gathered to stare at her as she approached the pharmacy door. A by stander whom saw Mattie when she exited the hospital door and crossed the street called the law. They were just around the corner and there in a jiffy. Tom, Jasper, Jack, Jane and Vince were in the lobby when Mattie came through. Vince walked over to the front window and watched her cross the street. When he saw the laws enter the store behind her he took off out the door. When the rest of them heard the commotion and loud noise outside they all headed towards the window. But when Vince hurried out the door they all followed him and pretty soon they were all in the pharmacy. By the time Vince had reached Mattie the law had almost surrounded her. When he walked up to her side she looked up at him with a tear falling from the corner of her eye and said," Oh dear, I'm afraid I have really made a mess of things. I just wanted to get some safety pins for the flowers. I didn't think about what I was wearing when I done it."

"It's alright Mattie. Everything will be fine. I'll explain to them," Vince said as he reached and patted her shoulder.

The officers that had took the call turned to look at Vince and saw all of them standing there in their gowns and pajamas.

"What is this PJ day in the streets," one of the officers asks him.

"No sir it's not, we are all part of a sleepwear wedding that is taking place in the hospital across the street in just a few minutes. She needed safety pins so she didn't think and came over here to get them. That's all it is. It's just a misunderstanding and nothing more," Vince told them. The rest of the gang started nodding their heads in agreement with Vince.

"This is my wife sir, and I can tell you for sure she didn't think before she left that hospital," Tom stepped up taking up for his wife.

The officer turned to Mattie and asks her," Did you see what you caused out there. People could have been hurt. Wrecks could have occurred. You stirred up quite a commotion lady. Don't you think you should start thinking before you do things like this?"

"I'm very sorry and it won't happen again. Thank God nobody was hurt. I just got all caught up in the excitement of the wedding and didn't think straight. I promise it won't happen again," she told the officers through her tears.

"Alright we're going to let you go this time and it better not happen again ever," he told her.

"Oh thank you so very much," she said and quickly turned to the clerk behind the counter.

"I need some safety pins and I don't have any money either as you can see I'm not properly dressed with pockets. And I don't have my bag with me. Please if you can see fit I swear I will come back after the wedding and gladly pay you for them," she pleaded with the clerk.

The officer pulled some change from his pocket and threw it up on the counter and said," Forget it and consider it a gift to the bride and groom." Mattie took the package of safety pins from the clerk's hand. She thanked the officer and hurried for the door with the rest close behind. When they all were safely back inside the hospital Mattie took enough of the pins for herself, Joanna, Trina, Jane and Emmy and told them she would bring Joe and Trina to the chapel and invited Jane to join her. Since she was Joe's best woman she would need to be with them.

"We will be ready when you all arrive," Vince assured her and they all went in their correct direction.

"I'm back finally. I caused a commotion but I'm back now," she said as soon as she entered the room.

"Oh thank God I was starting to get worried," Trina said with Joe right behind her as they approached Mattie.

"What happened anyway?" Joe asks her.

"Never mind that now dear, we don't have time. Their all waiting for us at the chapel," Mattie said picking up Trina's flower for her shoulder.

"I'll tell you all about it on the way to the chapel," Jane said as she was pinning Joe's flower on her.

"What about me? Who's going to pin my flower on me?" Emmy asks from her seat by the window.

"I will Emmy in just a moment," Trina quickly answered her.

"Okay I'll just wait here," Emmy said.

"Such a darling you are, Emmy," Trina said as she picked up the flower for her. Trina bent in front of Emmy and pinned her flower onto her shoulder. The rose was so big it stuck out as far as Emmys lips did.

"Oh my Emmy, it's too big. I tell you what why don't you just carry yours in your hands and hold it in front of your little tummy as you walk? How does that sound?" Trina asks her as she is removing the rose from Emmy's shoulder.

"Okay I can do that Madam. Trina," Emmy said.

"Good girl Emmy. Now when we get there you will be the one to walk in front so it's very important that you remember to walk slowly. Have you got the rings big Al and Vince gave you to hold onto before you came in here?" she asks her.

"Madam Jane has them but I'll get them from her when we get there. That way I'm sure I won't lose them and I'll hold them tight in my hand. And I promise I'll remember to walk slowly too," she anxiously told Trina.

"Alright Emmy," she said and gave her a big hug.

Trina stood and took a look around to make sure everyone was ready. "Well, I guess we're ready girls so let's go," she said.

"Oh boy it's time, it's time," Emmy said jumping up and down like she does when she gets excited.

"Emmy you settle down now. Don't jump up and down you'll mess your cloths up. Come on take my hand," Madam. Jane told her reaching out to her. The four ladies and Emmy walked down the hall to the chapel staying close together. When they arrived at the doorway George was waiting for them.

"There you all are and what a pretty bunch you are too," George said hugging Trina first and then the rest one by one.

"They are lovely dears aren't they," Mattie told George as he hugged her.

"Are they ready in there?" Trina asks him.

"Ready and waiting," George said.

"Well we are too," Joe added in.

"Alright I'll just let them know you are here now. Then we can get started," George said reaching for the door. He pulled the door open stepped in and peered at the head of the isle. Alejandro looked up and George nodded his head telling him the girls were all there.

They all lined up like they were to walk. First there was Mattie, then Jane followed by Emmy, then Trina with George in the middle and Joanna on the other side. The chapel had filled with the hospital staff. Word had gotten around that there was going to be a sleepwear wedding in the chapel and the workers had piled in to watch. When Emmy started down the isle some of the ladies in the back of the chapel started humming a lovely tune that Trina didn't recognize. But it made a very nice entrance for a wedding so she was thankful for them. When she stepped up to the door to enter Alejandro waved a hand at the ladies and the tune changed. They started humming hear comes the bride. They were wonderful and done a fantastic job Trina thought. They were all in the front now with Emmy standing one step out in front of George who was standing in between Trina and Joanna still and Tom was in front of her facing them ready start the ceremony.

The ladies stopped humming and Tom began. "Dearly beloved we are gathered here in the face of God to join this woman Trina Wright and this man Alejandro Azure, this woman Joanna Azure and this man Vincent Goldman in holy matrimony."

He drew in a deep breath and continued. "Who gives these ladies hand in marriage?"

"I do," George said and then he turned to Trina first taking her hand and laying in Alejandro's. Then he done the same with Joe's to Vince. He moved to the side and took a seat on the front row and Tom continued.

"Do you Alejandro Azure take this woman Trina Wright to be your lawful wedded wife from this day forward to have and to hold in sickness or in health until death do you part?" he asks looking at Alejandro.

"I do," Alejandro softly said peering into Trina's eyes.

Tom took a breath and continued with the ceremony. "Do you Trina Wright take this man Alejandro Azure to be your lawful wedded husband from this day forward to have and to hold in sickness or in health until death do you part?" he asks peering at her.

"I do," Trina said with her tears starting to whale up.

Tom again filled his lungs with air and then turned to Vince saying, "Do you Vincent Goldman take this woman Joanna Azure to be your lawful wedded wife from this day forward to have and to hold in sickness or in health until death do you part?"

"I certainly do," Vince quickly answered smiling at Joe.

Tom moved right along to Joe," "Do you Joanna Azure take this man Vincent Goldman to be your lawful wedded husband from this day forward to have and to hold in sickness or in health until death do you part?"

"Oh yes, I do," Joe answered just as quickly.

Tom looked at Mattie and gave her the smile he had used when she and he had gotten married. Just a little crook of the mouth to the side and Mattie's tears fell showing her love. Trina and Alejandro hadn't taken their eyes off one another since the ceremony started. Jane was looking over at her husband standing beside Vince and little Emmy was just looking back and forth from one to the other grinning a huge smile.

Vince and Joe were making faces at one another nobody could understand but them.

Tom began speaking again," If there are any objections present speak now or forever hold your peace." He paused for a brief moment and then continued when nobody spoke up," Marriage is not something we take lightly. We give ourselves to one another because we are in love. We share, care and love beneath our God in heaven always being considerate of one another," he said and then turned his attention to little Emmy.

"The rings?" he asks her. Emmy opened her little hand and Tom took the rings from her. He first turned to Vince and handed him the ring for Joe saying, "Take this ring and repeat after me as you slip it onto her finger. With this ring I thee wed," Tom told him.

"With this ring I thee wed," Vince repeated and slid the golden band onto Joe's finger.

Tom then turned to Alejandro and told him the same thing handing him the ring for Trina.

"With this ring I thee wed," Tom said.

"With this ring I thee wed," Alejandro repeated Tom sliding the golden diamonded band onto Trina's finger.

Tom then turned back to Vince and Joe and said," I now pronounce you husband and wife.

He then turned to Alejandro and Trina and said," I now pronounce you husband and wife."

Then he told everyone there watching the two couples wed that Alejandro and Trina had a few words they wanted to say to one another and turned it over to them.

"You are the bright ray to my everyday sun," Alejandro began.

"And you are the drop to my happy tears rain," Trina said back.

"Here today a new life we have begun," he told her dreamy eyed.

"And there will be no more unwanted pain," she said.

"We'll live together and always care," he told her.

"And our life we will always share," she told him back.

"I love you my precious wife Mrs. Trina Azure," his words showed much feeling.

"I love you my husband Mr. Alejandro Azure," she said and began to cry happy tears.

"What God has joined together, let no man tear apart. Gentlemen you may kiss your bride," Tom said.

Alejandro slid his arms around Trina's waist and deeply kissed her soft lips for the very first time.

Vince grabbed Joe and laid a lip locker on her holding her tightly close to him.

"Ladies and gentlemen I present to you Mr. and Mrs. Alejandro Azure," Tom said holding his arms and hand open towards them.

Then he turned opening his arms and hands to Vince and Joe and said, "Mr. and Mrs. Vincent Goldman.

"And, I am Emmy," she spoke up loudly saying and everyone laughed out loud.

Alejandro reached down and picked her up, carrying her in one arm and holding onto Trina with the other as they walked down the isle and out into the hall.

Vince and Joe followed behind them and then the rest of the party flowed out all in their own good time. Everyone returned to Trina's room where they would visit and have the best reception possible given the circumstance of Trina being hospitalized. Alejandro didn't mind, Trina had made him the happiest man on earth. When they arrived at her room Alejandro turned her loose long enough to push the door open and sit Emmy on the floor asking her to hold the door open for him. Emmy did as he ask and held the door wide open. Alejandro turned to Trina and picked her up carrying her through the door with her squealing all along and telling him," This isn't where you are suppose to do this."

"I'll do it here too," he said sitting her feet back to the floor once in side.

"Alejandro will you take a look at that?"Trina asks and pointed towards the window.

There was a table set up with a three tier cake with roses all over it and a big punch bowel full of punch. There were cups, plates, napkins and forks. The table was decorated in streaming pink and blue crape paper. Tied to the back was pink, green, blue and white hospital gloves blown up for balloons with big smiling faces drawn on them. Sitting on the floor in front of the table was a huge card opened up with signatures and congratulation notes all from the hospital staff. Everyone else, plus some of the hospital staff members, all joined the room by the time Alejandro and Trina discovered who had set the table. They all gathered around having a piece of cake and some punch chit- chatting about how pretty the sleepwear wedding turned out to be. Two hours must have passed by before the crowd in Trina's room started thinning down. But now all that was left was all the people whom had been in or took part in the wedding. Jasper decided he would draw the attention of everyone with a toast to the brides and grooms. Giving wishes of eternal happiness bestowed upon each couple. And then he took himself a seat by the door. Sitting and watching everyone move around the room and talk awhile and then cry awhile he was happy for them all.

The door opened and the chief from the law station stepped inside. Jasper quickly stood saying," No, not now. She just got married so please give her this day. Don't question her now."

"Relax, I'm not here to question her," the officer said and turned his attention to Trina who was looking absolutely beautiful.

"Madam. Trina can I talk to you please?" the officer asks. Trina looked up at him and instantly lost her smile.

Alejandro stepped forward asking," what about?" Trina joined Alejandro at his side never taking her eyes off the officer. George stepped to Trina's side. Tom, Mattie, Vince, Joe, Jack, and Jane all stood behind them. Jasper stood beside the officer and they were all anticipating what the officer had to say.

"Madam. Trina the man that kidnapped you was a wanted man," the officer said.

Trina grasped Alejandro's arm tightly and Alejandro spoke up saying," If you are here to question her forget it. It's not happening right now so you may as well go away."

"Relax young man and let me talk," the officer said. "As I was saying before the man was a wanted man. An investigation has been thoroughly completed. It was felt there was no need in questioning you. And the board of panel has decided that you Trina are entitled to the reward that was posted on him. I'm here to present you with a check for that reward," he told her reaching into his jacket pocket.

"Just how much are we talking about here," George asks.

"Trina I am very proud to present to you this check in the sum of five hundred thousand US dollars for the capture of one

Donald Dennison. The department is forever grateful to you for your aid in his apprehension," the officer said as he was handing the check to Trina who was so stunned she couldn't move.

Alejandro reached and took the check for her and then pulled her tightly into his arms holding her. The officer again thanked her and then he left.

"You did a good thing, Trina. Your parents would have been proud of you. Don't you ever forget it," George said and then hugged her and Alejandro from the backside of her.

"That's a lot of money Madam. Trina," Emmy said pulling at her gown cover from the side.

Trina turned lose of Alejandro and kneeled taking Emmy into her arms hugging her as she said,"Yes Emmy it is and when I get out of here I'll take you shopping and let you pick out whatever you want. That is of course if it's alright with Mr. Jack and Mrs. Jane."

She then stood and returned to Alejandro's side whispering, "If I ever get out of here that is."

"When you do get released, we'll go wherever your heart desires baby," Alejandro said taking her hand into his. The door opened just as Jasper had made his way to Trina and stood in front of her. They locked eyes and knew exactly what each was thinking. No words were needed. They understood so they just hugged.

"Well young lady. It seems you have had quite a day. Especially being in the hospital and all," Doctor. Jacobs said.

"I didn't know you were here," she said.

"My nurse and I just came in. I heard you got married. A double ceremony in the chapel is what I was told," he said.

"Yes I did, and so did this couple here," she said pointing towards Vince and Joe.

"My congratulations to all of you and may you find peace together from here out," he told her holding out his hand.

"Thank you," she said taking his hand.

"It's my pleasure. Now, what I come for is because I have your test results," he told her.

"What test results?" she asks him.

"The blood we drew earlier today once I found out you had awakened," Dr. Jacobs told her.

"Oh yes, I had forgotten about that. What are they?" she quickly asks him.

"It's good news. Everything is within normal limits. You are fine and as soon as you sign those papers, my nurse has there in her hand, you are free to go," he told her smiling knowing that was going to make her happy.

"Really, I am free to go right now?" she eagerly said.

"You are free to go," he repeated it again and then excused himself and left the room leaving his nurse to take care of the paperwork.

Everyone said their good byes except for Jasper, George, Vince and Joe and went home. George and Jasper excused themselves and headed for Jasper's flat. Vince and Joanna hugged them each and the four stood in silence for a moment before they excused themselves and went their own way.

Trina signed her walking papers and left the hospital on Alejandro's arm. Once they were in the jeep she turned to him and said, "I love you my husband as I know you love me." Alejandro reached across the jeep and took her hand into his raising it and lightly kissing the back of it. And then they drove off into the darkness. They were married. They both won and now they had money too. They were finally together happy for the first time in many years of their life. And eternity plus a day wouldn't be long enough for them to be, in love.

The End!

EPILOGUE

It had been eighteen months since Alejandro had darkened the doors of the hospital. Last time he wasn't sure of what he would see, or if he would be accepted. But this time he had a whole new meaning for being there, and he was ecstatic about it. He paced the lobby floor back and forth waiting. He tried several times to take a seat but was unable to do so. He couldn't keep still no matter how hard he tried.

"Sit down brother. You are going to walk a hole in the carpet if you don't," Joe told him grabbing his hand.

"It's been almost an hour since I was run-out of there. What's taking so long? I don't understand it I was there through the hardest parts. Why can't I be there now?" he nervously asks his sister.

"You go sit down and I'll go check on things," Joe said pointing towards a chair over beside her husband Vince.

Alejandro turned and glanced the way Joe was pointing and said, "Alright, I'll try. But you hurry up." He walked over and sat in the seat next to Vince and started looking around the lobby. The hospital was full of people today. They just kept pouring in from the streets. The lobby was filling up fast it seemed. It was January 28, 2010 and it was cold outside. Not as cold as it get's in some places but cold to Alejandro. He had lived on the islands for most of his life and like anywhere else when winter came around it was cold to him. Trina had relinquished her job in the city with her Uncle George and moved to the island after she and Alejandro were married. They had built a rather large house on the far side of the island that overlooked the ocean. Alejandro loved admiring the scenery from a big bay window in his writing room. He had pursued his writing and now had six novels published, and working on one that is to be turned into a movie! Trina had continued with her journalist talent, and took a job with the local newspaper. She had worked with them for a few months before her Uncle George had up and decided to move his paper business there as well. When he did she move back into working with him so she wouldn't have to travel away from home. She covered all the local news and she was happy doing it.

They built up quite a bank account that started with most of the money Trina has received as a reward for Donald's capture. She had some trouble accepting all that had happened but with time she overcame it quite nicely. She and Jasper had grown close after all that too. She looked at him as the father figure she had been without. She depended on him maybe more than she should. But he didn't mind and Alejandro thought he probably enjoyed it. After all he was still guiding the riding trials for the hotel and Trina gave him other things to think about.

"You sure are uptight brother-in-law," Vince said after Alejandro has sat a few minutes with no words exchanged.

"Yeah, I guess I am. I'm worried something has gone wrong," he told him turning to face him.

"Don't think that way. You'll drive yourself crazy if you do. Think positive man always think positive," Vince quickly told him.

"After Trina first got settled here and we were out looking for land to build our house on. She was so spunky that all the reality folks hated dealing with her," he said changing the subject thinking it might help him to cope.

"She was a spunky woman that's for sure," Vince said.

Alejandro laughed out loud and said, "Yeah one of them told her she was a land buyer from hell."

Vince joined him laughing out loud and said," I can see that too."

"Ah…but she was beautiful being spicy like that," Alejandro said.

"She is a beautiful lady Alejandro just like your sister is," Vince said.

"Sis is a spicy one too. They have a lot in common I think," Alejandro told him.

"They do and they get along quite well too. It seems their out to lunch and shopping everyday. I don't know when they get their work done," Vince said.

"Yeah and I made the mistake of asking Trina that very question one day. Man she got fired up. She thought I was complaining about them shopping and saying they weren't working. Boy did I make a mistake. She lit into me letting me know real fast that she and Joe would go shopping whenever they felt like it and their work was always done before they did. She was beautiful then too," he said rubbing his hands up and down the sides of his face.

"I hadn't made that mistake yet and now that you told me you have I guess I better not. I'm sure Trina told Joe about it," Vince said with a little chuckle.

"Knowing my sister, I wouldn't advise it," Alejandro told him chuckling with him.

Vince and Joe had bought them a place just over the way a short distance from where Trina and Alejandro had built theirs. So they were close by one another and access to town was not that far away. Trina and Joe took advantage of it as often as they could even if it was just for lunch. The word family meant a great deal too and both the ladies kept it close.

"Everything is fine brother. They are cleaning up and getting her settled. When they're finished then you can go in," Joe told him interrupting his thinking.

He was so deep in thought he didn't even see her coming.

"Alright I guess I'll just have to wait longer," he told her.

His phone rang and when he answered, it was Mattie on the other end inquiring about Trina. She and Tom had finished out their vacation on the island and returned home. Trina kept in contact with Mattie all along. She really liked Mattie. She sort of looked to her as the mother she didn't have. Yes Mattie had been good for Trina, and Alejandro was happy about that.

Joanna took the seat on the other side of Vince and the two remained quite while Alejandro was on the phone. When he hung up Joe asks him," How are Mattie and Tom doing?"

"Their doing fine, a nice couple they are. I'm glad we were blessed with meeting them," he said.

"Yeah when I think back about Mattie running off outside, and across the street to that pharmacy I laugh every time. She sure stirred up a commotion," Vince said chuckling.

"I missed out on that one but I wish I hadn't," Alejandro said.

"Me too but it all turned out for the good and that's all that mattered," Joe said.

"Yeah a sweet couple they are," Vince added.

"Have you seen Jack and Jane lately sis?" Alejandro asks.

"I seen them yesterday when I took Emmy over there," she said.

"Oh, how are they doing now?" he asks her.

"Their doing well they've gotten more children and they have a full house now," she said.

"It's a good thing them two are doing. There should be more people like them. They have big hearts and hard hearts at the same time. But its all for the good," he said.

"It's not a hard heart brother. It's called tough love. I'm assuming you were talking about when they have to let a child go. Is that right?" Joe asks him.

"Yeah, that's what I was talking about sis. I stand corrected," he told her smiling.

"Very well then, I'm glad it was me and Vince you were talking to when you said that. Someone else could have taken that the wrong way. Be careful what you say," she strongly told him.

"I will sis I will," he replied sarcastically and then became quiet getting lost in his own thoughts.

Emmy had become a treasure to Trina. They both had suffered an experience that was very closely related. They both lost their parents to a car wreck caused by a drunken driver. Trina was great therapy to Emmy, and Emmy to her. They grew quite close in a short period of time. Emmy was in school now and she was an A-student. Every report card she had brought home was honorary. She was a smart little girl and she had gotten so close with them, she had picked up some writing skills of her own at the age of seven. Alejandro was proud of her, and so was Trina.

"You can come in now Mr. Azure," the nurse called from the hallway.

Alejandro jumped up from his chair and headed that way when he heard," Wait for me," and he turned to see little Emmy running towards him. She had finally gotten dropped off. She was supposed to have been there an hour ago, but the traffic had been so bad there were some hold up and the sitter lady was late dropping her off. Oh well, she was there now and Alejandro stopped and waited for her to catch up with him. He took her hand and led her towards the room where Trina was. Once inside, Emmy ran over and climbed up on the bed beside her and peered down at the bundle Trina was holding.

"Oh Mum, he has hair the same color as big daddy Al's," she said.

"Yes sweetheart he does. Just like you have hair the same color as Mum's," she told her pushing the little blue blanket back and revealing more of Emmy's baby brother's hair.

Alejandro stood at the bedside and watched Emmy and Trina talk about him and his son as if he wasn't even there. What a beautiful sight it was seeing his wife, his daughter, and his son all together. He and Trina had adopted Emmy shortly after they were married. She had been a blessing to their life. And they had been to hers.

He painted a picture of his family in his mind that would last a lifetime. They were healthy and happy all together with him at his side. What more could he ask for and what more could she give?